Thrice the brinded cat hath mew'd.
Thrice and once, the hedge-pig whin'd.
Harpier cries:—'tis time! 'tis time!

# The Shadow Falls

## Witch-Hunter 3

K. S. Marsden

Printed by Amazon

Copyright © K.S. Marsden 2014

Cover art: Sylermedia

All rights reserved. No part of this publication may be reproduced or transmitted be any means, electronic, mechanical, photocopying or otherwise, without prior permission of the author.

ISBN-10: 1500358339
ISBN-13: 978-1500358334

**A letter from our hero…**

We are in dark days. I write this hurriedly at my desk, not knowing to whom I write, but wanting my story to be known. I hope it is found by one of my kind, and in turn gives hope…

My name is George Astley VII, known to my friends as Hunter. If it matters to you, I am 28 years old, English; and in a time of peace I would be the lord of Astley Manor, near the village of Little Hanting.

But this is not a time of peace, we have been fighting the losing side of a war for the past two years. Fighting against the witches. It all started when the legendary Shadow Witch arose - a witch whose magic was without limit, a witch raised to nurse a thousand years of insult and hatred. She plunged the world into darkness so that she and the other witch kind could claw above the stricken and powerless humans, preferably with as many casualties as possible to assuage their anger.

Where do I fit in with all this? In the very centre, shouldering both the blame and the hope.

I am a witch-hunter. As was my father, and his father and so on. I am the 7th generation of witch-hunters belonging to the organisation called the Malleus Maleficarum Council, which has successfully policed and hidden magic and witches for hundreds of years. Until now.

The Shadow Witch approached me in the guise of Sophie Murphy, a beautiful, intelligent woman that I thought was an innocent that I saved and sheltered from witches. With a grating stubbornness, Sophie demanded to join the MMC and train as a witch-hunter. I was the one that allowed her into our Council. I was the one that would let her learn all our secrets. I was the one that would later fall in love with her.

She finally revealed herself as the Shadow Witch, and the first of many battles between the witches and witch-hunters was fought, in which our side was nearly decimated.

What remained of the MMC regrouped, driven by desperation against this new and unbelievable force. We had only one advantage: the Shadow Witch revealed too much about the hidden talent born into witch-hunters - into me in particular. I don't know how I do it, I cannot explain it. Some liken my talents to magic, all I know is that I am strong enough to repel witches and protect those around me, amongst other useful skills. With my new skills, we initially managed to repel the Shadow Witch and destroy her followers. She seemed to vanish for the best part of a year and, as terrible and fierce as they were, we began to beat back the witches.

Then the Shadow Witch returned, stronger than ever, and even I was helpless in her path. She systematically destroyed the witch-hunters and their allies, returning power and victory to the witches in a devastating way. Those fateful days of battle will haunt me forever, as I watched brave men and women fall at my side.

There might be witch-hunters in hiding somewhere out there, but as far as I am aware, I am the only one left.

Friendless, alone, and the most wanted man alive, I've decided it's time to learn all I can about this mysterious power I have. I am going to find the Benandanti.

**Chapter One**

The small town was near deserted. Half the people had fled, or just plain vanished. The other half sat behind their locked doors, no one ventured out once the sun set. So, no one saw the sudden appearance of a man in the rough piazza.

One moment the square was empty, the next there he stood. He was tall, well-built and had perhaps been handsome, but now his clothes were creased, his face rugged, worn and wary, and half hidden by the short, dark beard and straggly black hair.

It was a very different image than the old, relatively carefree Hunter Astley. He'd been rich, good-looking and popular.

He'd been on the run for nearly eight months, ever since the last big battle in which the witch-hunters and their allies had finally been overcome by the witches. He hadn't dared stop anywhere for long, empty villages where no eyes could see him, or in the few dense cities that still existed where he could get lost in the crowd. He made his locations erratic and illogical, to throw off his hunters for a few peaceful hours.

Hunter had tried coming to Italy last summer, but found that wherever he went, the witches were close behind. Hunter didn't doubt that the Shadow Witch had a few spies permanently placed around here, for she knew how strongly Friuli would pull Hunter. For here was the region that had been the home to the Benandanti, centuries ago, the original anti-witches.

He eventually admitted defeat and fled to America, tracking down one lead in the library at Georgetown University; followed by Glasgow and Ulster. All he found were teasers and hints to what he truly wished to know.

As winter came around, Hunter kept his movements in the southern hemisphere. It was easier and safer than trying to find warmth and shelter – he could put no one in such danger.

But finally, spring came again, and Hunter was drawn back to Friuli. If the modern equivalent of the Benandanti existed anywhere, it would be here. It was dangerous, but Hunter had to find them, he was out of options. He'd started at the northernmost edge of Friuli and searched each town and village for hope. This one was close to the Lago di Sauris, a large landmark that allowed Hunter to gain his bearings in his speedy method of travel.

Hunter strode up to the nearest house and banged sharply on the wooden door. Dogs started to bark, but there was no sound of people.

"Per favore. Please, I need help." Hunter called out; his voice rough from disuse.

He heard the soft pad of feet and the creak of shutters. Hunter stepped back and looked at the surrounding houses.

"Please." He repeated to the dark, empty street. "I'm not a witch, I just need help. I'm looking for some people. They used to live here, many years ago. They did magic, good magic. Please."

Hunter's voice trailed off, he was used to the suspicion and wariness that now ruled every person's life. It was the way of the world under the rule of the witches. If this town couldn't help him, he'd travel to the next, and the next, persisting in his search.

"We want no magic here, signore." A warning voice came from behind a crack in a window shutter.

Hunter turned in the voice's direction. "No, I'm not here to harm you, and I'm not staying. But if you could help me by telling me anything, *anything* about the Benandanti…"

"I've never heard of them; they don't live here." The voice replied curtly.

Hunter frowned, it was a negative response, but at least someone was answering him - albeit through a blocked window.

"No, they might not live anywhere now. But they were in this region four hundred years ago."

"Four hundred years?" The voice spluttered. "Nobody here can help you, signore. It is too long ago. Now leave us in peace."

Hunter called out again but got no response. He even banged on the reinforced shutters but only set the dogs off again. It had been briefly promising but turned out to be less than helpful. Oh well, next village.

Hunter turned to leave the way he came when he suddenly stopped, seeing a pair of brown eyes peering around a crack in a door.

"Signore." A quiet woman's voice came. "It is true we know nothing but try the Donili monks. They have a small monastery a few kilometres south-west of here."

The door clicked shut.

"Thank you. Grazie." Hunter said quietly to the still night air.

He hadn't gotten any answers - hell, he'd hardly managed to get any questions out, but this was a start, a thread to follow. Not bad, he reflected as he left the village. Even a place as small and unimportant as this was dangerous - this close to the Benandanti rumours, it was best to travel unmarked paths and camp alone and untraceable. Which meant hunkering down in the lonely forest that rose to the hills. Not a comfortable prospect, but at least the weather was mild.

At dawn Hunter was on his feet once more, set resolutely south-west, detouring only for the most stubborn natural barriers. The woman had said a few kilometres. A few. What an ill-defined description. She could mean three kilometres, while he considered it seven, or vice versa. And did she mean precisely south-west, or bearing more to the left or right? He might walk right past the home of the Donili monks, or not walk far enough. The dismal beat of his thoughts matched his steady footsteps.

He replayed the steps that had brought him here. He had thought of nothing but the Benandanti for months. The focus allowed him to block out the nightmare of last year; investigating every dusty book, every story and myth was preferable than remembering the death and violence that was behind him.

The minutes seemed to drag by, and a mere hour pushing on exhausted him, but Hunter didn't stop, the distance passed slowly but steadily. He kept a keen eye for any sign of a monastery, anything to show he was on track, but so far there had been nothing man-made, there had been no sight nor sou--

A scream pierced the peaceful countryside. Shouts followed and worse, laughter.

Hunter stopped. The sensible part of him warned caution, those screams could only mean trouble and he shouldn't endanger himself. Unfortunately, he'd already set off in pursuit of the noise, self-preservation at the back of his mind.

Drawing closer, the trees thinned to reveal a lonely little cottage. In front of the humble building a woman stood before two young children, arms held wide to shield them with her own body. The three cried and begged while a man held onto an older child, seemingly playing a tug-o-war with the boy being pulled on the other side by a laughing duo.

"Please, no." The man begged.

"You know the law." The female aggressor said with a scornful laugh. "Sacrifices must be provided."

"No, please, not my son. Take me instead."

The heartless woman shook her head smiling, finding his distress highly amusing. They all cried and begged, and some even swore and fought back; but the result was always the same, when a witch demanded a sacrifice that demand had to be met.

Hunter had seen enough.

"Release him." He shouted with all the authority he once possessed.

The two aggressors turned, unimpressed by this scruffy stranger that dared to intercede.

"Move on." The male warned. "This does not concern you."

"Release him." Hunter repeated. "Or I will be forced to take action."

The crying father looked between the two witches and this unknown hero; his troubled mind slow to catch up.

"No signore, you mustn't, they... they will come, they will protect us." His strange mumblings faded into a whisper and he closed his eyes briefly in a silent prayer.

The man and his comments were ignored as the witches turned to the one individual willing to stand up against them, willing to fight even.

Hunter felt that familiar spark in his mind that sensed magic. Indeed, the build up from the two witches was almost tangible. He frowned, his hand clasping the metal amulet at his throat, his whole body reaching instinctively for protection. It had been years since Hunter had first used the natural shield that he was equipped with, and now it slipped over him with an invisible, but comfortable weight.

The first wave of spells hit, designed to blind and unbalance, a typical opening move. The magic distilled uselessly in the air, leaving Hunter unaffected and the witches disturbed and confused.

Hunter sighed, soon he'd draw his gun, he'd fight to destroy these ungodly creatures. But first he needed to protect the others in case things got ugly. With a simple thought he extended the shield to protect the cowering family.

Hunter snapped to attention, his shield was blocked, he pushed again but it felt like it had come up against a solid wall. This was unsettling, in the last two years, in the endless fights and battles his shield had been battered and weakened, but never blocked.

> *The spells came in from all sides, Hunter felt the shield buckle under the sheer pressure, he was half-aware of the witch-hunters at the very edge, no longer safe as his strength failed. Soon they began to fall, no longer protected from the lethal magic...*

Hunter shook his head, determined to stay in the present. Another spell dissolved against the shield. Hunter frowned, he hated blood and death and had seen enough of both to last ten lifetimes, but he duly drew his gun and steadily fired at both witches.

Hunter heard a feral snarl rip from one of the witches, but neither of them fell. Hunter froze - his aim was infallible, yet they weren't hit. Even more disturbing was the expression of confusion that was mirrored in the witches' faces. The bullets had been stopped and it was not their doing.

Beyond the sound of his own thudding pulse Hunter became aware of a low rumble of noise coming from the forest. He turned, automatically strengthening the shield about him. Out of the trees stepped two men, one grey-haired and wrinkled, the other younger than Hunter. Their eyes were closed in concentration and both chanted in low tones, the sound akin to a hum.

The older man suddenly fell silent and opened his eyes, facing the two witches. With a move of his hand there was a deep rumble and a bright flash of light. Hunter heard a scream rip from the witches, and he stumbled back, unbalanced and blinded.

It was over in a flash, Hunter felt his heart falter, then double its beat. The witches were nowhere to be seen. The father and son scrambled back to their family's embrace.

The two mysterious men turned to face Hunter, the old man locked his pale blue gaze onto Hunter and raised his hand… then faltered. His wrinkled brow creased further in a frown. He spoke quickly, but Hunter failed to follow his words, they were an Italian dialect he'd never heard before.

"Wh-what? I'm sorry, I don't understand." He stuttered breathlessly, unable to find his usual manners in this confusion.

The younger man looked at him with surprise. "Inglese." He said with some amazement, throwing a meaningful look to the elder.

"English? He says, 'you are not a witch'." The young man explained in broken English, the words flavoured with accent, while he gazed curiously at Hunter.

Hunter wavered beneath those bright blue eyes. "No… I mean, yes, I'm English. But I'm not a witch."

The older man whispered something to the young one, who nodded seriously.

"But you are using magic." He insisted, his eyes drifting along Hunter's aura, as though physically seeing the shield.

"Oh." Hunter turned his attention to his shield, reluctantly letting it drop. He was far from trusting these strangers, but felt he needed to show faith if he were to get answers. "That's not magic, it's something… different. I'm sorry, but who are you?"

"I am Marcus." The young man replied readily; a hand placed on his chest. "And my friend is Maurizio, we are Donili. And you?"

"Donili?" Hunter jumped at the word. "Of the Donili monks? But I came this way looking for you."

Marcus frowned, and relayed this to the older Maurizio, then turned back to Hunter. "And your name?" He insisted.

"Hunter Astley, a 7th gen witch-hunter with the British Malleus Maleficarum Council." Hunter replied.

Marcus hesitated at this stream of information, then repeated it to Maurizio. Hunter waited impatiently as they exchanged comments in that incomprehensible Italian, his nerves still sparking at every slight sound or movement.

"You will come with us, Signor Astley? Our council will have many questions. You have many questions also?" Marcus' voice rose, but Hunter couldn't tell whether in query or anticipation.

"Yes. Yes, of course." Hunter replied immediately, feeling truly hopeful for the first time in three months.

Maurizio, pleased with the outcome of this laboured conversation, turned to the family. The old man quickly exchanged words with the mother and father, and less quickly stood smiling as he accepted their thanks and blessings.

Marcus smiled indulgently, then hurried the older man along. They set off into the forest, trudging over the rugged terrain. Hunter, used to his above average stamina and physical ability, was surprised by Marcus, and especially the older Maurizio, who paced along swiftly and untiring. Hunter came up with mental excuses, that he was wearied from being on the run for so long, that he was further tired by the brief fight with the witches - but the truth was it was embarrassing that his breathing grew heavier and he felt sweat run down his face and neck.

Hunter stopped to take a much-needed drink from his old water bottle. He coughed and spat, feeling guiltily unlike a gentleman.

"How much further is it?" He asked his travelling companions, not quite sure what 'it' was. He took the opportunity to take a few deep breaths and kept his voice strong at least.

"Not far. One kilometre, no more than two." Marcus replied, patiently waiting for his English guest. He hesitated, obviously taking in Hunter's sweaty appearance and strained eyes.

Marcus turned and quickly fell into conversation with Maurizio. Hunter didn't even try to follow the flow of words, but he gathered from the stress in Marcus' voice that the younger man was trying to persuade the older.

Eventually Maurizio shrugged non-committedly and Marcus turned back to Hunter with a smile.

"We go the fast way - this is how we travel. Hold my arm. Trust me." Marcus said, holding out his hand invitingly, but an almost mischievous look in his eye.

Warily Hunter raised his hand. As soon as he touched the young man's forearm the world went black and Hunter felt a familiar shift.

**Chapter Two**

In no time at all, the world returned, and Hunter saw an array of stone and brick buildings and heard the small crowd of people that turned to gaze calmly at their sudden appearance. Hunter, so suspicious and tense himself, noticed that people looked at him with only a vague curiosity before moving on, as though their appearance were a common thing.

Next to Hunter, Marcus turned with an expectant look.

"Do you want to sit? It is disorie- dees… *disorientante* for new people." He said, but his smile faltered as he saw Hunter show no sign of distress from this almost magical form of transport.

"No, I'm fine thank you. Where are we?" Hunter asked, brushing aside the unnecessary concern and gazing about the settlement. The buildings were strong and sturdy and defied the forest which turned the horizon green in every direction. The land sloped gently downhill in front of him and Hunter could see the shimmer of a river where the houses gave way, and further the land rose again to the next sunlit hill. "Are we still in Friuli?"

"Yes." Marcus answered, still eyeing Hunter warily. "This is the village of Donili. Come, you must meet our Abate. He is at the abbazia."

Marcus led back up the hill towards a long, low stone building that looked down on the village like a guardian. Marcus glanced again at Hunter. "You sure you ok? Most people panico after their first travel."

"It wasn't my first time." Hunter said carefully, thinking this was enough honesty. There was no need to. He didn't know how much he could trust Marcus and decided that the less he revealed about himself the better.

Hunter ignored the quizzical look from his young companion, and kept his eyes trained on the path, the last thing he wanted was to trip, fall, and look a prat. At one point, Hunter finally noticed the absence of Maurizio. But they had just reached the doors and he had no time to give the old man any further thought. Marcus rapped on the wooden doors and they were pulled open from the inside by a monk who nodded them through.

They stepped into a large courtyard. Hunter was struck by the simple beauty of the place; the sun warmed the soft brown stone, and along each side of the courtyard, shadowed walkways were marked out with pillars.

Hunter heard the pad of soft shoes across the stone quad. He turned to see another monk approach them, the man looked young and strong, and he greeted them both with quiet confidence.

"Welcome to the Abbazia di Donili, Signor Astley. My name is Biagio, if you come with me, I shall show you to the padre."

Hunter was briefly taken aback by his fluent, yet accented English and could only nod in reply, before finally coughing out a thank you.

Biagio smiled indulgently, then bowed briefly to Marcus before turning and walking away.

Hunter hesitated, not sure if he were meant to follow. He glanced at Marcus, somehow trusting this Donili monk that he met first.

Marcus tried an encouraging smile. "Perhaps I see you later, signore." The young man bowed and backed away.

Hunter frowned, he'd been deprived of company for so long, it was tempting to latch onto the first friendly face he saw. He had to remind himself that, until he had answers and his life had gained some aspect of sense again, he should remain wary and taciturn; there would be time for friendships later, if there were time at all.

Hunter gripped the straps of his rucksack and stumbled along behind Biagio, looking like any other weary traveller behind the quiet, composed monk.

Biagio led indoors and down a narrow stone corridor. He opened the last door and invited Hunter in.

Hunter didn't know what to expect, he'd been so preoccupied with the finding of a link to the Benandanti that his mind hadn't considered any further.

The room was cosy, with an upholstered bench and several soft chairs. There was a grand fireplace, that was yet unlit, and the walls were lined with shelves of books. The atmosphere of the room reminded Hunter of his own private study or drawing room at home.

There were three men sitting in the room, all were grey-haired and bore signs of age. They were in quiet conversation, but broke off at Hunter's arrival, they looked in his direction and Hunter could see that age had not dulled those sharp, shining eyes that pierced him curiously.

Next to him, Biagio made an introduction in that bizarre dialect.

One of the monks rose from their seat and replied, his gaze flitting between Hunter and Biagio the translator.

"The Abate welcomes you, Hunter Astley. Please be seated, you must have many questions. And after Maurizio's account of your meeting, we too have questions." Biagio relayed eloquently, a slight air of smugness over his own fluency.

But Hunter paid him little attention, he glanced again at the two seated monks and realised that one of them was Maurizio. So, this was where the old man had disappeared to - coming to forewarn the boss while Hunter toiled with Marcus.

Ever since he had found out about his abilities, Hunter had steadily gained more questions and no answers. But right now, he was speechless. In the awkwardness of his silence, he acted upon the invitation to sit down, sinking into one of the heavenly comfortable chairs.

The Abate sat also and spoke again.

"The Abate would like to know what brings an English gentleman to the hidden valleys of Italy?" Biagio voiced eagerly.

"I... I came looking for the Benandanti." Hunter replied, getting straight to the point.

Hunter waited impatiently for this to be relayed.

"Benandanti? It has been a long time since any sought them. They were a branch of our family that were wiped out hundreds of years ago." The Abate said via Biagio.

Hunter sat up straighter, his pulse quickening as his hopes were realised. "The Benandanti were part of the Donili?"

"Yes, they were one of the largest families. They were discovered by Europeans and were killed by their narrow-mindedness. The Europeans saw the skills that were inborn and strictly trained to protect others, but instead of seeing it as natural they accused the Benandanti of devil worship and magic and punished them.

"Thankfully, the rest of the Donili remained undiscovered, and by the grace of God, have been able to keep protecting those that ask for our help."

Hunter sat there, absorbing this new version of history. He had hoped that perhaps some of the Benandanti had survived, he could never have dreamed that the Benandanti were only a small part of something bigger, older and perhaps stronger.

"Now, I have given you an answer, it is your turn."

The Abate frowned, equally displeased with the circuitous nature of speaking through a translator. He looked directly at Hunter, "Te parle italiano?"

"Si, fluente." Hunter replied, feeling those blue eyes pierce him.

The Abate quickly dismissed Biagio, who looked disappointed at no longer being needed.

"This is easier, no?" The Abate asked in steady Italian. "I dislike using a translator, but like many of my kin, I only speak the language of our fathers, and occasionally Italian."

"Si, padre." Hunter said, then couldn't help but lean forward. "But I have many things to ask."

The Abate raised a hand to stop him. "Of course, you do, but it is my turn. How else am I to ascertain if we should answer your questions, unless you answer mine?"

Behind the gentle words, Hunter saw the unyielding stubbornness of the Abate on this point, and he sat back reluctantly.

"Good. Now first, our friend Maurizio tells me you used a defensive shield similar to the Donili's. How?"

"It's a long story." Hunter sighed. "I'm a witch-hunter with the British Malleus Maleficarum Council. We discovered a long time ago that the sons and daughters of witch-hunters were born with certain advantages against witches and magic. Just small things really, they are faster, stronger, can perceive the use of magic and are immune to some spells - improving with each generation.

"I'm a 7th generation and a few years ago I was - ah - awoken to the fact that I could do *more*. I could travel anywhere in a blink; I can shield and block magic…"

Hunter broke off, there was more to it than a few tricks, his ability to shield himself and others had been a major factor in every battle. But Hunter was sure he was capable of more, there were times that things - inexplicable things - happened; what else could it be but an unconscious use of his power. He had a sudden image of a crumbling church, dead witches half-buried under the rubble. It was a dark and terrifying scene, but if he could harness that particular power, it would surely shift the balance of power away from the witchkind.

"Are there many like you?" The Abate asked, breaking into Hunter's thoughts.

"No." Hunter replied. "I'm the only one. That's why I came to find - well, you. There's so much I need to learn. And… and for your help."

The Abate brought his hands together and looked over his steepled fingers at Hunter, his bright blue eyes very serious.

"Certamente! We dedicate our lives to helping others. But the help they receive depends on the path they are willing to take." The Abate said cryptically. The old man then frowned, an edge of suspicion in his voice when he spoke again. "Surely the help and learning you seek are the same thing?"

Hunter dropped his gaze, suddenly inspecting the dirt on his hands, before remembering he was an English gent and witch-hunter and should not fear being assertive with anyone.

"Padre, I come to you as a representative of the Malleus Maleficarum Council. It cannot have escaped your notice that we are at war against the witches. I come to ask you to help us in any way you can. Become our ally and help us drive away the shadows."

The Abate sighed, as though Hunter had confirmed his low expectations.

"No."

The single word surprised Hunter. One word, with no deliberation or uncertainty.

"No?" Hunter repeated, as though the meaning of the word eluded him. "Can't you… will you at least consider it?"

"Signor Astley, we are not fighters, we are monks, we protect life. Oh, I am sure you have what you consider valid points to argue, but on this point, I will not be moved."

"You say you protect life - then protect those worldwide that are threatened by witches. Give your protection to those that will fight for a better world." Hunter leant forward; his speech impassioned.

But the Abate looked unimpressed and did not respond to this request. Instead he turned quite calmly to the other two old men in the room.

"Forgive my selfishness brothers, in hogging all the words. Perhaps you could voice your opinions to Signor Astley's request."

Hunter blinked, looking to the other aged monks that he had near forgotten.

The unknown monk spoke first. "Whether we are the shield or the sword, we shall not enter this bloody battle. Our prayers would be ignored, and our souls scarred if we stood by and watched you and your kin killing, knowing that we were the ones that enabled such murder and massacre."

Hunter could give no reply to such an answer; how could he, he'd just been labelled a murderer. He was surprised at how forgiving the Donili sounded about witches - surely, they couldn't turn a blind eye to such an evil force. Surely, they had been fighting witches even longer than the MMC.

"How can we help those that would turn on us?" Maurizio finally spoke, "It happened once before, when your people discovered a power, they did not understand in the Benandanti. The Donili have long memories."

Hunter looked with surprise at the old monk, for some reason feeling betrayed by Maurizio's harsh and unfair prejudice. How could they hold a grudge over something that happened five hundred years ago? Back when the MMC was a very different entity, its witch-hunters narrow-minded and devout on a religious scale. The modern MMC were much more controlled, fairly ruled by strict codes and laws. But... there came a seed of doubt. Hunter flashed back to when he had discovered his own unnatural powers, he'd been torn with fear that he would be condemned, even by those he called friends, so much so that he nearly kept this huge defensive bonus a secret as he and the other witch-hunters prepared for a suicidal battle against the Shadow Witch.

"That's ridiculous." Hunter retorted with a shake of his head, arguing against his own thoughts as much as the monks' words. He took a deep breath, frustrated, and ran a hand through his straggly hair. "It's not like it was, things have changed; the whole world has changed. I've travelled so far and seen so much, if you would just listen and-"

"We believe you, Signor Astley." The Abate interrupted curtly. "Indeed, you look so tired from your travels and troubles. Perhaps you would like to rest and gather your thoughts before we speak again."

At his words, Hunter felt a wave of tiredness wash over him, and was immediately suspicious of the three monks that sat with him. Hunter frowned and fought the fatigue.

"No, I don't need to rest, I need to keep moving." He stumbled over the words, concentrating on keeping his Italian fluent. "I must keep moving... they cannot be allowed to find me. I must move on to find those that *will* help."

"No, Signor Astley, I think you need to sleep." The Abate said with quiet confidence.

And Hunter felt the darkness of unconsciousness sweep him away.

**Chapter Three**

Normally Hunter's sleep was so fragmented, as he pushed himself daily beyond exhaustion. But in this forced slumber he slipped deeper and deeper.

*The colours were so bright and beautiful, as they only can be on a glorious spring day in the English countryside. The trees were in that transitional stage where the leaves gleamed green against the blossoms on the branches, waiting to fall. The sun was low and still hot, but the slight breeze was a cold reminder of the winter that was always slow to leave.*

*Hunter pushed open a small painted, wooden gate and stepped into a garden that was a half-tamed wilderness. With no control of his movements he walked up the garden path to a picturesque country cottage that inspired a vague sense of familiarity. When he reached the oak door, he opened it without hesitation, surprised at the feeling of possession that was sparked as he stepped over the threshold.*

*Hunter moved through the modern interior of the old cottage, wondering whether he'd ever visited this place in his life, and why he should feel so at home.*

*The cottage was quiet, but as he stepped into the living room, he found that it wasn't empty. A woman was standing at the opposite end of the room, as tense and expectant as he was. She was dressed casually in jeans and a simple maroon jumper. Her dark brown hair was pulled back into a careless ponytail, and her face was so beautiful and her eyes so sharp.*

*Sophie, the name leapt up Hunter's throat, but he didn't utter a sound. He just stood there, stupidly still and silent. It unnerved him that, even after all this time and chaos, his heart still leapt and he felt irresistibly drawn to this woman that had seemed so special, so important to him. But still he didn't speak, he didn't trust himself.*

*"Hunter?"*

*Hunter smiled; oh, his imagination was doing a good job of representing Sophie. That voice, quiet but confident. The expression on that beautiful face, an enquiring frown that gently creased her brow, and no compassion to be seen.*

*"Hunter, what's wrong?" She asked, before sliding onto the settee with natural grace.*

*Hunter was not in complete control but sat down next to her, his eyes not leaving her face, feeling suspicion and desire in equal measure.*

*"You need a shave." Sophie teased, with that familiar sneer that was the closest she ever got to smiling. To make her point she ran her left hand across the side of his face, her fingers gently stroking the coarse hair growing there. "You don't suit a beard."*

*Hunter felt an electric shock at her cool touch, and his hand flew to lay across hers. This all felt so comfortable, so familiar, Hunter experienced a sense of longing. Why couldn't he have this in his waking life, in a homey cottage with a beautiful woman.*

*He caressed her hand, his brow creased as he felt an unknown band of cold metal, then his eyes widened with understanding. A young, sharp cry rang across the room...*

Hunter woke with a start. His heart was pounding in his chest, but for once it wasn't with fear. The dream clung to him and he was disorientated as he opened his eyes. It took a few long moments for him to realise where he was - or where he should be - the last thing he remembered was that damn monk. He knew he was in a bed, with a soft mattress and light blanket, which seemed a safe place to be. Lying still, he was so wonderfully comfortable, and warm, and definitely not ready to be wide-awake. It's Sunday, Hunter thought lazily, it must be Sunday.

Quite happy not to move, Hunter ran through his dream, which was still bright and clear in his mind. He didn't often dream, and when he did his subconscious always steered clear of featuring Sophie Murphy, the human face of the Shadow Witch.

Hunter was slightly agitated by the whole happy feeling of the scene, compounded by the cry that had woken him - that cry had been one of joy, and he was pretty sure it hadn't come from either Sophie or himself.

Slowly his senses were reawakening to the world. To the bright light that filled the room, to the sound of birds outside... to the sound of another person's breathing inside.

Hunter jerked up and turned, getting twisted in the bed sheets in his rush to rise. But the haste was unnecessary. There was another narrow bed in the room, and upon it sat Marcus, legs crossed and calmly reading.

Quite unhurriedly, Marcus finished reading the page, then gently closed his book.

"I was thinking you would never wake." He said in his heavily accented English.

Hunter looked up to see the young man was only teasing.

"How long have I been asleep?"

"Twenty-four hours, signore. It is after noon." Marcus replied calmly.

Hunter swore beneath his breath and collapsed back on the bed.

Marcus smiled at the Englishman's reaction. "The Abate did not want you disturbed; he say you need rest. He also say when you wake, I am to give you a tour and give answer to your questions."

Hunter turned his head to look at the young man. "That's very kind of you."

Marcus smiled and waited patiently as Hunter pulled himself together and traipsed off to the washroom. When Hunter came back, he was clean and alert.

"Let's go." He simply said.

The Abbazia di Donili was old and strong, and somehow warm from years of sun on the white and brown stonework. The place sprawled across the hillside on several levels; it was a long walk from the accommodation quarters where Hunter had slept, through the corridors and courtyards, all clean-cut and well-kept. There were large rooms of varying yet specific use.

Marcus kept up a running commentary of the design and use of the buildings, only pausing to search for the correct word in English, often resorting to Italian.

Hunter listened, eager for any and all information, but his attention caught every time another monk passed them by. He couldn't help being curious about the many people that lived and trained in this abbazia.

"How many monks are there?" Hunter asked, breaking Marcus' monologue.

Marcus paused, thinking for a moment. They'd reached the foot of stone steps that Marcus promptly led up. Hunter followed, and soon stepped up onto a high walkway, with the hot sun shining brightly from above, and most of the abbazia laying out before them.

"There are perhaps fifty in the abbazia, and fifty in the town. The children of the Donili join the abbazia when we have thirteen years. We train, we pray and protect. Until we leave the abbazia to marry and have our own children." Marcus spoke calmly of this organised life, he leaned casually against a stone wall and gazed down at the green courtyard below.

Hunter followed his gaze and noticed a couple of monks going calmly about their business. Hunter frowned, suddenly realising something as he looked at the young slender 'monks' with their dark hair tied back.

"There are women?" He gasped. "In a monastery?"

Marcus laughed at the Englishman's amazement. "Certamente! The Donili daughters learn with the sons. It was common for male and female to live and pray together, a long time ago."

Hunter thought back on what he knew - or what he thought he knew, of the Benandanti. They were recorded as an anti-witch breeding cult, propagating and honing the genes that allowed them to repulse witches. A good idea in theory, but

Hunter couldn't imagine a less appealing life, amorously. He'd experienced a variety of women and relationships, from his childhood sweetheart whom he'd stuck with for convenience; his infatuation with Charlotte while at university, and so many meaningless dalliances. His thoughts stopped short before they arrived chronologically at Sophie, last night's dream still haunting the recesses of his mind.

"Will you have to marry one of them?" Hunter asked with a vague nod in the direction of the female Donili.

Marcus hesitated, looking at Hunter carefully. Then the young monk shrugged. "I do not know yet. I marry a Donili, or a girl from the village, or a girl from somewhere in Friuli. I do not know. Whoever I choose must be approved of by the Abate and the elders. But not for years, perhaps. I am happy training and doing my duty."

Hunter felt slightly uncomfortable. "Sorry, I didn't mean to ask something so personal."

Marcus looked away, but smiled, accepting the apology. "The Abate says to answer all your questions. You must be special, Signor Astley."

"Call me Hunter, please. And I'm not special." He said, modesty forcing him to voice the lie. Oh yes, he was very special, no matter how you looked at it.

"Hunter." Marcus repeated with a nod of his head. "It is nearly time for prayers. We will go down and join the others."

Marcus led back down to the lower level and along a stone pathway to the large church that was the head or heart of the whole abbazia. Inside the church opened up to a large, cool hall. They walked slowly between the rows of benches, and Hunter stared at the beauty of the architectural arches and the statues that stood watch. Beside him, Marcus would murmur the name of a particular saint or other; Sant Antonio; San Guiliano; San Pietro; all in hushed tones.

At the far end of the church the altar rose out of the ground, a large stone table. But behind was something to catch any man's attention. The walls were decorated in a brightly-coloured fresco. Staring up at it, Hunter could depict several suitably saintly men and women, standing with their hands placed serenely on their breast. But one picture drew his eye, a building struck by lightning.

"What-?" Hunter's voice failed as he pointed to the section of the wall bearing the image.

Marcus came up beside him and looked at the fresco. "Ah, that is importante. The old abbazia, hit by fulmini - lightning - and destroyed, in the year 1131 AD. We build again, naturalmente."

"Why should that be important?" Hunter asked quietly, not wanting to offend what they might consider vital.

But Marcus did not reply, the young monk had turned away and now bowed at the approach of another.

"Signor Astley." Came the voice of the Abate. "I hope you have enjoyed your tour, and Marcus has been helpful."

Hunter turned to see the Abate; the old monk was dressed in red and white robes, ready to lead his kin in prayer.

Hunter bowed to him, respectful of the position the man held as a representative of god. "Si padre, grazie."

The Abate looked at Hunter with an assessing gaze, his bright blue eyes very thoughtful. "Yes, we will speak properly after the service."

Hunter and Marcus both bowed as the Abate passed them by, Hunter felt his heart beat faster, harder, affected by the power of the old monk's office.

Hunter remained seated as the rest of the congregation filed out. As the church finally emptied, he got up and made his way back up to the altar to the fresco. The image of the lightning-hit church reminded him of the tower in a deck of tarot cards - a sign of disaster that overturned the old and welcomed the new. Unfortunately, Hunter could not remember whether it was a good sign or bad.

He sighed, shaking his head at his own thoughts. Tarot and other fortune-telling methods were the tools of wiccans, a laughed-at semi-religious sect that had been scorned by witches and witch-hunters alike, whom had seen true magic and power. If Hunter was seeing non-existent wiccan signs, it meant that Jonathan had succeeded in educating the stubborn witch-hunter.

Hunter took a deep breath to counter the pain of the direction of his thoughts. The wiccans had suffered greatly in the new regime. They had gone one of two ways; the darker obsessives had fallen to worshipping the real witches, fawning at their feet in hope of a taste of seductive, addictive power; the harmless majority had tried to use their practices to protect against, or even overpower the witches. Hunter had even managed to become friends with some of them, had started to respect them… before the Shadow Witch and her followers killed them.

"You admire our décor, Signor Astley?"

Hunter turned, taken by surprise at the old monk's silent approach. "Si, padre. The image of the old abbazia is very interesting."

The Abate came to stand beside him, gazing calmly at the familiar pictorial representation of the Donili's history. The old monk continued in Italian. "Ah, the old abbazia. Destroyed in 1131."

"So, Marcus told me. Destroyed by lightning."

The Abate smiled sadly. "How polite of him. It was actually destroyed by magic. The monks that survived the attack went on to discover all they could about witches and rebuilt the Abbazia di Donili, promising to protect the innocent people of the surrounding country. They could never have predicted that, after a few generations, certain skills would awaken within them."

"That was the origin of the Donili?" Hunter asked, amazed. The order of Donili evidently began three hundred years before the Malleus Maleficarum was set up; and they had been honing their skills since the very beginning, whereas Hunter was the first known witch-hunter in six hundred years to develop similar anti-witch power.

But that might have to do with the Donili's passive stance on witches, Hunter realised bitterly. They never brought on the outright wrath of witches that destroyed the witch-hunters' every bloodline, which was why no witch-hunter had ever reached the 7th generation before.

"Indeed." The Abate confirmed. "Come, let us walk in the sun before evening meal."

Without waiting for a response, the Abate led out of the church and into the courtyard. The bright spring sun was warm and blindingly low.

"I have been speaking with the other elders about what to do with you, Signor Astley." The Abate started, gazing out across the courtyard, rather than facing Hunter. "Your violent attitude towards witches, and your pride, both put you in bad stead. But the fact that you are so alike us in power enforces a certain responsibility on our shoulders. Indeed, it would be preferable that you learn here and perhaps tame your temper, rather than by experimenting alone."

Hunter stood quietly beside the old monk. As his character was slighted, he felt that same pride rear up, and he couldn't help but smile at that particular truth.

"And did you reach a decision?" Hunter asked mildly. During the service, he'd used the time to assess his position. He was no longer the renowned witch-hunter with the MMC to back him; no longer was he surrounded by loyal companions that would follow his every command, even if they thought it a bad idea; no longer lord of the manor with an extensive estate. He wasn't even special compared to these monks. The Abate had proven that by so effectively and easily knocking him out yesterday. And Hunter knew that he wouldn't get his way in this place by force or argument.

"Yes." The Abate replied. "You may stay; you will train with the young monks. As long as you do not try to persuade the others with your ill-formed prejudices. Do you accept?"

Hunter hesitated, but this was likely to be the best deal he would receive.

"Si, padre." He murmured, with a bow of his head.

## Chapter Four

After breakfast the next morning, Hunter followed Marcus down another identical corridor in the sprawling abbazia, heading to his first lesson.

"Catalyn teach you, today." Marcus explained, his English slow and broken. "Manipolazione di elementi, it is basic, but necessary."

Manipulating elements? It sounded far from basic to Hunter.

Marcus noticed the look of apprehension cross Hunter's face, and he patted his new friend on the shoulder. "Catalyn is good teacher, you will see."

Hunter nodded. "So, will you be joining us?"

"No Hunter, you will join the other novices." Marcus replied, his brown eyes flashing with amusement. "I will see you at dinner."

Hunter narrowed his eyes at the younger man's comment, but opened the door, stepping into what was effectively a classroom.

And immediately stopped in his tracks.

There were half a dozen students that turned to look at him. By their fresh faces, Hunter guessed they were only thirteen at the most. Hunter half-turned, but found Marcus blocking his escape.

"Seriously?" He hissed.

Marcus grinned, not understanding the word, but understanding the sentiment perfectly. "Catalyn - un nuovo studente."

A woman in her fifties drifted over, her eyes flicking over Hunter in assessment. "You must be Signor Astley." She commented in Italian.

"Please, call me Hunter."

"Join the others please, Hunter." Catalyn gestured to the others that stood in the middle of the room. "Grazie Marcus, I shall take it from here."

Hunter's shoulders drooped and he walked over to his 'classmates' as they milled in the middle of the room with the restlessness of youth. They all looked curiously at the Englishman, their scrutiny adding to Hunter's discomfort.

"Today we will be completing the practical of yesterday's theory work." Catalyn stated in quick Italian. She paused, her eyes turning to Hunter. "Normally I have students start with earth or water manipulation. But as you join us mid-course, we will see how you cope with fire."

Catalyn held out a hand and with a mere moment's concentration, a flickering flame hovered above her palm.

"Greta, what part of the air around you is responsible for manipulation of movement, and stops you getting burnt?" Catalyn asked, as the fire moved into a ball and hovered higher.

"Um, oxygen?" The girl replied.

The rest of the class tittered, and one of the boys raised his hand.

"Carbon dioxide. Oxygen is for the manipulation of size." He rattled off, looking at Greta with superiority.

"Good Francis. Now catch." Catalyn smiled and with a flick of her fingers, the little ball of flame flew at Francis.

The boy jumped, startled; but recovered to stop the fire before it hit him. He smiled, setting it spinning in front of him, before sending it across the room to a tall girl.

The girl laughed. Hunter watched, both amazed and discomforted to watch the children play with the fire, like it was nothing more than an ordinary ball. Every ounce of his witch-hunter upbringing screamed that this was an unnatural use of magic.

Noticing his distraction, one of the novice monks sent the fireball at the outsider.

Hunter staggered backwards and felt the searing heat fly past his chest and combust against the wall.

"Now Luca, that wasn't very nice." Catalyn stated in a very neutral voice. "I am sorry, signore, would you like to try again?"

Hunter hesitated, not sure what was going on, nor what he was supposed to do. "I am afraid I need your instruction, Signora Catalyn."

Catalyn looked stumped for a moment, then she brought more fire to life in the palm of her hand.

"Perhaps we should try something else. Come to the table please, Signor Astley." She motioned towards the long table that was the length of the back wall. Immediately a flame flickered from one of the tall candles on it.

"Now, I want you to extinguish the flame." Catalyn stated, breaking off as she heard some of the others chuckling. "Hm, if you will excuse me."

The female monk drifted back to the group, snapping in the Donili dialect that Hunter could not follow what she had said. But from the kids' blushes, he could guess.

Hunter sighed and settled to his task. Catalyn drifted over every now and then, giving tips and advice, but the candle stayed stubbornly alight.

Hunter looked over at the teenagers, feeling a stab of jealousy when one of the youths decided to play keepy-uppy with the fiery ball.

"Luca, stop showing off." Catalyn said, although the woman smiled at the boy's antics.

Catalyn seemed like such an open and easy to read; Hunter found it increasingly awkward whenever she looked at him. The female monk observed him like an interesting experiment.

Not soon enough, the lesson came to an end. Hunter thanked Catalyn and, feeling quite depressed over the whole ordeal, he made his way to the dinner hall.

Upon entering he noticed Marcus sitting with Biagio over to one side. With no better plan, he drifted over to them.

Both monks stopped their conversation and looked up to the Englishman.

"How was your lesson?" Biagio asked, managing to keep a straighter face than Marcus.

Hunter sat down next to Biagio, not saying anything.

"We exercise this afternoon. Many ages." Marcus said helpfully, not bothering to hide his amusement.

Hunter half-smiled but was already starting to regret all that was happening. For so long, finding the Benandanti meant finding answers to all of his questions. He had hoped for support, for miracles perhaps… but not this.

*****

*Hunter walked through the cottage, his hand running over the familiar furniture. He made his way to the living room – as often happens in dreams, he knew who he would meet there.*

*A young child sat on the floor with papers around him. As Hunter entered, the boy looked up guiltily.*

*Hunter noticed the wet paintbrush in his hand. "Adam… what did your mother say about painting indoors?"*

*Hunter's fake sternness slipped further as the boy looked up, with his dark hair and hazel eyes, he was the very image of Sophie.*

*Hunter tutted and picked up the newspaper from the sofa. He spread the broadsheets over the carpet and stepped back, letting his son carry on. Hunter watched the young boy painting with such rapt concentration, as long as Adam was happy, that was all that mattered.*

*"You spoil him."*

*The three words were softly spoken by his ear, as two slender arms wrapped around his waist.*

*Hunter turned his head to glance back at Sophie, taking in her calm and composed expression, her sharp features, the challenge in her gaze.*

*"You shouldn't encourage him." She added.*

*Hunter shrugged. "It's hard not to."*

*Sophie sighed and rested against him, moulding to his back. They stood together quietly for what felt like an eternity, before Sophie spoke again.*

*"Where are you?" She asked, the words barely passing her lips when she suddenly gasped, her arms jerking.*

*Hunter turned and caught her, before she fell into the side table. "Sophie? Are you ok?"*

*Sophie looked very pale, her hazel eyes standing out brightly. She wet her lips to speak. "I don't know... it was pain, just pain." She looked at Hunter accusingly.*

*"It wasn't me." Hunter said. "Maybe you're not allowed to know."*

*Sophie pulled away from him. "Don't be ridiculous." She snapped.*

*"Mummy, can I have more paper?" Adam's voice broke through, the young boy looking up at his parents, the picture of innocence.*

*Sophie glared at Hunter once more, then pushed past him to help her son.*

## Chapter Five

It wasn't too much later when Hunter was summoned to see the Abate. He had been relaxing in the company of Biagio and Marcus, trying to learn more of the Donili dialect when the message came. Hunter was apprehensive, but obediently made his way to the common room of the senior monks.

It was the same room to which Hunter had been brought when he first arrived, but this time only the Abate was present.

"You wished to see me, padre?"

The Abate, distracted by a heavy book, looked up. "Ah, Signor Astley. Please sit down."

Hunter did so, sliding into the comfortable armchair, with a sudden feeling of déjà vu. He looked across at the padre, aside from when leading the monks in prayer, Hunter had not seen the Abate, who left the teaching of novices to the other seniors.

"Now, how are you getting on?" The Abate asked, his bright blue eyes locking on Hunter.

"Very well, thank you, padre." Hunter replied quietly, and not quite convincingly.

"Really?" The Abate asked sceptically. "Aurelio tells me that you lack attention and Catalyn says you do not connect with the other novices."

Hunter grit his teeth. So, this was why he was here, to be castigated like an overgrown schoolboy? I am twenty-eight years old, came the bitter thought.

Although he hadn't said a word in reply, the Abate suddenly laughed at Hunter. "Your pride and your arrogance work against you, Signor Astley. Perhaps you have been spoiled by your heroic deeds and respected image. You are too sure of yourself and cannot take criticism. Trust me, there will be a time when you are fifty, or sixty, and you will laugh at your obstinate younger self."

Hunter sat, tense and silent. Yes, he may be proud and arrogant and aware of it, but it didn't help to be laughed at.

"I do my best, padre."

The Abate waved away his pathetic response. "Perhaps your pride is attached to some of your deep-rooted beliefs. Now you are here, perhaps we can break them both. What are you?"

Hunter frowned, honestly confused. "What do you mean?"

"It is a simple question." The Abate replied with a knowing smile, then repeated, slower. "What are you?"

"A witch-hunter." Hunter said without thinking.

The Abate shook his head. "No, you choose to be a witch-hunter. It was most likely a forced decision, but you could have chosen not to hunt witches. What are you?"

Hunter shrugged, not understanding this game. "A human." He tried.

The Abate considered this before responding. "A human? Yes, you could argue that. But you aren't the same as those we call human in any ordinary sense. Hm, for example, I am Donili, a different class of human. What would you call yourself?"

"An anti-witch." Hunter replied hesitantly, voicing the term he'd often used amongst the Malleus Maleficarum Council and other witch-hunters.

"Anti-witch?" The Abate repeated. "I do not understand this term, please explain it."

When Hunter obeyed, the Abate smiled. "Anti-witch. Yes, I like this term. But to understand it fully, what is a witch?"

Hunter frowned, finding this all too patronising. But he played along, quoting almost word for word the definition that was in the modern Malleus Maleficarum - the witch-hunters' handbook. "A witch is a man or woman that can wield magic and is born of at least one witch parent. They are a sub-human species recognised as *homus maleficarum*. As such they have every appearance of being human and can cross-breed.

"A witch is born with latent powers that emerge at some time between childhood and puberty. These powers are varying in strength and use, from controlling natural forces; creating illusionary and solid threats; dominating the minds of men; and many other varied and inventive ways of undermining the natural order of a magic-free world."

"That is enough, Signor Astley." The Abate didn't look too pleased at the official MMC opinion, and to be honest, Hunter had stressed certain points, half hoping to open the Abate's eyes to the real world.

"If you want my opinion, and I know you won't like it." The Abate stated. "Anti-witches and Donili have a lot more in common with witches than normal humans."

Hunter's eyes blazed at this. "We are nothing alike. It is like comparing the Night and Day and saying they are the same because they are opposites."

He was angry at this assumption, it clashed against everything he'd ever been taught, everything he'd experienced, had learnt for himself.

*Sounds like magic to me.* The voice came rushing from the past, and he remembered it so clearly, how Sophie had dared to say such a thing, and his and James' responding anger at such outrageous thinking. But Hunter finally saw it in a new light. After all, it was not he, but Sophie, that had discovered the nature of the witch-hunter's evolution into something that rivalled the witches they fought. How much had she known, there in the library, when her questions gained an extra fervour? Had she already guessed what was in store for Hunter; Sophie already binding his affections to her.

"That argument did not spare the Benandanti from persecution." The Abate's voice pulled Hunter back to the present.

"That was four hundred years ago. Things are very different now." Hunter replied, irritated by the Donili's refusal to drop this grudge.

The Abate sat back in his chair, observing Hunter. He sat silently for so long that Hunter began to think this uncomfortable meeting was over. But then the old monk spoke again.

"You are an anti-witch that chooses to hunt witches. I am a Donili that chooses to be a monk. Do you not think that witches choose their own paths also?"

"No." Hunter replied quickly and honestly. "They are inherently evil and think nothing of killing and torturing and destroying anything that displeases them. They are addicted to power, whether it is power over populace, or the power they gain internally by draining the life of a sacrifice."

The Abate nodded, considering this. "So, you have never met a witch that was good?"

"No." Hunter replied again, too quickly this time. Unbidden, his mind dredged up one figure, a witch named Beverley who had risked everything to save Hunter and James from the Shadow Witch and her followers. Even more amazing was the fact that Beverley was Sophie's mother. But dear old mum had her reasons - she feared the torment it would cause Sophie if she had to kill the man she loved.

"Witches have their reasons for everything they do - even mercy."

"Well, I think I will let you think over all we have said." The Abate said, almost affably. "I think we should have more of these debates, it is most invigorating."

Hunter, taking this as a dismissal, rose and after a courteous nod of his head he left swiftly. He did not look forward to another tête-à-tête with the Abate, he was disturbed by the awakening of old memories, and of the harsh contradictions against everything he knew in this world.

## Chapter Six

Over the following week, Hunter did his best to learn the new role he had been set. Getting up before dawn every morning for an exercise regime that required utter control of the body and precision, Hunter had not thought that such practices were carried out this far into the western world. This was followed by breakfast and morning prayer, led by the Abate or another senior monk. The rest of the day would be devoted to understanding their skills, both theoretically and physically, only to be broken by meals and prayers. In the evenings they were free to meditate but were encouraged to read history and foreign languages.

Hunter was still irked by the fact that he trained alongside boys and girls that were ten years his junior. But soon he relaxed, comforted by having a regulated day. Also, after being put in his place by one or two of the 'juniors' that obviously possessed more skill than he did, made Hunter re-evaluate himself.

It was true that the young Donili had been training all their lives, but Hunter still felt wounded by the fact that he was the dunce of the class. He listened to the droning voices of his teachers with the same enthusiasm he'd had in those dreary Oxford lecture halls. The monks placed so much importance on theory, on the background and morals attached to every detail. And Hunter sat, impatient to test himself and improve, to get on with the whole damned reason he was here.

As the Abate had promised, he sought out Hunter again, insisting that the Englishman accompany him on a walk.

Hunter was somewhat relieved to have the excuse to get outside, the old abbazia soaked up the sun, and the air was stifling with the first heat wave of the year. The monk and the witch-hunter walked along the top of the wide walls that encased the Abbazia di Donili.

"How are you settling in, Signor Astley?" The Abate asked.

"You tell me, padre. You have your monks making reports on me." Hunter replied in a dull tone.

The Abate gave Hunter a shrewd look. "My fellow monks can tell me of your progress. They cannot tell me how you feel, George. I am guessing that you are still less than happy."

Hunter opened his mouth to argue but thought better of it.

"Correct me if I am wrong, but is this not where you want to be?" The Abate asked. "Why so unhappy?"

Hunter felt a flush of guilt. "No, it is padre. I am honoured that the Donili have accepted to teach me. It is just the frustration of being so inadequate compared to the others."

The Abate stopped and leaned against the parapet, looking down over his abbazia. The older man stood quietly for some time, until Hunter began to wonder whether this meeting was over.

"Naturally the Donili have tried to teach you the basics. But by all reports, you struggle with the simplest tasks."

Hunter grit his teeth, reminding himself of his previous promise of humility.

The Abate looked up to read the expression Hunter could not entirely hide. On another occasion, it might have amused the Abate; but now he was only concerned.

"You misunderstand my concern, Signor Astley. Tell me, how are you able to shield against magic?"

"I don't know, it just happens. It's a reaction that becomes an extension of me." Hunter said, thinking of how many times he had explained it to James, to the MMC, to the wiccans… he still didn't understand it, hence seeking the monks for answers.

Hunter sighed and leaned against the wall next to the Abate. "Why does that matter? Surely the Donili know both the theory and practice of such a thing. I saw Maurizio and Marcus use a shield when I first met them."

"Si, certamente. It is a useful defence we teach to all of our monks." The Abate replied. "But you never *learned*. And unless you were grossly exaggerating the part you played – you stopped a *Shadow Witch*."

Hunter shrugged, no he had never learned, per se. He had simply opened his mind to the possibilities, and there it was. After that, it was just like any muscle: the more he practised, the better his control.

"Do not shrug your shoulders at me, George. Your Shadow Witch is magic without limits, perhaps the Donili monks together could repel her."

Hunter glanced over at the Abate. Now that sounded impressive. "So, you're saying that I am powerful, even by

Donili standards?" Hunter asked, both thrilled and disappointed. It was always nice for his ego to have his skills praised. But at the same time, Hunter couldn't help thinking that he had come to the Donili seeking an ally stronger than himself – one that would succeed where he had failed.

"You are as weak as a child born yesterday." The Abate replied curtly. "Except for your gift with shields and transporting yourself and others."

Hunter gazed out without taking in any of the scene. So, he was a freak here too? "Have you any theories as to why?" He asked reluctantly, not sure he wanted the answer.

"It may be a simple matter of genetic diversity." The Abate answered, his voice betraying how he was not sold on the idea of his brothers. "Your family evolved in a different country with different pressures. It is perfectly possible."

Hunter accepted this easily enough but waited to hear the rest of what the Abate had to say.

"The more fanciful of us think that your powers are linked to the Shadow Witch. She has chosen – probably unconsciously – to connect with you."

Hunter jerked straight, as though stung. "Why should what happened between Sophie and I – I mean, the Shadow Witch and myself – have any bearing on my abilities?"

The Abate smiled at the younger man's reaction. "Think, signore, you can protect yourself against magic and bullets; when you are incapacitated by loss you unlock a very destructive, but very defensive power; you can transport yourself anywhere – which is a unique ability of the Shadow, no? And Signor Astley, we must accept that you only came into your powers after you became close to Sophie."

"Yes, because she was the one who opened my mind to such an idea!" Hunter argued. He pinched the bridge of his nose, trying to stem the headache that suddenly kicked in. "So, I'm basically the Shadow Witch's toy? Are you telling me that I'm nothing like the Donili?"

"I cannot imagine you being anybody's toy, Signor Astley." The Abate replied with dry humour. The old man sighed. "I believe that as a 7th generation witch-hunter you are capable of using anti-magic, although not as naturally skilled as the modern Donili. Perhaps you are more like the Benandanti were four hundred years ago. It is just your fate to be linked with the Shadow Witch."

"Fate?" Hunter echoed.

"You do not believe in fate? That there is a bigger picture in which the threads of our lives entwine?"

"Not really, padre." Hunter answered honestly. "I like to believe that I am in charge of my own life."

"Good!" The Abate replied, surprising Hunter. "God has enough to do; we should not just sit back and let the tide of time carry us."

## Chapter Seven

After his meeting with the Abate, Hunter did his best to appear humble and accepting. Outwardly he strove to be open-minded, and as he became more adept at controlling his powers, it became easier to maintain a relaxed persona. But on the inside, he kept his stubborn streak that he was right. Perhaps if this had been a time of peace, he could have considered the possibility that witches could be forgiven. But this was a time of war, and Hunter had seen every person he'd ever been close to killed by witches, he'd seen hundreds of brave men fall, and he wasn't about to stop fighting for their cause - otherwise their deaths would have been in vain.

The Abate and his monks could be as forgiving and pacifist as they liked, it was easy for them, repelling the odd threat from their beloved Friuli home. They didn't know about the wider world in ruins - and sometimes Hunter thought they didn't care.

It was frustrating to stay in this environment, watching the days and even weeks speed by, while the world struggled on.

Hunter felt guilty, in this safe haven. But it was necessary, he told himself repeatedly.

Today had been bearable, after struggling for a month, Hunter had finally succeeded in breaking through the barriers into another man's mind. After a month of straining nothingness, Hunter got a thrill from the sudden web of colour and images that brushed his own consciousness and begged him to look closer. But the Donili monks were forbidden from viewing the private thoughts of others and trained strictly to avoid such temptation. The use of the exercise was used instead to remove memories or plant ideas. Hunter had already seen both uses, without knowing it at the time. During that brief confrontation with witches in the Italian forests, Maurizio had delved into their minds and removed every trace and memory of the Donili monks, of Hunter, of the intended victim and his family; all in the space of a second before transporting them beyond the borders of the Friuli. After his own struggles, Hunter marvelled at the speed and precision of the old monk.

The second time, Hunter had been the victim. The Abate, impatient with his arguments, had invaded his mind and planted the idea that it desperately needed sleep. Hunter yawned at the mere memory of that induced slumber.

Hunter wondered, guiltily, what else could be done with such control. He knew that his teachers, the older monks, wouldn't encourage such questions. Hunter could already see the patronising smile, and the sorry shake of the head whenever he stepped out of line. But just because today's monks were spotlessly clean, unquestioning lambs, didn't mean that previous generations hadn't had such thoughts and had investigated and experimented - even if to only understand the limits better. Their writings were stored alongside many scrolls and heavy books written by the Donili over the last nine hundred years.

And Hunter had access to them. In fact, he told himself, the monks encouraged extensive reading during free time. Of course, that didn't stop him taking the precaution of reading in the privacy of his room.

He sat in front of the fire, the books and papers scattered around him. Hunter wrapped the blanket tighter around him, trying to block out the biting winter that invaded the draughty old abbazia.

Suddenly his door was flung open, the fire stuttered in the cold wash of air, and a figure stood in the doorway. Hunter started, one hand darting to the metal dog tags that hung around his neck, the other to his side, instinctively reaching for the gun he no longer wore.

"You are nervous, Hunter." The man said, unravelling the scarf from his face.

"Bloody hell, Marcus, you made me jump." Hunter gasped, looking up at his friend. "Close the damn door, it's freezing."

Marcus pushed the heavy door shut, then turned back to Hunter with an air of suspicion. "What are you doing?"

"Just reading." Hunter replied calmly, gathering a few errant sheets. "The Abate encourages us to read."

Hunter drew the open books to him with feigned innocence, but Marcus moved quickly and picked up a thin volume. His eyes darted along the written word, picking up the topic and frowning.

"I do not think he would approve of this." Marcus muttered, closing the book gently.

Hunter shrugged, gazing into the fire rather than face his friend.

"I stand by my promise not to share my unrighteous views, but I cannot change who I am or why I am here." Hunter said honestly, one hand idly tracing the heretical page. "But perhaps it would be best if you told the Abate nothing of this."

Hunter looked up at Marcus. He was sure the Abate had his monks spying on him and reporting any signs of dissent. The only question was, how far could Hunter trust Marcus. The young monk looked innocent enough.

"You really believe you are doing the right thing?" Marcus asked with a sigh. He frowned and slumped into a chair near the fire.

"Yes." Hunter replied. "If you had seen what I have seen... there would be no question. The witches are more dangerous now than they have ever been. I couldn't stop them from taking over, but I will do anything and everything I can to correct that."

Marcus sat quietly, contemplating this and more.

"How was guard duty?" Hunter asked casually, wanting to change the subject.

Although he was proving a fast learner and naturally gifted, Hunter had yet to go on a patrol with the Donili monks into the Friuli region. It was obvious that the Abate didn't trust him, that he feared Hunter would revert to his violent methods when finally confronted with his old foe.

Part of Hunter regretted this bitterly, for he longed to test his new skills for real. But deep down he knew that he could not promise to control himself.

"Quiet, no sign of witches today." Marcus replied, quite bored with a long cold day's patrol for nothing. "We think that winter has driven the witches back to the comfort of the cities, it is not likely they will roam these sparse hills and valleys."

The two men fell into silence, the only noise the cracking of the fire in the grate.

"You know, there have been so many more confrontations with witches the last few years, compared to earlier times. I was talking to my grandfather about it. I think you are right; they are stronger and more dangerous than ever."

Hunter looked up, surprised. This was the closest any Donili had come to admitting that Hunter's vision of witches had any truth. "You do? Does this... does this mean you're on my side? That you'd be willing to fight?"

Hunter's voice dropped to a whisper over these conspiratorial words. The idea of not being alone when he left the Abbazia di Donili; that he might be joined with both a friend and an ally excited him. And if Marcus were brought on side, others might follow, might open their narrow minds and take up arms. The only niggling thought was Hunter's promise to the Abate, to not try persuading his monks.

Marcus gazed down at Hunter with that familiar, condescending smile that ignored the fact that Hunter was nearly a decade older than him. "I said that I think you are right about the witch threat. That is a very big concession for me. But I will not abandon my home, my responsibilities, and my morals."

Marcus looked past Hunter to the untidy stack of scripture. "I think I should leave you this evening, before the Abate suspects me as a sympathiser to your rebellion."

The young monk stood up, grabbing his scarf from the back of the chair and left with a sorry smile. Another cold gust came through as the door opened briefly, leaving Hunter very much alone.

## Chapter Eight

After this honest exchange, Hunter and Marcus never spoke openly again on their truce. But throughout winter, when guard duty was typically quieter, Marcus began to travel further into towns with the task of meeting and blessing the citizens in his role as a Donili monk. Then he would return to the abbazia and casually tell Hunter about his day, including sharing all the news and rumours he had heard regarding witches.

It gave Hunter a safe link to the outside world, although it was sometimes hard to hear about. It seemed that now they were no longer hampered by the witch-hunters and their allies, the witches were consolidating their position, creating new laws that placed them firmly above the human populace. Each big town and city had been gifted to a particularly strong, or high-standing witch, and they were charged with controlling their borough. Hunter found out that this included providing regular sacrifices from their subjects. The witches had always performed sacrifices, boosting their powers via the draining of life from innocent victims. But now they could act without fear of discovery and persecution.

The worst part of Marcus' news was the sway in public opinion. Now the Malleus Maleficarum Council no longer existed to resist the witches, it was harder for the average person to rally against them. Hunter couldn't blame the normal people that kept their heads down, trying to salvage what they could from their new life, the survival of their families much more important than playing the hero. But it transpired that there were a few ambitious characters that did more than merely survive. They sold their souls to the devil and worked for the witches. It sickened Hunter to learn about this, he longed to be out there, stopping such weasels and unsettling the reign of the Shadow Witch. Each new story hardened Hunter's resolve. He filed them all away and gradually his anger cooled into something stronger and harder.

It became easier to appear unaffected during the day, when surrounded by the other monks, following the same patterns of learning and training. Hunter spent a lot of his time in the company of Marcus and the artistic Biagio. He was aware of the wary glances the older monks sent their way, as though the trio were rebellious youths, about to graffiti or vandalise as soon as none were looking.

Although they followed the rules and said nothing that could be remotely rebellious, there were occasional questions that came up. Biagio in particular was curious about Hunter's culture, what life was like back in England. He would ask constant questions over the towns and cities, the buildings and the lifestyle - which was alien and hard to understand for the innocent monk. Only when they came close to the subject of witches would Biagio's questions falter, his curiosity tempered by the forbidden topic of Hunter's previous career.

Yes, the days went by swiftly and fluidly, in a daze of learning and friendship. But the nights... the nights Hunter would stay up reading until his eyes could no longer focus, desperate to learn all he could, and also desperate to hold off the dreams. They did not come every night, sometimes they only came once a month, but Hunter came to crave and dread them. They were set either at the cottage or in a village, he was always accompanied by Sophie, who continued to look at him with a steady love, and a small, dark-haired boy - their son. Hunter had never seen the child that he had with Sophie, and had only heard vague reports of the Shadow Witch having a son, but in his dream the boy was fleshed out to be an active and beautiful child, who looked like his mother, except with warmer Astley eyes. Adam. That was the name that rang in Hunter's mind every time he saw his son, the name that Sophie spoke out loud. And as time passed, in his dreams Hunter saw the subtle shifts as Adam slowly grew older in real time.

**Chapter Nine**

"How long have you been with us, Signor Astley?"

It was a bright summer day, with the warm sun shining down on the Abbazia di Donili. Hunter stood on the high walkway, looking down the hillside to the town and the shimmering river in the distance. He closed his eyes and breathed deeply the sweet-scented breeze.

"How long have you been here?" The Abate repeated gently.

"Nineteen months, two weeks and a day." Hunter reeled off without hesitation.

It seemed such a long time, and he hated watching each day pass. But each day there was something more to learn, and he became that much stronger.

"How long do you plan to stay?" The Abate asked softly.

Hunter shrugged, "There is so much to learn, padre."

"I know." The Abate agreed. "I have dedicated my life to the Donili, and I cannot claim to know everything. But I wonder if this is where you belong…"

"You want to get rid of me?" Hunter was a little hurt that the Abate might finally be giving up on him. It was true that Hunter always had to work that little bit harder to fit in, he always had to control his temper and hide all his heretical research. It hadn't been too bad a life, until Hunter lost his close friend and almost-conspirator. Marcus had left the abbazia at the beginning of spring to marry and take his place in the village. Hunter thought back on a conversation with Marcus, only a year ago the young monk was focused on his duties and studies and had no desire to leave. But he was so young, a year could drastically change his ambitions.

The Abate gave Hunter an amused glance. "You know that is not true, my son. But I wonder, what are your plans?"

Hunter didn't reply but continued to stare out across the hills as he leaned against the sturdy stone wall. He didn't know what his plans were. During meditation and sleepless nights, he would run over scenes and scenarios, but failed to see what could ultimately work. And the longer he put it off the more daunting a prospect it became.

"You no longer speak of your old friends, your Council, your home. I fear that you are forgetting them and forgetting your reason for coming here."

Hunter sighed. "It's difficult to talk about them, they don't belong here. Anyway, I thought you wanted me to give up my old life. Congratulations, you've won."

The Abate smiled sadly. "Perhaps I did, I wanted you to abandon your violent past and adopt our ways. But I see that you are giving up everything and taking on nothing. What are you afraid of George?"

Hunter looked up, surprised by the use of his Christian name, when the Abate had never strayed from calling him Astley, and the other monks only knew him as Hunter.

"I don't know." He muttered, turning away again. "I'm afraid that the world has moved on and is beyond repair. I'm afraid that they'll think I've abandoned them. Most of all, I don't know that I can actually do anything."

Hunter fell silent, and the two men stood in the spring sunlight as the minutes drew by.

"So, if you think I don't belong here, kick me out." Hunter finally said. "Or I'll devote my life to the Donili, as a monk; or at a word from you I'll marry within the Donili and have children, I am not too old."

Hunter looked to the Abate and there was desperation in his eyes. The Abate stepped closer to Hunter and placed a frail hand on his shoulder.

"I am sure that you would make a fine monk, Signor Astley… if you could give up the inbred self-righteousness of course." The Abate suddenly smiled. "You are thirty-years-old, I am sure you do not need to be told what to do! Very well, my instruction to you is to take the first step. No one can predict the outcome, but don't let that stop you."

Hunter nodded, knowing that the Abate was only saying what he already knew.

"So, the question is, what is your first step?" The Abate asked.

Hunter took an unnecessary moment to think. "The first thing is to head home, preferably without alerting the Shadow Witch. Then I want to find my son."

"Then I suggest you go, my son. There is nothing more we can teach you. You will always be welcome back."

Then the austere Abate did something that shocked Hunter, he reached out and embraced him warmly like a son.

"Grazie, padre." Hunter managed to mumble.

**Ten**

Hunter left the very next day. Now that he had made up his mind he wanted to leave before it became more painful to abandon the comforts of the Donili life. He made a few brief goodbyes amongst the monks and villagers. Hunter wished he could take Marcus, or even Biagio on this new adventure, he had become so accustomed to company and friendship and he was loathe to give it all up again.

But after a restless night's sleep; and a rushed, solitary breakfast, Hunter slung his pack of meagre possessions onto his back and closed his eyes. He had rarely thought of home for a year, but the image of Astley Manor rushed in with such strength and clarity that Hunter almost felt homesick for that brief second before he opened his eyes and the reality of the Manor overwhelmed his senses.

It was cold and dark in the sitting room in which Hunter had materialised. The brittle light of early morning seeped in at the seams of heavy drapes. Hunter's eyes grew accustomed to the dim light and he moved over to the window, peeking through a gap in the curtains. Outside the world was silent; there was no sign of life across the stretch of land that belonged to his family's ancestral estate. From the light and time of year, Hunter guessed that it was not yet 6.00am - he wondered if there were any residents still asleep above his head.

Hunter turned back to the room, there were no obvious signs of habituation; dust covered the surfaces and there was cold ash in the fireplace. Even in the darkness he could see the familiar layout of the room. He hadn't been here for two years and he felt sorry for how he'd abandoned the old place.

Astley Manor was an unusual place. For years the grand estate was owned by the very private and reserved Astley family. The residents of the local village had seen it as part of the landscape, impressive but boringly traditional. Until all hell had broken loose at the Battle of Little Hanting.

People were increasingly aware of the fact Astley Manor was filled with seven generations worth of objects confiscated from witches, all sort of occult and ceremonial items that could be both protective and offensive. There was also the largest privately-owned library on witchkind in the country. The information and artefacts that Hunter had at his disposal rivalled the MMC - no wonder the Council had feared his ability to work independently.

But what was most amazing about Astley Manor was the basic fact that it was still standing. The more successful a witch-hunter was, the more he and his family were targeted by revengeful witches. Families struggled to reach 5th generation status and lived in constant fear of near-inevitable destruction.

But Astley Manor stood untouched for seven generations - and it was hardly a discrete safe house.

Hunter didn't know what enchantments or miracles had been invoked by his ancestors, but no magic could penetrate the borders, and no witch could step onto the estate without having their powers stripped. And no witch would enter a witch-hunter's lair so defenceless - Hunter grudgingly marvelled at Sophie's courage in doing so for so long.

After the witch rebellion, it became the rallying point and makeshift base for witch-hunters after the fall of the Malleus Maleficarum Council. It protected them against magic, even that of the Shadow Witch. But all this protection and information wasn't enough.

Hunter still remembered the evening the witches drove the witch-hunters and their allies from the Manor. The night that Anthony Marks, the leader of the MMC, had sacrificed himself to give the others time to escape.

Hunter didn't know if there was any organised rebellion left. And if there was, he had no idea where they were, and only a vague idea where to start looking.

Hunter heard a creak from upstairs and he tensed, his hand straying to his gun, which felt familiar even after so many months of absence in the peaceful abbazia. There were three possibilities: his charming mother had survived here alone for years; a remnant from the MMC was using the famous Astley Manor; or a witch or two were stationed here in case Hunter or his allies returned. As much as Hunter wished for someone on his side, he pessimistically assumed the worst. After all, Sophie knew him so well, she would definitely station someone here.

Hunter drew his gun and moved silently towards the ajar sitting room door, then slid into the hallway. Quickly glancing up the wide staircase, Hunter took a deep breath and purposefully slammed the door behind him. The sound was booming in the silence and echoed through the familiar corridors. Hunter heard the shuffle of feet upstairs and pressed himself into the shadows, his gun aimed steadily at the stairs.

There was the sound of feet treading slowly and carefully onto the bare boards, more than one person, trying to be silent. In the darkness of the heavily panelled hallway, Hunter detected two figures moving down the stairs. The way they moved and the fact that they carried guns echoed of witch-hunter training, making Hunter hopeful.

"Who goes there?" A voice called out.

Hunter frowned. "You first. Who are you?"

The man whipped around, staring blindly in Hunter's direction. "I am a first gen with the MMC, this property is under the Council's authority, you are trespassing. Now, who are you?"

Hunter watched as the speaker reached the bottom step and stared wide-eyed to try and detect anything in his near-blindness. Hunter, who had no trouble seeing thanks to his 7th gen status, considered bringing a little bit of light to the proceedings; but lord knows where any candles were, and he doubted that this man and his colleague would appreciate a very magical-looking but harmless ball of suspended light.

"I am not trespassing." Hunter replied quietly. "Come into the sitting room and we shall talk."

Hunter turned back to the sitting room and opened the heavy door, before promptly whisking open the curtains to allow in the strengthening morning light. He watched as two men in their thirties stepped into the room, squinting in the sudden light.

"Who-"

"I am Hunter Astley, 7th gen, lord of this manor." Hunter said quickly, cutting across the inevitable question.

The two men stood staring formlessly at Hunter. They obviously hadn't expected that answer.

"Do you, ah, have any ID?" One man managed to choke out.

Hunter laughed, suddenly released from tension and amused at how things were playing out.

"I haven't had identification on me for years - an unfortunate result from being constantly on the move and not wanting to be known, of course." He smiled, oh yes, how handy would that be, if he were caught by enemies that could quickly check his passport to discover who he was. "But if you won't take my word, go to the portrait room. Unfortunately, I don't have one, but if you look at my father's I am sure that you will see the family resemblance."

The two men continued to stand there, looking nonplussed. But one eventually managed to speak.

"We thought you were dead." He breathed. "After the battle of Salisbury Plain, we thought none had survived."

So, it suddenly made sense, why they looked at Hunter like a ghost. He supposed that it was a natural assumption, especially as Hunter had no way to contact any surviving MMC, even if he had thought it safe to do so.

"I am very much alive and well, I've just been off the radar. But who are you, gentlemen?"

"Shaun Williams, 1st gen." The first man replied.

"Jack Lowe, 1st gen." The second man added. "We're part of the MMC, stationed here to defend Astley Manor and its contents for the good of the Council."

"So, the MMC still stands? I feared there would be no organised resistance. Where are they based? Not here, obviously."

"They're currently at a secure base within travelling distance." Shaun Williams replied obscurely.

"I think I should go to them." Hunter suddenly decided; he was likeliest to learn what he needed to know from the MMC directly. "Where are they located?"

The two witch-hunters exchanged a look.

"Sorry sir, we aren't authorised to disclose that." Jack Lowe said formally, "But we can take you."

Hunter paused, considering this offer. He would prefer to blink straight there rather than spend potentially hours in a car. But he doubted he could learn where the MMC were located without breaching the privacy of the witch-hunters' minds. Plus, as he thought about it, blinking and suddenly materialising inside the anti-witch headquarters might not be the most sensible entrance.

"Very well." Hunter said with a brief nod of agreement.

The witch-hunters shared a brief conversation, with Jack taking the task of driving Hunter, and Shaun staying to keep charge of the manor. Jack left the room to get the car ready, leaving Shaun with Hunter. Shaun stood uncertainly, obviously in awe of the legendary 7th gen, returned-from-the-dead, Hunter.

"We're not really supposed to leave only one guard on duty. I mean, we're due to return to base when the next team relieve us, but I'm guessing you'd rather go now, sir." Shaun rambled on.

"It's fine." Hunter cut across, something else on his mind. "Mr Williams, can I ask… do you know anything of my mother? Is she still here?"

Shaun hesitated. "I don't know for certain, sir, but I think Mrs Astley is in MMC care."

Hunter found it hard to believe that his proud and fierce little mother (who had very little respect for witch-hunters) would give up her family home, no matter what the danger. And Shaun's flimsy answer did nothing to comfort him.

Outside there was the rumble of an engine, and Hunter went out towards the drive to find what looked like an old army jeep. Jack Lowe was already sat at the wheel and eyed Hunter curiously as he hopped into the passenger seat.

Jack coaxed the old jeep forward and they crunched over the gravel until they got to the long drive. Hunter looked out at the beautiful, familiar landscape that was his estate. They passed through the village of Little Hanting, a picturesque place that Hunter had always taken for granted.

Hunter sighed, watching the scene pass by - too slowly for his liking. Hunter tried to surreptitiously glance at the speedometer. He frowned as he saw the needle wavering over the 45mph mark.

"Sorry." Jack suddenly apologised.

"What for?" Hunter asked, looking up at the older man. Closer to, Hunter could tell that his initial guess of mid-thirties was a bit young. Jack looked closer to his late-forties, or even early-fifties.

Jack looked back, unconvinced with Hunter's innocence. He nodded to the dashboard. "I'm sure it's slower than what you're used to, but it's MMC rules. Diesel is rationed, so we have to drive conservatively. Not that this old piece of crap could go fast anyway."

"It's fine. It's faster than walking." Hunter replied unconvincingly. What would be faster and more fuel economic would be to blink over there.

They drifted back to an uncomfortable silence that allowed Hunter too much thinking space.

"So… how long have you been a witch-hunter?"

"Nearly two years." Jack replied shortly. The older man glanced unnecessarily in the mirror, and his grip tightened on the wheel. "I joined the MMC after I lost my son to the witches. He was a witch-hunter, see. Fell at Salisbury Plain."

"I'm sorry." Hunter mumbled.

"He was only twenty-year-old, he said he'd save the world or die trying." Jack smiled bitterly at his late son's bravado. "Maybe you met him? Darren. Darren Lowe?"

Hunter saw the gleam of hope in Jack's face, the hope that his son lived on in one more memory, and he felt sorry for letting him down.

"I'm sorry, I didn't." Hunter replied quietly. "There were… so many men and women at Salisbury Plain. I wish I could say I knew him."

"It's ok." Jack mumbled, to himself. "It's ok."

**Chapter Eleven**

The jeep rumbled on for over an hour, until Jack nodded and spoke up.

"Nearly there."

Hunter looked out at the surrounding countryside but saw no sign of life. Jack swung the jeep off the main road and down a private track. Hunter finally saw an old barbed wire fence running around what looked like an airfield. Across the cracked tarmac were a couple of derelict hangars.

"Just... wait and see." Jack said, watching Hunter's expression with amusement. Jack drove straight into the hangar and parked the jeep alongside several vehicles of similar antiquity.

"This way." He jumped out of the driver's seat and led the way to an internal concrete bunker. Jack pushed back his sleeves and grabbed the handle of a small iron door, with a grunt he managed to drag it open wide enough for them to enter.

"After you, just mind your step."

Hunter frowned and stepped into the dark. Immediately before him was a set of steps leading down, faintly lit from far below. Hunter had taken a few steps when he heard the door clang shut behind him, blocking out all daylight.

"The MMC has gone underground. Literally." Jack said as he squeezed past to lead the way.

The faint light grew stronger as they neared the bottom, until they came to its source - a single oil lamp next to another door. Jack paused to pull out a key and quietly opened up.

On the other side there was more light provided by extra lamps. Hunter could see a desk set up with a man and woman quietly discussing some dreary matter. They both looked up at Jack and Hunter's entrance.

"ID?" The woman asked automatically.

"Jack Lowe, 1st gen." Jack replied, handing over an old driving licence.

"Lowe." The woman mused, glancing down at the desk. "You're not due to return for another week. Is there a problem?"

"Not exactly. I had to escort someone here." Jack said. Hunter had the strange feeling that Jack was relishing the moment. "Mr Hunter Astley."

The effect was immediate and a little unnerving for Hunter. The expression on the woman and man's face were identical. Hunter doubted if they could have looked more shocked if Jack had brought along the Shadow Witch, or even Father Christmas.

"H-Hunter? Astley?" The woman gasped. Her eyes flicked over Hunter hungrily, matching the actual person to the name.

She suddenly turned to the man standing gawping behind her. "Go - tell the Council. Go now."

The man staggered away then, with one more disbelieving look at Hunter, he broke into a run and disappeared down the far end of the corridor.

"Um, radios don't work, so the fastest way to send a message is with a runner." The woman explained.

"I know, I remember." Hunter said with a smile.

The woman blushed and looked rather breathless; Hunter wondered whether it was his sudden appearance that caused this reaction, or was his old charm still in perfect working order? It would be flattering if it were the latter.

"Y-you're really him, Hunter Astley?" The woman breathed. "I never thought... I've heard so much about you, we all have-"

Jack coughed in the background, breaking the woman's rambling.

"Oh, sorry. Why don't I take you through to the Council?" She offered with a glowing smile.

"It's ok Lesley, I know the way." Jack said softly to the woman. He clapped Hunter on his back. "Come on, it's this way."

Hunter politely bid the woman goodbye then followed Jack down the corridor.

The underground base was like a warren with numerous corridors and rooms, Hunter could only marvel at the scope of it. As they walked along the empty corridors gradually filled with the faces of people wanting to see Hunter with their own eyes. Obviously gossip and rumours still travelled fast. He heard his name being passed in whispered voices and he felt the energy and excitement that was connected to it.

There was the sound of rushed footsteps and Hunter saw several people rushing towards them. One man pushed in front, limping heavily, but smiling widely.

"It is you! How the hell?!" He laughed and grabbed Hunter, wanting physical confirmation. "You are a bloody miracle."

It took a second for Hunter's brain to process that the person before him was someone he knew. "Toby? Christ, I never expected - I thought you were dead!"

"Likewise, Hunter, likewise."

"It's good to see you again, Mr Astley." A reserved voice broke through.

Hunter looked past his old friend Toby to see another familiar face. "Sergeant Dawkins? It's good to see you too."

"Actually, it's General now." Dawkins commented with a wry smile. "Not that that matters here."

Hunter took a moment to look at his old acquaintances. They looked so worn and aged since he'd last seen them, they had obviously had a rough time these last couple of years, and Hunter felt guilty over his own safe life.

"So, where have you been?" Toby asked.

"Ahm..." Hunter hesitated, aware of all the keen eyes and ears in this cramped corridor. Even after all he'd done, and all he'd learnt, he was still uncomfortable sharing information on his almost-magical abilities. Especially to strangers. And especially in the official witch-hunter base.

There were obviously stories told about him, but Hunter didn't know how accurate they were.

Dawkins accurately read the hesitation. "Come through to the Council rooms, Mr Astley."

It was a relief for Hunter to follow the General to a quiet, empty room. It was lit by the yellow light of an oil lamp on the wall, casting shadows from the table and chairs.

Toby limped over to a chair and dragged it out, dropping into it heavily. Hunter sat opposite him, glancing enquiringly at the leg that stuck out stiffly.

"Broke my leg pretty bad." Toby explained, hitting his thigh with frustration. "Got caught by witches a week before Salisbury Plain - was so mangled I missed the mission. Two years and I'm still limping."

Hunter shook his head, "I still can't believe you're alive! I thought all witch-hunters over the 2nd gen status had been hunted down - especially those unlucky enough to have met the Shadow Witch during her time undercover."

Names and faces of those that had been on the list of the Shadow Witch came to mind; Brian Lloyd, Matt and Dave Marshall... James Bennett. They had made the mistake of making themselves known to Sophie Murphy. Toby Robson, as a 4th gen was also on the list and it was a miracle that he'd survived.

"I can't explain it, I've been lucky." Toby said with a shrug. "Besides, you're still alive and kicking, surely you top every list!"

"Yes, how did you survive?" General Dawkins broke in, the army man leaning against the table. "Where have you been, and why?"

Hunter glanced briefly at Dawkins, before staring resolutely at the wall. "I thought there was no one left. I saw the last of our men fall before I resolved to leave to continue the fight. I was on the run for months, trying to shake any followers."

Hunter paused, taking a deep breath. "You both know what I'm capable of, well I went to find the Benandanti…"

Hunter went on to tell of his meeting with the Donili and explained all the time he'd spent with them and all he had learnt.

## Chapter Twelve

"So, you've finally returned to us?" Dawkins asked after Hunter had finished.

"I had to find out what was going on." Hunter replied, somewhat off-topic, not wanting to admit that re-joining the MMC wasn't on his list of priorities.

"What do you want to know?" Asked Toby.

"Everything." Hunter said with a shrug. "What's the current status of the MMC and its allies. Even what the witches have achieved - I've been out of it for so long."

"Well, the witches are consolidating their position, so we're busy protecting our last strongholds and trying to find their weaknesses. It's not easy. You're right about the MMC, we've hardly any real witch-hunters left, most of the people here are 1st gens. As for the army, well…"

Toby broke off and looked to Dawkins, allowing the General to take over.

"The army is split in two." Dawkins sighed. "The majority are with us, integrated as 1st gen witch-hunters. But there is still a standing British Army - working for the person running Britain."

"The Royal family?" Hunter asked, vaguely hopeful.

"In a secure location in Scotland." Toby said with a shake of his head. "I'm afraid our country's leader is the Shadow Witch and her council."

"That's not good." Hunter muttered.

"No, it's not." Dawkins agreed. "Look, I have rounds to do. Can I leave this to you, Toby?"

Toby assented and the General left with a brief goodbye.

Hunter stared at the closed door. "I remember him being a lot more fun."

"We all were." Toby said bleakly. "Colin was the natural successor after General Hayworth, but he still feels like he has to prove it."

Hunter looked about him at the bland room. "So, what is this place?"

"An abandoned RAF base. We can only guess why there's such an extensive underground run, we can't find any record of its existence - it was either above top-secret, or completely forgotten. It's a miracle we found the place." Toby explained. "We've been using this place for nearly a year now. I miss windows and daylight, but at least it's safe."

"How can it be safe against witches? How can you put the MMC in danger by staying still so long?" Hunter felt his temper rising, angry at his old friend's complacency. Hunter didn't think he had to tell Toby of all people how the witches had chased them out of Astley Manor; out of their bases in Manchester and Newcastle.

"Relax Hunter, it's ok." Toby said, smirking at Hunter's expression. "The witches won't find us here."

"How? How can you know that?" He demanded.

"It's... hard to explain." Toby said with a sigh. "You wouldn't understand unless you saw it for yourself. Then again, I'd love to see what she says to you."

"You are not making any sense at all Toby." Hunter said curtly, very aware that the other witch-hunter was laughing at him.

"Come with me." Toby said, suddenly standing and hobbling to the door.

Toby walked down the corridor with a pronounced limp, and Hunter could feel his excitement.

"I'm going to introduce you to someone very special, Mythanwy Elspeth Lughnasa - but everyone calls her Mel." Toby explained. "She's not a witch, as far as we can tell, but I want you to keep an open mind."

"This isn't filling me with confidence." Hunter warned. "Nor is it explaining anything."

"Look, Mel is... Mel. She found this place, swore it was safe." Toby said, gesturing vaguely with one hand. "And don't look at me like that, Hunter. You just have to meet her to understand. She's very truthful, I don't think she knows how to lie, actually."

Hunter frowned, not liking this, but said nothing as he followed Toby through the warren of corridors and doors. They eventually stopped at a door guarded by a witch-hunter, as they approached, he nodded them through, closing the door behind them.

The room was exactly like the one they had just left, except there was a sofa along one wall, with a neat stack of folded bedding beside it. A table took up most of the space of the room, and at it a young woman was sitting alone, with pale blond hair held back with a blue ribbon. When she looked up, it was with big blue eyes, and seeing her guests she smiled widely.

"Hi Dave!" She gushed, jumping up eagerly.

Toby, smiling in fond response to her enthusiasm, turned to Hunter and explained quickly and quietly. "We don't know who Dave is, she calls all men Dave."

Then he turned back to the girl. "Hello Mel, it's nice to see you again. But my name is Toby, remember. Now, I have someone I'd like you to meet, Mel, this is my good friend Hunter."

Hunter felt his scepticism suspended as he faced the mysterious Mel. It was hard to tell her age, she must have been at least twenty years old, but her open and innocent expression made her look younger. She wore a pale blue blouse, and knee-length white skirt, her outfit modest and old-fashioned. Mel's face lit up as she saw Hunter.

"George!" She gushed, then pouted. "You're late."

Hunter saw that Toby was as confused as he was. So much for every man being called Dave, he could only assume someone had told Mel about his unused Christian name.

"I'm sorry I'm late, Mel." Hunter said slowly, "I didn't mean to be."

Mel smiled again, obviously satisfied with his apology. She stepped up close to him, her blond head barely reaching his shoulder. Mel reached out and gently placed one small, cool hand in his. She bit her lip and rocked up on her toes, so very excited that he was here.

"Sit down, sit down, we shall have tea and cake and all things nice." Mel rambled on, drawing Hunter to the table and chairs.

Mel danced around the table, making sure her two guests were seated before skipping to the door and yanking it open.

"Hello Dave." She trilled to the witch-hunter on sentry. "We're having a tea party. Can you bring the tea? Mother doesn't let me use the kettle; she says I'm clumsy."

"Sure thing Mel." The witch-hunter chuckled, and to Hunter's surprise, the guard left to fetch tea.

"Is she sane?" Hunter whispered to Toby.

Toby shrugged in response, smiling and relaxed. "It doesn't matter." He murmured back.

"Rustle, rustle, little mouse." Mel suddenly popped up between them, joining in the whispering. "We shall have our party, but quietly, quietly, for papa is working and cannot be disturbed."

"Mel?" Toby said, trying to gently get her attention. "Hunter wants to know about this place, why it's safe from witches."

Mel frowned, as she obviously tried to work out who Hunter was. Finally, she looked at Hunter with a vague understanding.

"Georgie Porgie, pudding and pie; killed the witches, made them cry. When the truth came out to play, Georgie Porgie ran away."

"That's very nice Mel, but we came to talk about this place. Be a good girl and tell Hunter."

Mel beamed at Toby with her bright blue eyes and white smile. "Yes, I am a good girl, I always eat my greens and brush my teeth before bed. But witchy-witches aren't always good; sometimes they stay up past their bedtimes, or spill blood on the floor." Mel looked momentarily scandalised at the thought. "Naughty red stains make mother so angry."

Mel got to her feet and moved about the small room, almost with a dancing step, she tilted her head to skywards.

"Starlight, star bright, first star I see tonight-"

"Mel, that's the ceiling." Toby interrupted with the first sign of impatience. "And it's daytime."

"They can hear me." Mel promised. "But the witches can't. Their ears are deaf, their eyes are blind they cannot see, they have not found their specs with me. And in their hidey-holes, the mice are safe and have tea."

As if on cue, the door opened and a witch-hunter entered, carrying a tray of tea. Hunter enjoyed the sight, having been without this very British custom for so long. He leant forward to share a private word with Toby. "You know, I'm not too keen on being referred to as a mouse."

"Me neither." Toby concurred. "But it's just her way of seeing the world."

Mel acted the good little hostess and served the tea, before sitting next to Toby. She gazed unflinchingly at Hunter with those strange, innocent eyes.

"Mel, how do you know that you are right?" Hunter asked carefully.

"I…" Mel hesitated, looking uncomfortable. "I open the book and read the words where no lies can be written. But not everyone likes it. People are scared of me and shoo me away."

Mel took a sip of tea and beamed again, her moods so very changeable, but also infectious. "But Dave is nice to me, and I have so many friends here."

**Chapter Thirteen**

They left shortly afterwards. In the narrow corridor, Hunter found himself wishing he was outside, just to be able to breathe again.

"She's something, isn't she?" Toby asked casually.

Hunter shook his head in disbelief, struggling to find words. "Definitely. I mean... all that nonsense. At least, it seems like nonsense except I felt like she was trying to communicate something to us."

Toby smiled wryly at his friend's attempts to understand. "You see what I mean though, once you hear her you cannot doubt her honesty."

"I know, you're right, I don't think she can lie." Hunter said, pausing and looking back down the corridor. "She's so innocent, childlike even. Yet enigmatic - I swear I'd do anything to keep her safe."

"Don't worry, she has that effect on everyone." Toby said, almost guiltily. "Just be careful. She's an emissary of the truth.

The Truth. Something beyond good and evil, right and wrong. She can be dangerous."

"Dangerous? But you told me to trust her."

"I told you to trust what she says to be true, nothing more." Toby countered.

Hunter sighed, finding this all a little bit hard to assimilate. "So that's why she has a guard, to keep everyone safe? She's effectively a prisoner?"

"No, no, the guard is to keep her safe, and to keep track of who sees her." Toby hurried to explain. "We could never keep her prisoner. She comes and goes as she pleases."

"Isn't that a risk to security?" Hunter asked.

Toby sighed. "We tried to force her to stay once, she got upset and refused to talk to anyone for days. Then one evening she'd vanished, we couldn't tell how, but she wasn't on base and no one had seen her leave. She turned up a week later, as happy and chirpy as though the whole thing hadn't happened."

Toby saw the doubtful look on Hunter's face. "I know, it sounds bloody dodgy, but there's nothing we can do."

Hunter sat in council with half a dozen witch-hunters. The only people he recognised were Toby Robson and General Colin Dawkins. The rest were senior members of the MMC, though none were more than a 1st gen status.

Hunter sat there, listening to them go over the boring fine detail of missions he had no knowledge of. He'd never been a fan of fine detail, of paperwork and dull updates; Hunter used to give such menial tasks to his right-hand man, a very capable 1st gen called James Bennett.

"So, Mr Astley." A stern woman addressed him, "To get straight to the point, what are your intentions? Are you here to help? To assume a role of leadership?"

Hunter felt all eyes descend on him. "I'm not here to take over."

"Then you're here to work for us?" The woman asked doubtfully. "From what we hear of the stories, you don't follow orders very well."

"Theresa…" Toby warned in a low voice.

"No, it's ok." Hunter said, knowing that his past unease with authority was bound to arise. "But that was then, and this is now. I'll be here to help, I'll do what I can, and I will be here to advise, but sometimes I'll have to go my own way."

"You sound like you already have something planned." One man voiced.

Hunter looked round the table, eyeing each member of this Council. He wondered how much to share, how much to keep back.

"The Shadow Witch has a young son." Hunter said, then stopped.

"Devil's spawn." One voice spat.

Hunter looked round with surprise.

"Enough, Mr Andrews, we don't need those common rumours." Toby said, stepping in to mediate again. He then turned to Hunter to explain. "The child was probably conceived during a ritual, but most whisper that his father is the devil himself."

Hunter felt frozen inside, as he wondered how much his old friend knew, or had guessed. More worrying was how everyone would react when the truth inevitably came out. But he would put off that unsavoury moment for as long as possible.

"You have a plan concerning this witch-child?" The woman, Theresa asked.

"I'm going to kidnap him." Hunter said calmly.

The room was deadly silent as the shock statement set in, then suddenly it erupted. Several chairs scraped back, and six voices all clamoured and argued. Hunter sat quietly, patiently waiting for them all to finish their indistinguishable rants, many expletives filling the air.

"Are you finished?" Hunter asked mildly.

"Hunter, you can't be serious." Dawkins said, still standing and leaning across the table to make his point. "Even if such a thing were possible, why would you do it?"

"Surely you can see that we could use him as leverage." Hunter lied. "And if the boy has even half the Shadow Witch's power, he could be very useful. He's still young enough to influence."

Hunter felt a stab of guilt, for lying to these people, and for even daring to say such cruel plans. But all he wanted was his son, safely with him before any real offensives began. If he had to tell a few falsehoods and bend a few rules, so be it.

"It can't be done. Such a mission would be suicide." One witch-hunter argued, struggling to keep his cool.

"I hate to disagree, but I know that I could do it. All I need to know is where the boy is." Hunter spoke with such certainty and authority that the others were momentarily cowed.

"We shall consider giving our permission, Mr Astley." Theresa said coldly, motioning towards the door.

"You're crazy, you know that?"

Hunter was sitting on the floor in the corridor outside the council rooms, he didn't care about the cold or discomfort, he actually liked the distraction. He raised his head out of his hands as he was spoken to. The Council were behind a closed door deliberating his fate. All except Toby, who stood staring at Hunter with sheer amazement. Good old Toby, just like he always had been, he never got mad, even when Hunter contemplated insanity. Would the rest of the Council think he was crazy? Most likely, but they still might let him go ahead with this mission. Not that it mattered how they voted; Hunter had already made his mind up.

"You're crazy." Toby reiterated.

"I'm just doing what I have to do." Hunter replied calmly. "Shouldn't you be with the Council fighting my corner?"

Toby sighed and dropped in down onto the floor next to him, inelegant and awkward. "Dawkins will deliver my vote. As if the others don't know already. I'm a witch-hunter through and through. The legendary Hunter Astley turns up and wants to lead a suicidal mission, I'm in."

"I don't know about legendary." Hunter said with a crooked smile. "And I'm not leading anyone, I'm going alone."

"You can't! I-"

"You are not coming." Hunter said firmly. "I know what you're capable of Toby, you know I respect you, but I can't risk you slowing me down."

At this the amiable Toby swore beneath his breath and cast a dark look down at his bad leg, cursing it. "Fine. Fine, we have others that can go."

"A group of 1st gens?" Hunter asked bitterly. "No thanks."

"They're the best we have." Toby replied in a half-hearted argument.

"I'm not taking 1st gens into the Shadow Witch's lair." Hunter said adamantly. The last thing he wanted was a bunch of ill-trained, noisy and slow wannabe witch-hunters botching his one and only chance to get his son.

"You used to trust 1st gens." Toby said quietly, then glanced anxiously at Hunter. "I'm sorry about your team. And about James, he was a good man."

Hunter tensed, waiting for the familiar lurch of grief and guilt that came whenever he thought of the people that he had lived and worked with for so long. It had been General Hayworth and Anthony Marks that had put them together; Maria, the unflappable Ian, sweet little Alannah, and of course James. They were all ghosts now.

James had been there when Sophie Murphy had appeared on the scene. James and Sophie had never gotten along, and that combined with his friendship with Hunter and his unique authority with the MMC had made James an obvious target. Hunter would always regret not being able to save him in the end.

The Council door flew open, interrupting the uncomfortable silence. General Colin Dawkins walked out unsmiling and went straight over to Hunter.

"You've still got a strong influence, Hunter. You have permission to go." Dawkins said, strangely cold.

## Chapter Fourteen

Hunter didn't waste any time. He insisted on going that night, before the Council changed their mind. Dressed in black, with a balaclava to hand, he felt himself slip into the mode where his actions were reflexive. It felt good that it came so easily after so long.

Even though he was going into the witches' den alone, Hunter left the Warren with ten witch-hunters. They broke the surface and travelled in the cloudy darkness for a couple of miles. It was part of the agreement that Hunter would not blink directly in and out of the safe headquarters in case he could be followed. They made their way across the silent countryside, scrambling over fences and brushing through fields of high grass, Hunter's trousers becoming cold and damp as he strode through. Eventually one of the witch-hunters called out, marking this spot as a safe distance from the warren.

While the others checked the safety of the designated area, Hunter did a self-inventory, then pulled up his hood. He touched the metal dog-tags around his neck for luck, tucking them inside his shirt. Then he was gone.

One second, he was standing in the middle of a dark field, the next he was stood in the middle of a dark field, only a change in direction of the wind to confirm his change of location. Hunter looked up to see an excessive scattering of stars in what was a very clear sky. He looked about to get his bearings, and saw a building hunched in the darkness to the west.

Hunter moved quickly, every nerve tingling, ready to sense guards or traps in the darkness. The house began to loom as he drew nearer, a great black block against the inky, starred sky. Several windows were filled with warm yellow light that flooded out weakly into the grounds.

Hunter sat in the shadows, listening intently, looking, feeling. He was pretty sure most of the house was sleeping, with only those on guard duty awake. He heard the quiet buzz of conversation of two people in the entrance hall. He thought he heard the shuffle of feet that might mean more security pacing corridors.

Hunter moved closer, then crouched by the door. He closed his eyes and opened his mind, reaching out to the two witches in the hall. It was too easy, to break into their minds and distract them. Witches were unprepared to defend against magic, for who would use such skills against them?

Hunter carefully opened the door and slipped inside soundlessly. The two witches stood there, strangely vacant in their expressions as Hunter drifted by. Once he was out of sight Hunter released them, and they took up their conversation, none the wiser that any time had passed.

Hunter headed upstairs, crouching silently in the shadows whenever a guard passed close. He held his breath when one walked particularly close by, he then darted across the corridor as soon as they had gone. Following his gut, his instincts, his heart; whatever it was that drew him along, Hunter slipped into the nursery.

Even in the darkness, Hunter could see the mess of toys strewn across the room. He heard a half-noise and turned to see a female witch rising from a chair. Hunter barely had time to feel panic, before he met her gaze. The witch's eyes fluttered closed and her body slumped. Hunter dashed forward to catch her before she hit the ground with a thud and laid her sleeping self down softly.

He should kill her now, while she was defenceless. After all she'd seen him (balaclava or not), and all his witch-hunter training demanded it. The knife in his belt felt heavy and demanding, but Hunter reluctantly turned away. He wasn't here to fight and kill, he only wanted his son.

The witch had been sitting next to a door, and Hunter opened it, letting himself into the night nursery. There was a small bed in the middle of the room, and there, oh there in the pale sheets was a small, dark-haired boy.

Hunter drifted closer to him; his eyes locked on his son. He looked so peaceful and so beautiful as he slept.

Hunter paused as he sensed something else, a gentle breath and steady pulse, a rhythm of life that was so painfully familiar to him. Not here, but in the next room, just beyond that wall, he was certain Sophie slept.

He'd not been this close to her since the battle of Salisbury Plain, when he had tried to bind her powers; and she had killed his friends before vanishing. Hunter felt a physical blow at this revelation, that the Shadow Witch was mere feet away.

Hunter's pulse stuttered as he heard a distinct change in Sophie's sleep, as if she too, were disturbed by their closeness. Fearing his time was running out, Hunter scooped up his son from his bed. He felt the little boy stir in his arms, and an alarm went off in his head.

Hunter held his son close and thought of the meeting point. It only took a moment and he felt the cold breeze cut through his clothes, and in the cloudy darkness he could see men carrying lamps as they moved in towards him.

The boy cried in his arms, squirming to get out of his hold, and punctuating with high-pitched screams. Hunter put him down before he dropped the struggling boy, setting him on his feet. The boy staggered away from him; his face frozen with fear having been dragged from sleep to be surrounded by strange men. His cries were continuous, and the other men shouted to one another over the noise, hardly helping to calm the poor witch-child.

Hunter pulled off his balaclava and bobbed down, holding out his arms. "Adam, Adam, it's me."

The boy suddenly stopped crying at the sound of his voice and turned.

"Daddy!" He shrieked, then threw himself into Hunter's arms.

"It's ok." Hunter mumbled into Adam's hair, holding him tightly. "It's ok, no one's going to hurt you."

After a minute or two, it dawned on Hunter that the rest of the world was silent. He looked up to see a ring of horrified eyes gazing down at him.

## Chapter Fifteen

The reaction of the Council to the news that Adam was Hunter's son was everything Hunter had predicted. They were initially silenced by shock and disbelief, and more than a little disgusted. This was swiftly followed by anger.

Hunter didn't know what they were angrier about - the fact that their shining hero had taken the enemy to bed and fathered a son; or the fact that Hunter had lied about his motives in reclaiming Adam. But it all faded into the background as Hunter revelled in knowing his son for the first time. Adam was exactly how Hunter imagined he would be; exactly how he appeared in his dreams. A dark-haired, bright-eyed little boy with a ready smile. Hunter wondered how anyone could think Adam was evil or the son of the devil.

What was amazing was that from the very first moment Adam had seen him in the middle of that field, the boy had recognised Hunter as his daddy and had clung possessively to him. Hunter tried to discover the reason for this and had tentatively asked Adam how he knew. But the little boy had shook his head, not understanding the question. Hunter didn't push the point, but just enjoyed spending the next few days playing games and telling stories in the privacy of the quarters the Malleus Maleficarum Council gave him. Well, it wasn't exactly a generously given homely quarters, it was more similar to a minimal-comfort house arrest while the Council debated Hunter's punishment and future with the MMC.

Hunter knew that he could take Adam and blink them both far away at any time, but for now he was content to stay as the MMC's 'prisoner' in an attempt to mend those hastily burnt bridges.

Adam didn't mind being cooped up, there was so much to preoccupy a four-year-old mind. He had a very definite sense of games one should play with a father, and it seemed as though the little boy had saved them all up in anticipation of this meeting.

It was on the third day of their exclusion that they finally had visitors. The door opened and Mel ran in, heading straight for Adam and descending upon him with a great bear hug. Hunter raised a brow but didn't say anything as he heard his son giggling at the sudden attack.

"She's been waiting to do that for days."

Hunter looked up to see Toby enter in a more dignified fashion and close the door behind him.

"So, I offered to bring her after you'd settled in." Toby added, sitting on the sofa next to Hunter with a sigh.

"You look tired."

"Molly's ill." Toby shrugged, then realised that Hunter probably didn't remember who Molly was. "My daughter. She's got a bit of a fever and kept us up all night."

Toby smiled bitterly and nodded to Adam. "You've got all that to look forward to, you know."

"Did you know?" Hunter asked.

Toby sat silently for a while. He understood exactly what Hunter was asking. "I had my suspicions. It seemed like too much of a coincidence for Adam not to be your son. But I didn't want to say anything, and then it seemed that everyone who knew the Shadow Witch as Sophie Murphy had gone, and there was no point in saying anything."

Hunter sat there, digesting this. Toby was one of the few people that knew Hunter and Sophie had been a couple. But at Toby's words, Hunter realised that Sophie Murphy was no longer recognised as a beautiful, intelligent woman that he had fallen in love with; people only knew the terrifying and unlimited power of the Shadow Witch.

"And the Council?"

"Are pretty pissed off right now." Toby said, smiling as he watched the childlike Mel bob down to talk to Adam. "You have a talent for frustrating authority, Hunter. You provide a unique advantage against the witches, but the Council wonder whether you're worth the trouble."

Hunter smiled bitterly. "Déjà vu." He muttered.

Toby laughed at this, obviously thinking the same thing. Once, before all chaos had broken loose, Toby had brought the news to Hunter that the Malleus Maleficarum Council were turning against him in what amounted to a political struggle.

"Speaking of which, what happened to Halbrook?" Hunter asked. Gareth Halbrook had long been a thorn in Hunter's side.

"That cockroach is still alive, as far as I know." Toby said, not meeting Hunter's gaze. "He survived Salisbury, but hasn't been seen since."

They were distracted from their conjecture by Adam running up to them with his hand outstretched.

"Look, daddy, Mel gave me a pet!" The boy said excitedly. "He's called Incy."

Hunter looked down and inhaled sharply at the sight of a large spider in Adam's little hand. His eyes snapped up to Mel, who was sitting silent and serene in the middle of the floor, obviously pleased with her present.

"A spider?" Hunter asked with exasperation. "Fine. Why don't you get Mel to teach it tricks?"

Adam grinned, and held Incy carefully close to his chest as he took it back to the ever-smiling Mel. There was a knock at the door and Hunter looked up to see a very sober face pop round the door.

"Excuse me, Mr Astley, the Council want to see you."

Hunter glanced at Toby and sighed. Here they went again. "Can you watch Adam for me?" Hunter asked, not wanting to take his little lad before the Council, and not trusting him in the care of anyone else.

"Sure thing, mate." Toby said, looking across at Adam and Mel, content in their games with Incy.

Hunter got to his feet, already weary at the thought of what the Council might throw at him next. But he obediently followed the messenger out of the room and through the warren. The man was silent and was either unable or unwilling to answer Hunter's questions.

They carried on walking until they reached the stairs that led to the exit. Hunter went up them, frowning at what might cause the Council to hold an outdoor meeting.

It was only mid-afternoon, and it was a reasonably fine day, with pale grey clouds covering the sky with a few brief breaks of sun.

Hunter marched across the fields to the same location they had used the night he had abducted Adam. His sharp eyes focussed on the group of people in the centre of the field. A few Council members stood off to one side, deep in discussion. The rest of the witch-hunters formed a wide circle, all standing to attention, their guns aimed at a single female figure within. The woman stood with her back to Hunter, but there was something familiar about the dark brown hair that was lifted by a passing breeze, and the tall, elegant figure.

"Ladies, gentlemen, what's going on?" Hunter asked as he drew close to the Council members.

He was fixed with several pairs of cold eyes.

"We have taken a prisoner. And she demands to speak with you." Theresa explained, her voice miraculously calm and even.

Hunter glanced again at the woman that required such a heavy guard. He automatically began to walk in a slow, wide circle outside of the witch-hunters, slowly bringing himself into the eye line of the prisoner. Hunter was aware of the Council falling into step behind him, but they were the least of his worries when he finally faced the woman.

"Bev?"

"Good afternoon, Hunter. It's been a while." The woman replied civilly.

Dear god, Beverley Murphy, the mother of the Shadow Witch, and one of the last people that Hunter wanted to see. Hunter felt his pulse speed, and he was very aware of the audience he had for this special reunion.

"It has. Must be four years now." Hunter replied conversationally. Had it really been four years? He remembered the last time he had seen Bev like it was yesterday. When she had been playing the messenger, bringing news of Adam's birth. "What brings you here?"

Bev smiled coolly at his weak questioning, as though he couldn't guess. "The Shadow Witch sent me, to ask you to return her son."

Hunter stood with his arms folded across his chest as he swiftly processed the information behind the words. "She knew it was me?"

"Of course, who else could have done it - would have dared do it? Even after all this time, Sophie still recognised your work." Bev replied.

Hunter stood quietly, his initial worry that he should be so easily recognisable was dwarfed by the thrill of hearing someone else say Her name aloud. Oh boy, that was wrong.

"And she expects us to just give him back? And everyone stays friends?" Hunter said bitterly.

Bev sighed, annoyed by his attitude, and clearly unmoved by the many guns aimed directly at her. "It is her right; she is his mother."

"And I am his father." Hunter returned swiftly, ignoring the tenseness, ground teeth and dirty looks from the other witch-hunters. "Adam stays with me."

Hunter grimaced at what might come with this stubbornness. He had to know what was coming, and only Bev Murphy could answer him. The main question was, would she be forthcoming, and would she be truthful.

"Now tell me Bev, how did you find us, and how many more are coming."

Bev eyed the gathered witch-hunters with an assessing gaze. She seemed to be weighing her options. "Our intelligence showed this area to be void of witchcraft. It was an educated guess that your base would be somewhere in the region. I have been wandering for two days in hope of crossing paths with a patrol. As for how many - the Shadow Witch sent me alone. For now."

Hunter nodded as he assimilated this information, and took a step back, turning to the Council members. "What now, sirs?"

General Dawkins watched Bev carefully, fixing the witch with a scrutinising gaze. "She'll be taken into custody and held until we arrange a trial. She'll be given a chance to offer information for leniency."

A bitter lump rose in Hunter's throat. He could not imagine Bev being put through whatever strict trial had been developed in these harsh times. But he nodded again, he might as well agree with the Council for now.

The witch-hunters moved in to escort the witch under guard into the cell-like rooms in the warren.

Hunter stepped back, out of the attention of every man. His dark brown eyes fixed on Bev with a sudden intensity, as his thoughts reached out to brush across the surface of hers. Bev's eyes widened with shock and she glanced at Hunter as she was led past.

*'I will meet you later. You are under my protection.'*

Bev's expression hardened, and she gave an imperceptible nod.

"So, you recognise this witch?" Dawkins asked, his voice coloured with disgust as he watched the witch walk past them.

Hunter frowned as his eyes lingered on Bev. Yes, he knew her. He was suddenly assailed with the memories of meeting Ms. Murphy, it had been a fine summer's day when he, Sophie and James Bennett had landed on her doorstep by chance. She had seemed like any other mother; welcoming, but cautious of the men that accompanied her daughter. Hunter almost smiled as he remembered how Bev had warned him off Sophie - he had initially thought her over-protective, but he now saw that she had been trying to protect him.

Hunter nodded in response to Dawkin's question.

And the General looked unsatisfied with his answer. "And what of her? You crossed paths and you failed to kill her? What is her position with the witches?"

Hunter grimaced at the General's presumption. Obviously, it must be expected that he killed any witch he met. It was only a few years ago that it had been common practise to imprison witches and bind their powers. But all that had changed when the Shadow Witch had opened the prisons and returned the powers, and the witch-hunters had suffered for their previous leniency.

"I didn't know that Bev was a witch - she was one of the bound when I met her. She was the Shadow Witch's point of contact when she was undercover - a liaison to the other witches." Hunter replied convincingly. It sounded like the truth and was believable. Hunter wasn't about to tell this frankly austere Colin Dawkins that Bev was Sophie's mother.

"And when I was held prisoner at the witches' headquarters, she was-" Hunter broke off. He'd been about to say that she was the one to help him escape, when he suddenly realised that this Council might see him in Bev's debt. "-she was a mediator in the group, I'm not surprised that she should be sent."

Hunter ignored Dawkin's sceptical look and turned to walk back towards the warren. The rest of the Council fell into step, the party finally deserting the field.

"So, what do we do about the boy?" One asked.

Hunter felt anger flare up. The boy - his son. He was annoyed at how narrow and close-minded these people were; they wouldn't even call Adam by his name.

"I don't know. We knew he could be a beacon for the Shadow Witch to find us. But it might be worth it if he shows some real power." General Dawkins replied, cold and logical. He turned to Hunter. "Does he?"

Hunter didn't reply immediately. He knew that he'd promised the Council a chance to have a mini-witch with all the power of his mother, but he wondered, did Adam's anti-witch paternity cancel out Sophie's power? "No, not yet anyway. It's perfectly normal for witches not to display power until puberty."

"So, we may have to wait ten years!" The Council member, Theresa, stressed. "Ten years of danger for a flimsy promise of power - is it worth it?"

"Depends on how you see it." Hunter replied warningly.

He stopped walking, glaring at the Council members. How could they talk about such a sweet, innocent boy like that?

Hunter turned his mind to Adam, playing in their quarters. It was so tempting to blink away from these fools and back to his son. But Hunter stopped himself. It would only upset the Council more if he started blinking about the place. And maybe it would be better if he did not draw any further attention to that particular ability for a while.

Hunter walked on again, striding out so that he did not have to walk with the Council. He just wanted to get back to his rooms. Hunter was not stopped as he entered the warren, and no one crossed his path as he made his way through the dim and confusing corridors towards his comfortable prison.

Hunter flinched as he threw the door open with unintended force. Three faces stared up at him.

Toby stood up, frowning. "What's happened?"

Hunter closed the door behind him with more care. "Look, can you stay here for another half hour? I have to go somewhere, and I can't let the others know."

Confusion and suspicion clouded Toby's face at this request. "I have no idea what you're talking about, Hunter."

"Look, Toby, I swear that I will explain everything later. But I need to go. Now. I just need you to hang around, and if anyone comes in, tell them I'm - I'm in the bathroom. I'll be listening for that one. Thanks mate, I owe you."

Hunter clapped Toby on the shoulder. Toby opened his mouth to respond, but it was too late, Hunter had already blinked out.

Hunter took a deep breath as he left, he always got dizzy when he had to guess where he was travelling. He locked onto Bev and pulled himself through the cold and dark. When he opened his eyes, Bev was staring at him calmly. Of course, for a woman that had seen frequent miracles from her daughter, to have a man materialise in her cell must mean nothing.

"Hi… are you ok?" Hunter asked weakly. He looked about the small room that had nothing in it, no chair nor table wasted on this witch. Hunter glanced at the door and reached out with his mind until he confirmed the presence of two witch-hunters standing guard outside.

"I am a prisoner to our ruthless enemy. But other than that, I am fine." Bev said bitterly, automatically keeping her voice low. "You are taking a risk."

Hunter shrugged; some risks were worth it. "Why did Sophie send you?"

"To get her son back. My grandson." Bev replied, finding the answer obvious.

"No, I meant, why you? Sending her own mother into the lion's den. I haven't told the Council, by the way, they think you are a regular witch."

Bev didn't respond immediately; she folded her arms protectively in front of her. "She sent me because she knew that I was the one witch that you would listen to. And also… because she can afford to lose me."

Bev looked sharply at Hunter, her green eyes glinting with a pain that had hardened over time. "She never forgave me for what I did, for daring to steal her powers to save you and your friend. And I think… I think she suspects the other part I played."

Hunter frowned at Bev's words. "What part would that be?"

Bev dropped her gaze, her fingers twisting together as she fortified herself. "How… how do you think Brian Lloyd found out about the return of the Shadow Witch?"

Brian Lloyd had been a highly-respected 5th gen witch-hunter; he had been Hunter's own trainer after his father died. Brian had been Sophie's trainer when she pretended to be a fresh recruit. Until the Shadow Witch had killed him for getting too close to the truth.

Hunter felt the breath knocked out of him at the realisation of what Bev was admitting. "The papers; that was you?"

He opened his mouth to speak but stopped. Sophie had noticed Brian disappearing every couple of weeks but had assumed he had a woman to visit.

"Brian didn't know who I was." Bev said quietly. "He did not know I was Sophie's mother, there was no reason to connect us. I feared what Sophie would do, and I had to warn somebody. Amongst the witches, Brian Lloyd was a famous witch-hunter."

Hunter took a deep breath. "Well, I suppose that explains why Brian hid his research so far north…"

Bev tucked her dark hair behind her ear. "Yes, though I wish he hadn't. From then on Sophie has been suspicious of me and my motives. A crack in our relationship that the more ambitious in the Witches council have played upon. Shortly after I brought you news of Adam's birth, I was stripped of all trust and respect and reduced to being a face, frequently ignored in her house. I became no more than a carer for Adam.

"This is my chance to redeem myself. It has been made clear to me that if I do not return with Adam, I should not return at all." Bev sighed, resigned to her fate, then spoke again beneath her breath. "Yet if I do return victorious, they will all question how I persuaded you to give him up."

"Bev, I'm sorry." Hunter replied quietly. He had never considered what consequences her lenience might yield. He almost felt guilty for what had happened. "How can Sophie treat you like that?"

Bev looked directly at him, with no shame. "It's not so much Sophie these days, as the other witches at council. My daughter is little more than a figurehead, now that the witches have what they want. There to cow the populace while the council are the real power."

Bev shook her head at her own daughter's place. "After all those years of hatred, of wanting revenge... I don't think Sophie ever gave serious thought to what would happen afterwards."

Hunter stood quietly, feeling pity towards his old lover; and then disturbed that he should so naturally feel sorry for the bane of his life.

"So please, give Sophie her son back. Adam is all she has in this world."

"Likewise, Bev, likewise." Hunter muttered, feeling that he had much less than Sophie at this point.

"But she is distraught, you have not seen her! She fears what the witch-hunters will do to a half-witch child."

"I would never let any harm come to him." Hunter replied, hurt that Bev thought he would ever let that happen. "Why shouldn't she trust me with my own son? I am the good guy after all."

Bev smiled bitterly at the honest answer that she left unspoken. She gently shook her head. "You are the enemy Hunter, capable of atrocities in a time of war. And even without that, Sophie would never put her trust is paternal affection!"

"But..." Hunter stopped; Bev's comment made him pause. What did she mean by paternal affection? His brow creased beneath this little mystery. "What do you mean?"

"Sophie never told you? Why she hates witch-hunters. Why she distrusts men, you above all?" Bev replied quietly, musing over an old torment. "Because-"

Hunter suddenly jumped. He heard Toby saying his name, as clearly as though he stood beside him, though he remained in another part of the warren. This mystery would have to wait.

"I have to go; I don't want them to know I'm here." He explained, then blinked out.

Hunter was in a small dark room, and through the door he could hear Toby talking. Hunter reached out, fumbling in the dark until he found a chain. The toilet flushed and Hunter opened the door into the main room of his quarters.

Adam and Mel were still sat in the middle of the floor, and Toby sprawled comfortably on the sofa. All just as Hunter had left them. Except for the fourth person in the room.

Hunter looked towards Colin Dawkins, who stood near the door, wearing that seemingly permanent sceptical expression.

"Can I help you, General?" Hunter asked mildly.

Dawkins didn't reply immediately but took in the scene suspiciously. "I came to see if you were alright."

"To check up on me, you mean." Hunter corrected, suddenly tired with the pretence of friendship and deciding to jump straight to the point.

Dawkins made a half-hearted effort at being affronted at Hunter's assumption, then just shrugged.

"Can you blame me? You knew that witch by name." Dawkins said coldly. "You're hiding something Hunter; you had a familiarity with that witch. I saw your concern over what we might do with her."

Hunter stood silently, not sure how to respond to this. Even if he denied it, the obvious lie would throw fuel on the fire of suspicion. Hunter gazed at Dawkins, trying to work him out. Had he been too eager to presume that a familiar face meant a friend and ally in these times? He realised that Dawkins had been cool, even negative, ever since he arrived at the warren.

"Look, Colin, is there something I have done? For I thought we were friends, you and I?" Hunter asked quietly and sincerely.

The General smiled bitterly and shifted his weight. "You jump to conclusions, Hunter. I was never in this to be anyone's friend. I followed orders from General Hayworth, regardless of my own opinion." Dawkins shook his head and paced away with restless energy. "He saw something in you that he was willing to die for, but forgive me, for I see nothing."

"I'm not asking you to die." Hunter responded, a subtle anger and distress colouring his tone. But the General continued as though he had not heard him.

"I see nothing, save a power that is unpredictable and limited in its use. I see the person that wields it as a man lacking all sense of duty, who thinks himself free of all the restraints and rules of our society, a man that can *beget a son* by the enemy! And a man that, when we go for that hard push, will probably run and hide again in the Italian hills."

Dawkins voice grew colder throughout his rant, and he glared at Hunter with a finally unveiled revulsion. The General stood for a moment more, then wrenched the door open, suddenly leaving the room.

Hunter and Toby were left speechless in his wake. The only sound came from Mel, who was singing quietly…

*"Fuchs, du hast die Gans gestshlen, Gib sie wieder her!"*

Hunter frowned at what he recognised to be a German nursery rhyme; he was quickly learning to not be surprised by anything Mel might do. But her little voice did make him shiver.

*Hunter pushed the cottage door open and struggled through, his sports bag slung over his shoulder.*

*"Sophie, I'm home." He called out, aware of the noise of the television that floated through from the living room.*

*There was the sound of thumping feet, quickly followed by the appearance of Adam, all black hair and pale skin and very big bright eyes as he greeted his father.*

*"Daddy!" He squealed, promptly throwing himself at Hunter and clinging fiercely to his legs.*

*"Hey little man, I brought a visitor too." Hunter said, giving Adam an awkward hug, while trying to keep his sports bag balanced. Hunter shuffled down the hallway, to let his guest in, hampered by his son.*

*Another man came limping in behind Hunter, his eyes gleamed at the sight of his favourite little boy. "Hey up, mate."*

*"Uncle James!" Adam shouted, immediately releasing his father and barrelling into James, his noisy hug quickly followed by ear-splitting laughter.*

*Hunter chuckled, not sure who was the biggest kid, and he turned away to see Sophie hovering in the doorway. She was always more reserved when James was around. Hunter dropped his bag and walked over to her, kissing her in greeting. She pulled away and looked pointedly at the floor.*

*"I hope you're going to clean that mud up, Hunter. How was rugby?" Sophie dragged her cold hazel eyes from the mess on the floor*

*and looked directly at Hunter, a deep need in her gaze that almost distracted him.*

*"It could've gone worse. We only lost by six points. But I had to take James for stitches afterwards."*

*In the hallway, James kicked off his shoes and, holding a giggling Adam upside-down, he pushed past his hosts into the living room. He tilted his head as he passed, showing off the red area above his brow.* "I still say I didn't need stitches - a plaster would've done. Nowt a cuppa tea can't fix, anyway."

*Sophie sighed, rolling her eyes at the Yorkshire man. From the very first time they'd met, Sophie and James had never gotten along. But she moved grudgingly into the kitchen. Hunter paused to untie his boots and kick them off; from the living room he could hear the cartoons on the television, and the sound of Adam laughing and James' funny accent; from the kitchen he could hear the clink of mugs being set out, and he could just imagine Sophie's expression.*

*Obedient to his heart, Hunter walked into the kitchen and wrapped his arms around his Sophie, he breathed in the scent of her hair as he murmured a few choice words in her ear. Sophie took a shuddering breath, savouring the moment. But as the kettle boiled, she pulled away from Hunter's arms and played the perfect hostess, taking through the steaming hot tea for Hunter and James, just as she used to back in Astley Manor, back before all the madness. Hunter followed her like a shadow through into the living room. Adam was quieter now and sat on the floor in front of his Uncle James. James turned to accept his mug of tea and Hunter could see fresh blood on his face, seeping out from the stitches, much more than he expected. A red drip rolled down James' cheek, and the Yorkshireman caught it before it dropped onto the clean sofa.*

*"Why are you always bleeding when I see you these days?" Hunter said with exasperation. But half of his consciousness tore away with sudden fear, his eyes were fixed on the wound on James' face, the bruises on his arms and legs, all of which became large and glaring under Hunter's scrutiny. James' eyes looked back at Hunter, empty.*

*"I'm sorry I couldn't save you." Hunter murmured. Then awoke, bathed in cold sweat.*

**Chapter Sixteen**

More than anything, Hunter wanted to see Bev again, to ask her more about the danger they were in, to ask her what she had meant before. But he could not risk it, the Council were more alert than ever, and Colin Dawkin's enmity had thrown him.

The next day Hunter was summoned to the Council again. He came, reluctantly leaving Adam in the care of Toby's wife, Claire. Robinson. Claire had looked less than thrilled at the prospect of babysitting the half-witch child but had agreed for her husband's sake.

When Hunter arrived at the Council's rooms, he found them all seated about the long table, awaiting his arrival.

"Ah, Mr Astley." Theresa greeted warmly, looking up as he entered. "I'm glad you could join us. There are certain matters in which we require your help. One in particular, actually."

She motioned for Hunter to join them at the table, and a folder of hand-written documents was pushed towards him. He flicked through them, some pages stirring a certain familiarity in him, although on a whole they made no sense.

"After your disappearance we claimed Astley Manor and its extensive collection for the good of the Malleus Maleficarum Council."

Hunter looked up at this, a flash of anger that anyone should take what belonged to him and his family. Theresa gave him a sympathetic look, then continued.

"We found documents, arranged and researched, pertaining to this Shadow Witch, and one we did not know existed in 1940. We wondered if there might be some information about the last one, how she was contained, how she was released, that might aid us now. Of course, your documents were incomplete, but they did point to a German source. The Council decided to send a small party of witch-hunters to investigate this source. Yesterday we received word that they have failed and been killed."

There was a shared murmur of condolences and regret from the Council members. But they all fell silent again.

"I hope you understand our predicament, Mr Astley. Good men and women have given their lives trying to discover a weakness in the Shadow Witch, and I do not want their sacrifice to have been in vain. Yet travel between the UK and the rest of Europe is slow; communication is slower still."

Theresa fell silent, and Hunter sat there with a vague impression that this was where he came in.

"And what do you want from me?" He asked hesitantly.

"You can travel anywhere, can you not?" A man to his right asked.

"Yes." Hunter replied slowly. "Well, as far as I can tell."

"Well then, you could be in Germany at a moment's notice." The man continued. "And find out what we all need to know."

"I know you no longer follow Council orders." Theresa added, noticing Hunter's reluctant expression. "But this could be the breakthrough, the information that you came back for. Also, you can see it as repaying our help in recovering your son. And you needn't do this alone, you'll have the best witch-hunters with you."

Hunter grimaced. "I can't take anyone else-"

"Nonsense." Colin Dawkins interjected coolly, the first time he had spoken. "I've seen you transport a whole bloody army when the need arose for it - and travelled with you myself I might add."

Hunter waited for Dawkins to finish and did his best not to fix him with a scathing look. "Thank you, General. But I did not mean I was physically incapable, just morally. I can't risk a group of unprotected first generations, no matter how good they are." Hunter had expected some resistance or argument against his statement, but instead he was met with silent, knowing stares.

"We thought you might say that. And perhaps you are right, anyone would be in double the danger if you were around them, and we should not inflict that on any first generation." Theresa agreed. "Which is why we've assigned a higher gen to you."

Hunter wavered; he had not expected to win that argument so easily. Then he froze. A higher gen? "Not Toby!" He blurted out, shocked at the idea that his invalid friend might be dragged into this.

"I wish." Toby grunted. "But thanks for the vote of confidence."

"No, not Toby." Theresa replied with a vein of amusement in her voice. "A sixth gen, due back at the warren today. We will send them along to your quarters once they are briefed."

Theresa nodded at the file beneath Hunter's fingers. "You had best spend your time memorising that. We expect you to leave as soon as possible."

*****

Hunter was sat in his room, trying to wrap his head around the documents before him. It was stodgy reading material and jumped from English to German (and even a piece in Russian); and his concentration was not aided by Adam and his new best friend Mel, equally jumping between games and quiet time, where Mel tried to teach Adam German.

*"Wo ist vater? Es ist der vater! Wo ist mutter? Es ist der mutt-"*

"Mel-" Hunter snapped, then immediately felt guilty beneath her hurt blue gaze. "Sorry Mel, it's just you are disturbing me, and I have to…"

"Ok, George." Mel mumbled, looking away, obviously not forgiving him easily this time.

Hunter thought back to the last time Mel had come around, and something suddenly struck him. "Mel… did you know that I was going to Germany?"

*"Sonst wird dich der Jäger holen, mit dem Schießgewehr…"* Mel murmured tunefully, still not facing him. "Or the Hunter will fetch you, with his gun."

Hunter leant forward, about to speak when there was a sharp knock at the door. Hunter jumped, and cursed his nerves, before going to open the door.

"Toby, come in." He said, unsurprised, standing aside for his friend.

But before Toby could limp in, a blond girl pushed through impatiently. Hunter watched in shock as she took a blatant gander about the room and then turned to him with an assessing blue gaze.

"So, this is the famous Hunter Astley?" She remarked in a ringing American accent. "I thought you'd be taller."

Hunter opened his mouth to reply but found himself dumbstruck.

Toby (biting back a smirk) nodded to the new girl. "Hunter, this is Kris Davies-"

"Kris-*ten*." The girl stressed.

"Sorry, Kristen. Kristen Davies, 6th gen. She'll be accompanying you to Germany." Toby finished.

Still short on words, Hunter held out his hand to shake, a gesture Kristen ignored.

"So, it's true then? You can, like, just blink and be there?" Kristen asked, her blue eyes bright and excited at the thought. "But I mean, it just sounds magical."

"Ahm." Hunter managed a non-committal sound, as he let his arm drop back by his side.

"The Council suggests meeting in the field and setting off at dawn tomorrow." Toby interjected helpfully.

"Dawn?!" Kristen scoffed. "What's wrong with you people? Instantaneous travel at our disposal and we can't sleep in 'til a reasonable hour? Whatever. I'm gonna go crash."

The girl sighed heavily and without any further explanation she left the room.

Hunter stood there baffled. "That was… interesting."

Toby chuckled. "Oh, you have no idea mate."

\*\*\*\*\*

The warren had quietened down for the night, as those within settled for sleep. Hunter watched silently as Adam slept soundly on the fold-out cot, looking ever so peaceful as he dreamt.

Hunter knew that it might be days before he saw his son again - longer if things went wrong. He also felt that tonight would be his last chance to finish a certain conversation. Hunter sighed, not wanting to leave Adam alone, but knowing that he had to, so as not to draw attention. He closed his eyes, the blackness enveloping him tightly, and when he opened them again, he was in the small cell-like room, the faint light from an oil lamp showing that addition of a camp bed someone must have dragged in. Hunter walked over and gently touched the sleeping Bev's shoulder.

The woman awoke with a start, snatching back from Hunter, eyeing him fearfully. But after a moment, she managed to calm herself.

"What are you doing here?" She hissed, brushing her long dark hair out of her eyes, to see him better.

Hunter frowned as he looked at her, something about her had changed, her very aura altered. "They… they bound your powers?" He asked hesitantly, referring to the old witch-hunter practise of binding a witch's powers with the use on an artefact that would then be catalogued and stored. A practise that had ended when the Shadow Witch had broken the key and released every bound witch in the world, to wreak havoc and revenge.

Bev sighed, looking weaker and older than she had just a day ago. "At least they let me live. Not that it matters, nothing does now. My magical heritage has never brought anything but trouble."

Hunter could only feel pity for this woman that was a shadow of her former, proud self. He moved to sit on the single, hard wooden chair in the room.

"You once told me that you could have been the next Shadow Witch. What happened?"

Bev looked at him with a faint smile. "You have a good memory."

She sat quietly on the camp bed, pulling the covers snugly about her. Bev gazed at Hunter for a while, as though assessing whether or not to be honest with him. But then she shrugged. After all, she had already admitted that nothing really mattered anymore.

"I remember when they first approached me - the witches. It was my 30th birthday when they just turned up. They said that they were heir hunters, trying to find the descendent of Sara Murray. They asked a lot of questions, many I didn't understand, but seemed satisfied with my answers. When I asked what I was due to inherit, they turned to one another and became conspiratorial. They told me what they were - witches - I didn't believe them of course, so they cast a few showy spells to make their point. They told me what I was, what I could become. But I... I was wary. Up until that point I knew who I was, I was happy with my simple life and didn't want to take on their fight and their cause.

"They perhaps read my reluctance, but their eyes lit up with an intense greed when my daughter suddenly walked in. Sophie was thirteen and very angry back then. Always in trouble at school, disrespectful and challenging authority."

Hunter was caught by this little insight to Sophie's youth. Up until then he had never considered what she had been like as a girl, but her mother's description sounded very believable, that she had always been proud. Hunter half-smiled at his thoughts, and kept silent, not interrupting Bev's story.

"I hoped that it was just teenage rebellion, a passing phase. But I didn't trust the way those witches looked at her, and I forbade them from approaching Sophie until she was at least sixteen. Much good it did. Soon after, Sophie changed, becoming quieter and more secretive. She'd always been proud, but she became almost arrogant. I was in a difficult position. I couldn't come down hard on her, because I knew that would just push her straight to the witches, and I wanted to keep some influence over her, make sure she kept even a fragment of humanity and morality.

"Then when she was sixteen, they gave her another witch's power, a small taste of what she was to gain. And Sophie was hooked. Then finally when she was nineteen, news came through that the Shadow Witch's power was to be returned. And… well, you know the rest." Bev finished, her voice hollow and eyes empty, as though she had nothing left to live for. But then a small spark was remembered. "How's Adam?"

Hunter hesitated, still absorbing Bev's little story. "He's fine, reasonably settled and happy. I, ah, didn't tell him you were here."

Bev blinked, but slowly nodded. "Of course, no need to upset him." She mumbled, more to herself than to Hunter.

"You said that Sophie would never put her trust in paternal affection, or men at all." Hunter reminded quietly, gently pushing for information.

"Well, she hardly had a good role model." Bev almost snapped, then fell silent again.

"I'm sorry, Sophie never mentioned her father, I don't know…" Hunter replied, suddenly embarrassed at how little he knew about the woman he had claimed to love.

Bev stared at him with that assessing gaze again, then eventually sighed. "Sophie's father wasn't there, because…"

Bev broke off and looked away, into the darkness as her eyes gleamed with an old hurt. But after a minute's composure she spoke again, quieter this time. "When I was sixteen years old I… I was raped by my boyfriend. Sophie was the result of that rape, but I kept her, and I loved her. I thought to keep her parentage from her, but secrets have a habit of coming out in the end. She grew very angry, and she blames you. Your family anyway."

Bev broke off, gazing curiously at Hunter, bemused at how things worked out. "As she sees it, if my grandmother, Sara Murray, had not been forced to strip her descendants of power to save them from George Astley V and others like him, then there would have been no way that a mere mortal man could… could…"

"Bev… I didn't know." Hunter choked out after this shock confession. "I'm so sorry."

Bev waved a hand dismissively. "Oh, *I* don't blame you. It's in the past, and after all, I got my Sophie. Yes, I have learnt to come to terms with it."

"But Sophie?" Hunter asked gingerly.

"Sophie is still torn between hating your family and loving you." Bev replied with a smile. "And she got her revenge. After the witches delivered the Shadow power to her. Her father was the first person she killed."

Hunter sat in quiet shock. He could just imagine that sinful father taking a lone walk, when suddenly the shadows came to ensnare him and there - there would be the daughter he knew nothing of, a fierce and beautiful woman, driven by hate and vengeance.

"I..." Hunter tried to start talking but found his voice unwilling. He coughed and began again. "I'm leaving in the morning on a mission. I'll hopefully be back within the week, and I will return. We will talk again."

Bev half-smiled, her tired hazel eyes locked on Hunter as he rose from his chair. Her gaze did not falter as he stood there in the middle of her cell. And then suddenly he vanished, and Bev was left staring into space.

## Chapter Seventeen

It was a grey and dismal dawn, with wispy mist-like rain clinging to their hair and clothes. Hunter stood in the middle of the field, with Kristen beside him. The girl yawned, and huffed, and stamped her feet against the cold, making her displeasure against this early departure very clear indeed.

Hunter was a little more awake, although he'd hardly slept after last night's revelations. Instead he'd stared unseeingly at Adam as he slept, watching how peaceful his son was. Although he didn't want to admit it, even to himself, Hunter feared that Bev's confessions would bring another dream upon him, tangible and real, and having the pain of seeing Sophie and understanding her a little better.

During those sleepless hours, Hunter had allowed his mind to turn over those dreams. They were disturbingly real - he remembered the panic he had felt after the first dream, last year at the Abbazio di Donili. The Sophie in his dreams was the Sophie he remembered, but he still couldn't explain how the Adam of his unconscious imagination matched the real Adam perfectly. The location had confused him for a while - why would their pretty family picture not be situated at his Astley Manor? But finally, the realisation dawned on him that they were at Beverley Murphy's cottage near Keswick.

But dreams were dreams, and no real answers came, though his mind ran over and over it.

"Are we going or what?" Kristen snapped, fed up with waiting in the cold.

Hunter blinked, dragging himself back to the present. "Yes, yes." He muttered.

At that moment Toby limped forward, hand outstretched. "Good luck, Hunter."

Hunter shook his hand. "Thanks. And you'll…"

"Look after Adam, yes I promise." He confirmed with a reassuring smile. His wife Claire wasn't fantastically happy with the arrangement, but she was slowly accepting that Adam was a sweet and innocent young boy, despite his unorthodox parentage.

Happy that his son would be in safe hands Hunter swung his backpack over his shoulder and stepped back, holding his hand out to Kristen. The girl took it nonchalantly, but Hunter smiled at the cold sweat on her palm that she could not hide. With a nod to the Council members, they vanished.

Hunter opened his eyes to a wooded area.

"Woah, shit." Kristen exclaimed, staggering back as her knees buckled.

"Steady." Hunter murmured, "Maybe you should sit down."

He frowned at how pale she was looking. Kristen obediently lowered herself to the ground shakily and stuck her head between her knees with a groan.

"Ugh, god, is it always like that?" She moaned.

"Only the first few times. You get used to it pretty fast." Hunter answered, remembering how his previous team had adapted. He crouched in front of her, waiting patiently for her to recover.

Kristen groaned again, obviously dismayed at the idea of doing it again. But she finally lifted her head and flicked her blonde hair back over her shoulder.

"Where are we? Why is it so bright?" She moaned, squinting against the unexpected light.

"We're a few hours north of Berlin, in the Bioshärenreservat Schorfheide Chorin, I used to holiday near here. And it's light because we're an hour ahead of where we just set off from. Hence why we set off so early." Hunter replied patiently, relieved that she was recovering quickly. His method of transport affected people differently. Hunter remembered the first person he'd blinked away, a young and still-optimistic Colin Dawkins - the then sergeant had been pale and winded, but not as dizzy as poor Kristen. Now that Hunter knew that she was ok, he couldn't help but find her reaction amusing.

"We'll, ah, start trekking to civilisation once you're feeling up to it." Hunter added, smiling bitterly that he should be hampered by this witch-hunter the Council promised wouldn't slow him down.

"Nah, I'm good, I'm ok." Kristen argued, and got back to her feet, looking a little pale, but very determined.

Hunter watched her carefully, but just shrugged his backpack straight and began to walk due south. Kristen kept up with him without complaint, occasionally having to jog every few steps to keep up with Hunter's longer stride. They kept marching until the trees dropped away and the morning sun beat down on them, and then continued still over the varying terrain. They kept away from roads and settlements as much as possible. After an unrelenting pace for two hours, Hunter had to admit that he was impressed with Kristen's fitness, the girl wasn't flagging. Of course, maybe that had something to do with her 6th gen status. By the 6th generation, a witch-hunter had earned a little extra strength and stamina beyond the average man. Hunter glanced at the blonde girl again, curious at how a 6th gen could have survived the witches' purge of any and (almost) all witch-hunters above a 2nd gen status. Hunter moved to ask her, but Kristen opened her mouth instead.

"What? Do I look funny to you?" She asked toughly, as she caught the older guy staring at her again. "Or maybe you're thinking something else. Bet it's been a while since you saw a woman, cooped up in that monastery?"

Hunter raised a brow at the girl's attitude and laughed when she actually had the cheek to wink at him. "No, I promise I wasn't thinking that, not that I wouldn't be flattered, you're a very pretty young… I mean."

Hunter broke off and kept his head down, marching along. What the hell was wrong with him, once upon a time he had been the most charming young man, he'd been able to banter and tease with any number of women. Kristen had just caught him off guard.

Hunter coughed and brought his thoughts back to where they'd jumped from. "For your information, the Abbazia de Donili was home to men and women. No, I was wondering how you are, well, alive? How did you survive, being a 6th gen?"

Kristen walked along quietly for a couple of minutes, trying to coordinate an answer that made sense. "Just luck, I guess. I was never registered with the American Malleus Maleficarum Council, so I slipped under the net."

Hunter continued to stare at her, trying to work her out, until he nearly tripped. "But how? Forgive me, but surely your MMC would pounce at the chance of having a 6th gen working for them. And if they're anything like the UK Council, they keep stringent records of all witch-hunter bloodlines, whether they join or not."

"Yeah, you're right, except they didn't know about me." Kristen replied, a little smugly. "My mom fell in love with this English witch-hunter that saved her, and she stayed with him for a while. But it didn't work out, so she moved back to America and didn't know she was pregnant with me. I didn't even know what I was until I was a teenager, and I started getting these headaches and it was obvious I was different from everyone else. Mom finally had to tell me about my father and all about witches. I mean it freaked me out, seriously. But I was even more scared of the idea of this Malleus Maleficarum Council coming along and taking control of me."

Hunter nodded, in silent agreement with her comment. He'd never been keen on the politics and double nature associated with any council.

"I couldn't ignore it though, when I realised the headaches was my mind detecting magic, so I worked rogue, just small stuff, not alerting the MMC. Then that night came, when everything just crashed, and the world was turned upside down. I knew it was witches, and I felt guilty as I watched the MMC destroyed and I couldn't do anything to stop it. The witches set themselves up as authority figures and began to hunt down all the witch-hunters listed with the MMC. I wasn't on the list, but I wasn't about to hang around doing nothing. I joined in a few rebellions, but with only 1st gen hunters it was pretty desperate, especially fighting those average witches. I realised that I would be more useful fighting the epicentre, so decided to follow the rumours of the Shadow Witch to the UK. Jumped on a boat to Spain, then travelled up Europe, keeping out of trouble best I could. I finally met your MMC last year and have been working with them since. They were pretty happy to get a 6th gen. Took them no convincing after I mentioned my father's name, either."

Hunter listened quietly and stopped to grab his water canteen. He offered it to Kristen first, before taking a drink himself. "And who is your father?"

"Brian Lloyd." Kristen replied, with a tilt of her head.

Hunter choked on his drink, spluttering so water dribbled down his chin. He gasped and wiped his sleeve inelegantly across his mouth. "What?" He rasped, his eyes red and watery.

"Mm, guess you've heard of him then." Kristen replied innocently, although a mischievous smile touched her lips. "Turns out he was something of a hero."

"You're *Brian's daughter*?" He stressed, trying to take in this bizarre turn.

Kristen nodded slowly; eyeing Hunter like he was an imbecile.

"But..." Hunter frowned, he thought he'd known Brian. How could he not know that he had a daughter? "Brian was my mentor, after my dad died, he taught me almost everything I know. And I thought I knew him - he never mentioned you."

"He didn't know about me." Kristen said with a shrug. "You really knew him?"

"Yeah, as well as anyone." Hunter replied. "He was this big, stubborn, fierce man with impossible standards, but he was loyal and one of the best damn witch-hunters we had. He was world-famous amongst witch-hunters, you should have seen how many people honoured him after his death. He, ah, was killed by the Shadow Witch."

"I know, your MMC told me, when I first came, half hoping to meet the father I never knew. But they also told me that he was the one that uncovered the Shadow Witch and made sure the world was ready for her." Kristen said, quieter now, as she thought about the greatness of this mystery father figure that had lumbered her with these gifts and the duty that was bound to them.

"He did." Hunter confirmed. It had indeed been Brian that had put together the clues and worked out that the Shadow Witch was returning. Or so Hunter had thought; that conversation with Bev made Hunter look at things in a different light.

And now here was his daughter. Hunter gazed at her again, with new eyes. Kristen looked nothing like Brian Lloyd, but Hunter thought he saw some of his stubbornness and hopefully his courage.

He smiled and tucked away the canteen, picking up the pace again, as they headed for Berlin. Kristen walked alongside him, quite pleased with herself.

"So, you know you're a 7th gen and have all these extra gifts... does that mean if I have a kid, they'll be the same?" Kristen asked.

Hunter thought for a moment. "I don't know, I guess so. But there have been so few 6th gens and I'm the first known 7th gen that I can't promise they would." Hunter looked resolutely ahead. The Abate had thought 7th gens special, but only on the first step to being truly evolved anti-witches. Was it truly only Sophie that made Hunter more than that?

"Well… I know how to make it much more possible." Kristen replied, nudging Hunter with her shoulder as they walked together. "You know, if you ever fancy it."

Hunter laughed, "You don't give up do you?" He shook his head, he had to admit that Kristen was pretty, but this was hardly an appropriate time for flirting. Plus, now all he could think was this was Brian's daughter…

## Chapter Eighteen

It was nearing evening by the time the city of Berlin was finally in sight. They had trekked for near twelve hours. Kristen had been energetic and chatty for the first six hours, but after they took a brief midday stop, she became quieter, her fewer comments taking on a sarcastic and annoyed edge. Hunter didn't rise to her jibes, but just kept walking. Yet even his legs were beginning to burn, and he cursed the fact that he'd decided to be overly cautious in where they transported to. He told himself that it was still a shorter journey than if they'd had to travel by normal means from England, but that was little comfort. Hunter looked up at the quiet streets as they walked into Berlin, he took a deep breath, but said nothing and the two witch-hunters continued to march in silence up the tarmac roads of the outer boroughs. It was eerily quiet, in this once heavily populated area, that there was so little noise. Once there would have been television and music rolling out of the houses and flats and clashing in the background noise of the estates of people talking, children laughing and playing and the constant drone of cars rumbling through. But the cars stood as unused relics at the curb, no more technology threw out noise, and the children and families alike stayed quiet behind their doors. Hunter and Kristen passed a few pedestrians, people that kept their heads down and hurried home before dark.

The atmosphere was enough to make Hunter and Kristen only whisper sparse words as they kept walking. Hunter kept a sharp eye out for the street signs, following the directions from the file he had memorised last night. Glauben Strasse was the address he had been given. Glauben Strasse, Glauben Strasse, the name of the street pounded in his head in time with his footsteps.

Eventually they came to the road. It was unremarkable, the same as every other in the estates that clustered about Berlin. Hunter glanced over his shoulder to visually check that they were not being followed, while his other senses stretched out to confirm it. Satisfied that they were alone, he led the way to the house number he had been given and rapped sharply.

There was a noise of movement inside as someone shuffled towards the door. There was a pause as the occupier probably looked through their peephole, for who could possibly be visiting at this time, so close to night.

"Wer sind sie?" *Who are you?* A voice came out bluntly, muffled by the door.

"Herr Holtzmann?" Hunter said, leaning in towards the door so he did not have to raise his voice, he then continued to give the barest of their background.

At the mention of the MMC, the man gasped and unlocked the several bolts on the door and pulled it open. He stood before them as an older gentleman in his sixties, but with sharp eyes that took in their faces, then checked the street was empty before ushering them into the narrow hallway.

"Danke, Herr Holtzmann." Hunter murmured as he stepped through, the dim hallway was losing the daylight and was relying on the old oil lamp that was set on a side table. "Ich bin Herr Hunter Astley, und das ist Fräulein Kris Davies."

"Kris-*ten*." Kristen hissed.

"You came! And much quicker than I had anticipated, I only sent the message to your Council a month ago." Herr Holtzmann said, still gazing at their faces with an unsettling light.

"We knew the importance of this assignment and came as quickly as possible, Herr Holtzmann." Hunter replied, quickly skating over just *how* they had travelled so quickly. "The last British witch-hunters stayed with you, ja? Do you have any of their documents or information?"

"Please, call me Max." Holtzmann insisted, then paused, putting his thoughts into words. "Unfortunately, no, your witch-hunters were very careful not to share any details with me, for their safety and mine. Over the six months they were here, they never brought papers home, never spoke of their work. I knew that they were researching the background of the Shadow Witch and looking for her weaknesses, but nothing more."

Hunter inwardly sagged, that they had travelled so far for this. "Is there no one else that helped them; that could help us? The German Council?"

Max shrugged. "Our Council is not as strong as yours, and they have moved their base away from Berlin in an attempt to survive the persecution of witch-hunters. Berlin is reigned over by the witches and we are left to cope as best we can. But I know that your men had a contact, an important one, at the Reichstag."

"Ok, well that's a start." Kristen said, the first words she'd spoken. "Let's go there."

Hunter looked at her with askance, worrying that this was just the first of many silly blonde comments he might have to deal with. "Kristen, do you know what the Reichstag is?"

"Sure, it's the old parliamentary seat of Berlin, now used as the witches' headquarters, locally known as the Witches Rat, home of the most powerful witches in Germany, currently headed by a female witch called Laura Kuhn." She replied with a haughty flick of her blonde hair, and a challenging look in her flashing eyes. "I'm not as dumb as I look."

Hunter sighed, looking back to Max. "Are you sure there are no other contacts or leads we could take?" He asked. Hunter was not a coward, but if he could avoid walking into the epicentre of witches in Germany, then he would.

"No." Max replied immediately and confidently. He had had a month to think about what the British witch-hunters could do, after his friends had been killed.

Hunter shrugged. "Fine, then yes Kristen, we're going to the Reichstag."

Max smiled sadly at the young people before him, that were so ready to go into danger, just like the last poor souls. "You are both welcome to stay tonight, Herr Hunter, Fräulein Kristen; and seek the contact tomorrow in the safety of daylight."

"Danke." Hunter replied, accepting the offer. He was tired after the trek and if he needed to rest, he was positive that Kristen would be feeling twice as bad.

Max showed them to the spare room, where several mattresses covered most of the floor, the blankets and pillows all clean and set aside since their last users needed them no longer. Max hesitated at the door; he never came in this room; not since he lost the British witch-hunters that had been his friends. And then the old man brought up what he could muster for a supper and left the two witch-hunters to rest.

Hunter sat down on the furthest mattress and helped himself to the bread and cold meat that Max had brought them. Expecting that Kristen would settle likewise, he raised a brow when she came over and sat beside him, picking off his plate. He had to admit that he did enjoy the warmth and comfort as she leant against his arm, and the very scent of her, and she was right that it had been a long time…

"Kristen." Hunter warned coldly.

The girl sighed, sitting up straight, and eyeing him undecidedly. "What? I'm not hurting anyone."

"We're working." Hunter replied, getting to his feet to get a little more distance between them.

Kristen gave a crooked smile, and her eyes gleamed with a mischief that Hunter recognised from his own youth. "Technically, we're not working until tomorrow."

Kristen's smile faltered as she saw that she wasn't winning, she wrapped her arms about her knees and looked innocently up at Hunter. "You know, if you don't find me attractive, you could just say, I wouldn't be offended, promise."

"It's not that, it's…" Hunter paused, wondering how to phrase it. "I've got a bit of a psycho ex, and I don't want to get you in any more trouble."

"Come on, how can any ex of yours cause trouble to 6th and 7th gen witch-hunters?" Kristen said with a yawn, and without waiting for a reply she lay down and tried to sleep, with the happy knowledge that Hunter at least found her attractive, by his own omission.

Hunter stood staring at Kristen as she settled, then realised that the American had been away during the whole realisation that Hunter and the Shadow Witch had been a couple and had a child; and he and Kristen had probably left before she had chance to hear the gossip. Poor girl. Hunter sighed and dropped down onto the mattress furthest from Kristen, and as he closed his eyes, he realised that he was far too tired to hold back the inevitable dream.

*Hunter was lumbered with a heavy satchel and he was glad to dump it in the hallway when he reached home. It had been a long day and he was weary. He kicked off his shoes without unlacing them and shrugged off his coat, hanging it on the coat stand before trudging through to the living room. Sophie was curled up on one half of the settee, quietly reading, but she looked up as he entered.*

*Without a word, Hunter collapsed on the settee next to her, giving a small sigh of contentment at the soft seat. Sophie rested her book and continued to gaze curiously at him, wondering what on earth could be troubling him.*

*When it became apparent that he wasn't going to say anything, she finally spoke. "Hard day at work?"*

*"Hmm, about average these days." Hunter replied in a monotone voice.*

*"Anything interesting happen?" Sophie enquired with a too-perfect innocence.*

*Hunter turned his head against the back cushion, to gaze at his dear Sophie, who did not fool him one bit. There was not a chance that he was going to let her hear anything of value, whether this was magic, a dream, a delusion or any other kind of madness. "No. Same old, same old. Though we've had a new girl start. Very annoying. Very American."*

*"Very pretty?" Sophie asked, jumping straight to what she considered important.*

*"Don't know, didn't really notice." Hunter replied.*

*"That's a yes then." Sophie replied with a chuckle, amused at Hunter's attempt to not give the wrong answer. She turned back to her book, convincingly uninterested with this new girl. "What's her name?"*

*"Oh no, no." Hunter replied, "You're not learning that. All I need to do is give you a name, and doubtless you'll track her down. I haven't forgotten Gabriella, and neither have her family. All we did was flirt and you had to go in there with your curses..."*

*Poor Gabriella, Hunter thought. An innocent girl from the Donili village that hadn't known that her innocent flirting would bring on the wrath of the Shadow Witch. There had been no solid proof of witchcraft or foul play after the accident, but Hunter was convinced that it was too much of a coincidence.*

*"I don't know what you mean." Sophie replied airily, turning the page of her book.*

**Chapter Nineteen**

The Reichstag was an impressive building set in the centre of Berlin. Hunter, Kristen and Max stood in the shadows of the Sheidemannstraße, looking out at the building. People moved with business-like haste to and fro in front of the Reichstag, in fact only the lack of tourists distinguished it from pre-witch Berlin.

"There is Herr Beerbaum." Max muttered, nodding to one gentleman who marched past in a fine suit. "Calls himself Bürgermeister der Leute - Mayor to the People, the ambitious Saukerl. Beerbaum is not a witch but is one of their main supporters.

"There is Fräu and Herr Shaudt, they are witches on the lower council." Max continued, pointing out another couple who walked into the Reichstag. "The Witches Rat is made up of the lower and upper council. From what I gathered; your witch-hunters had a contact in the upper council. How do you propose to get in touch with them?"

Hunter looked up at the daunting Reichstag, the morning sun glinting fiercely off the glass dome. "I was thinking of walking up and asking." He replied unconvincingly.

"That's a shit plan, Hunter." Kristen said with half a laugh, unsure whether he was joking or not.

"Look, the last guys took six months to find this contact, we don't have that long, we need this source now. We need to let that contact know we're here." Hunter argued quietly.

"So, what you got in mind?" Kristen prompted.

Hunter paused, gazing at the young, energetic witch-hunter. "You trust me?"

Kristen shrugged. "Sure, why not."

"I'm going to hand myself in, be the bait to draw out the contact." Hunter said simply.

Kristen thought about it for a moment, then nodded. "Ok, I'm in."

Hunter smiled at her willingness. He felt the necessity to talk her out of it, but then he'd never been able to counter the stubbornness of those that aided him: Toby; Marcus; James; even Sophie. Hunter seemed to attract the most iron-willed people.

"You are going through with this?" Max asked with exasperation. "You are crazy, you both are!"

Hunter turned to the old man. "Max, thank you for your help over the last year, the British Malleus Maleficarum Council are in your debt. But you need to go home now and forget all about us.

Hunter held out his hand, and when Max took it to shake, the old man froze in shock. Hunter looked deeper into those bright eyes and pushed further until he could sense the presence of thought...

The two men stood there for no more than a minute, when Hunter finally let Max go. Max stood for a moment, disorientated, then wandered away.

"What did you just do?" Kristen asked quietly.

"Altered his memory, removed everything to do with the MMC." Hunter muttered, shaking his head to get rid of the ghost of another man's memory.

"Huh, one of your party tricks?" Kristen asked warily.

"Something like that." Hunter replied. "It's for his own safety, and ours - I don't want to leave a trail."

Cutting off the moral argument he was sure was brewing, Hunter led across the street straight up to the Reichstag. There were two armed guards at the main door, and they eyed Hunter and Kristen warily as it became apparent that these two people weren't passing by.

"Guten morgen." Hunter called out as he climbed the first few wide steps. "We'd like to see the Witches Rat."

"You have appointment?" One guard asked.

"No, but they'll want to see us, we're witch-hunters." Hunter replied helpfully.

The effect was immediate. The guards both aimed their guns at the unwelcome visitors. The first guard snapped at Hunter and Kristen to raise their hands, while the second shouted the alarm in frantic German. Hunter glanced at Kristen and raised his hands as half a dozen armed guards came running out. Their force was well-trained, and four men secured the two dangerous witch-hunters and marched them inside, while the others carried the bags and weapons, they had taken from them.

The Reichstag wasn't designed for holding prisoners, but Hunter and Kristen found themselves thrown into a room with small, high windows, and the door locked behind them.

"What happens now?" Kristen asked, rubbing her arms where the guards had held her.

Hunter walked calmly about the room, which seemed to have no real function. "We wait." He replied, feeling a certain déjà vu. This wasn't the first time he'd walked into a witch headquarters, unarmed. It was a miracle he was still alive.

Time passed slowly, the two witch-hunters sat in silence, afraid to say anything prying ears might hear or deduce. Hunter paced the room at first, testing the defences. A powerful witch had put a block over every window. But after years of fighting the Shadow Witch and developing his own powers, he could read the flaws of this comparatively average magic. It was a relief to know that there was nothing physically stopping Hunter from leaving at any point.

By the time the door eventually opened again, Hunter was beginning to feel offended at how low a threat and a priority he and Kristen obviously poised to the witches. Two people appeared at the door, Henric Beerbaum, whom Max had pointed out earlier, hovered with dark flickering eyes that Hunter immediately distrusted. He had the air of a man that had done well at the expense of others. It made Hunter seethe - it was weasels like this that made the fight so much harder.

The second figure stood before Beerbaum radiating power that sang in tune with the defences that Hunter had been probing earlier. The female witch stood staring at the captives; her eyes narrowed.

"Why are two British witch-hunters seeking the Witches Rat?" She asked in fluent English.

"We came to find out what happened to our friends." Hunter replied conversationally.

The witch hesitated, not sure how to take this very calm man. "The six we caught nosing around last month? They were arrested and executed, which is the fate of any witch-hunter we find." She spoke slowly, clarifying the unfortunate position of the two new witch-hunters that were so ridiculously stupid as to hand themselves in. No wonder the witches had won, if this was an example of their enemy.

"Yes, but before that, we believe that they had an inside contact at the Reichstag." Hunter replied, casually pushing aside the threat.

The witch froze, shocked by this announcement. In her silence, Beerbaum shook his head and simply said, "Impossible."

"Nothing is impossible, trust me." Hunter replied dryly.

"Why are you telling us this?" The witch asked suspiciously.

"Because we think that this contact has important information."

The witch hesitated again, and Beerbaum took the opportunity to add another snide comment. "You are hardly in a position to make use of any such information."

The witch suddenly came out of her daze and snapped at Beerbaum in rapid German. The man replied with false humility, then without notice they both left, the door being closed and locked behind them.

The two witch-hunters stood in silent contemplation for a long moment, then Kristen stepped up, looking imploringly at Hunter.

"What the hell was that Hunter?" She fumed. "Are there any other secrets you want to share with them? No, don't shush me Hunter!"

"Be careful using names, we don't know who's listening." Hunter hissed, his paranoia kicking in. He didn't mind taking on a building full of witches, but if they worked out exactly who they held captive, the Shadow Witch wouldn't be far away, and Hunter wasn't ready for that.

"Of course, I told them. What do you think the witches are going to do now they know there's a traitor in their midst?" Hunter explained. "They'll hunt them out - doing our work for us and getting a result much faster."

"It's risky though, what if they kill them before we can do anything?" Kristen asked quietly, unsettled by being the sensible one.

Hunter shrugged. "Trust me." He knew he was being rash, but he was already nervous after one day away from Adam.

*****

Barely ten minutes had passed when the witch returned, alone this time.

"Fraulein Kuhn wants to see you." She said calmly.

The witch looked between the two witch-hunters and with a sigh she raised a hand. Hunter suddenly felt his wrists drawn together behind his back, as though ropes pulled tight. He struggled against the unnatural feeling, but his elbows felt like they were about to pop under the strain. Hunter glanced back and saw Kristen struggling likewise. Hunter concentrated on the vein of magic around him, he could sense the strength and the weakness, and he knew he could break it –

"Come quietly and you will not be hurt." The witch said with mild amusement at their plight, not knowing that Hunter was a mere breath away from breaking her bonds. But Hunter remained passive, turning to Kristen and meeting her fierce gaze he nodded, not saying anything but hoping she took his lead.

The young witch-hunter visibly relaxed before his eyes. Hunter always found it unsettling when people trusted him unquestionably; it was a big responsibility on his shoulders. But it sure as hell made it easier to get through the tasks ahead when there were no arguments or lengthy explanations to waste time on.

"Move." The witch snapped, pointing through the open door.

Hunter led the way; Kristen close behind him and their captor bringing up the rear. Hunter grimaced, suddenly struck by the realisation it wasn't his first time bound and captive in a witches' headquarters. Only this time he doubted there would be a miracle rescue, as there had been by Bev Murphy. Oh well, the plan had seemed like a good idea this morning.

The witch-hunters walked obediently down a dark corridor of the Reichstag, before finally reaching a set of double doors. The witch pushed past them and knocked.

"Ja?"

At the sharp female voice, the witch pushed the doors open and nodded Hunter and Kristen through. Hunter walked in, immediately taking in the scene. The room was an office, official and almost clinical in appearance. Photos of previously important people adorned the walls, along with the German flag.

And at the broad, polished desk, a woman sat, looking up expectantly. Fraulein Laura Kuhn, the strongest and most feared witch in Germany. She was an attractive woman in her mid-forties, her light brown hair scraped back in a severe bun and shocking blue eyes locked fiercely on the witch-hunters. Fraulein Kuhn rose from her desk and walked over to the bound witch-hunters, assessing them with a detached, impersonal gaze.

Hunter saw Kristen flinch as Kuhn drew near, and as the witch passed him, he shivered at the strength of magic that rolled off her. It took every effort on Hunter's part not to raise his shield against her. He didn't doubt for a second, she'd be able to read it and work out who he was.

"You seek a spy in our ranks." Fraulein Kuhn snapped in rapid German, no question in her voice. "You will tell me everything, their name, other sources."

"We cannot." Hunter replied mildly, looking back at the witch that had brought them.

Kuhn followed his gaze and paused as she regarded her colleague. "Danke Erica, you may leave."

The witch nodded and left immediately, trusting that her boss could handle the two bound witch-hunters.

As soon as the door closed, Hunter felt a bubble of magic rise about the room, it was thick and cloying and Hunter guessed it was to keep what was said in this room firmly private.

"What are you and the Amerikaner here for?" Fraulein Kuhn demanded.

Hunter paused, thinking how to play this. Kristen leant towards him; her curiosity caught by "Amerikaner".

"She wants to know why we're here." Hunter muttered, translating quickly.

"Well why don't you tell her." Kristen replied quietly, rolling her eyes. She then turned to the witch and spoke louder, enunciating each word. "We are here to find out about the Shadow Witch."

Fraulein Kuhn looked scathingly at the blonde witch-hunter, then spoke in clear English. "I am German, I am not deaf."

She then looked at Hunter, obviously marking him as the brains of this operation. "You are fools, you follow your friends' fate by coming here."

"Yes, that has already been pointed out, thank you." Hunter replied politely.

Kuhn shook her head and walked back to her desk. She held her hand over a drawer and closed her eyes. A moment later there was an audible click, and Kuhn opened the drawer and pulled out a thick sheaf of paper. She immediately held it out to the witch-hunters.

"Yes, me. Although I may have to find a scapegoat if I am to keep my position." Kuhn mused. "Well, make what you will of it." She snapped back to attention and thrust the papers in Hunter's direction.

Hunter looked down, momentarily shocked into silence, but then wet his lips to speak. "Ahm, perhaps you could be so kind as to remove our bonds." He commented, straining against the magical restraint at his wrists.

Fraulein Kuhn smiled. "Remove it yourself, Astley."

Hunter froze, then immediately raised his shield, not needing to hide it would seem. "You know?"

Kuhn did not reply straight away; her eyes followed the lines of his shield and as she read the strength of it, she looked mildly impressed. "Yes, Herr Beerbaum did not take long to work it out – you are quite famous, Hunter Astley."

While she spoke, Hunter broke the magic that bound his wrists with a simple channel of thought, then freed Kristen.

"So, what does this mean?" Hunter asked warily.

It means that the Shadow Witch is on her way, and I cannot help you." Fraulein Kuhn replied sadly. "Our Burgermeister has likely contacted her people already, the ambitious little pig. The house will be sealed, and I doubt even you, Herr Astley, can break out, when it is designed to trap you in."

"But… you are the most powerful witch in Germany." Kristen broke in. "Can't you do something?"

"Against the Shadow Witch? I highly doubt it." Kuhn replied, a frown creasing her brow. "And if I tried, I would be revealed as a traitor, and would lose my place. And then who would curb the violence against my people? Who knows what monster my successor might be?"

Fraulein Kuhn walked away from them, looking at one of the large windows, yet not seeing the stretch of green and grey ahead. "I was happy with life before the Shadow Witch. Since her rise, Germany has been in ruins, the average person treated as nothing more than cattle. As the most powerful witch I was offered this position and took it in the hope I could make life easier. But I have to hide my own husband for fear he will be targeted, and I have to counter the malicious moves of some witches and people like Beerbaum. I have thought about finding equally sympathetic witches, but it is too dangerous. And then the witch-hunters came, and I felt new hope... until they were caught by the others. And now you."

Hunter was left silenced by her confession.

"You have to hide your husband?" Kristen echoed.

Fraulein Kuhn half-turned from the window. "He's not a witch, just a normal man. Under the new regime I am permitted to... take up with such a person to procreate. But to love such a man would be frowned upon indeed. Albert's very existence is hidden, and I have to answer to Fraulein Kuhn twenty times a day instead of Frau Gren as I long to be."

Kuhn walked back to the witch-hunters, looking much weakened, even though her magic still rolled off in powerful waves. "Please don't reveal any of this when She comes for you. I'm trusting you to find a way."

Hunter tightened his hold on the folder and nodded.

Kuhn took a deep breath and composed herself. "I'll take you back to the holding room. Good luck. And remember – once we are outside this room, we are not shielded from eavesdroppers."

Hunter and Kristen exchanged a look, neither feeling confident at this point. But Laura Kuhn opened the door, shattering the bubble of privacy. The witch looked suddenly fierce and daunting; all softness washed away once more.

**Chapter Twenty**

Back in the holding room, Hunter stood, waiting for the sound of footsteps on the other side to fade completely before he turned to Kristen. "Ready to leave?"

"Hell yes." She replied with a dramatic sigh. She eagerly grabbed his hand and closed her eyes, prepared for the pulling, rushing sensation that... didn't come.

Kristen opened one eye, then seeing the same room, she opened the other. "Hunter?"

Hunter was pale and panicked. Shit. He tried again, but nothing, he was completely blocked. Shit. Even with Kuhn's warning he had arrogantly assumed he could still get out.

"I can't..." He gasped, his eyes roving skywards as his senses pushed out. They were met by a wall of magic infinitely more complex and stronger than the other witch's defence. And Hunter could read the pattern of the magic, it was as familiar to him as his own.

"The Shadow Witch. She's trapped us, I can't find a way out." Hunter said, dropping Kristen's hand, guilty at the fate he had sealed for her. "She's coming."

The two witch-hunters stood in a shocked and fearful silence. Hunter became gradually aware of a quiet voice singing, akin to a radio far away.

> *"...Alle Leut', alle Leut' geh'n jetzt nach Haus'*
> *Grosse Leut', kleine Leut',*
> *Dicke Leut', dünne Leut'"*

"Mel." Hunter suddenly blurted out, remembering where he had heard it before. As soon as he spoke, the singing stopped.

"Hi George." That familiar chirpy voice came out.

Hunter turned and, beyond all comprehension, Mel walked over to him. She still looked like an innocent angel, wearing a modest pale blue dress and a white cardigan. Her pale blonde hair was held back with a white headband.

Hunter stood gaping, wondering if this was madness, or his desperate imagination. But Kristen moved closer to him, her eyes locked on the strange girl.

"Mel, what are you doing here?" Hunter asked, remaining tense and defensive.

"You're not glad to see me." Mel replied, faltering at her friend's less than friendly welcome. "Adam was worried about his daddy, he wanted me to make sure you are ok."

Hunter noticed that Kristen looked at him oddly, and he realised that he hadn't told her about his son.

"Yes, I am glad to see you, of course I am Mel." Hunter replied, remembering how easily hurt this immature girl was. "But Mel, how... did you get in here?"

Mel paused, her brow furrowing in confusion. "I don't understand."

Hunter took a deep breath to calm himself. Getting frustrated at Mel wasn't going to help.

"That's ok Mel. But are you able to come and go as you like? Just like in the warren?"

Mel bit her lip but nodded slowly.

Hunter took another breath to calm the nerves that threatened to overwhelm him. The Shadow Witch was close, she was so very close, and Hunter didn't want to meet her just yet.

"And can you take Kristen and me with you?" Hunter asked quietly.

"Of course, George, if that's what you want." Mel replied, taking a moment to work out who Kristen was. Oh, she must be the other girl, the one with the blonde hair that was so much yellower than Mel's. Mel fiddled with a lock of her own hair, contemplating which was prettier…

Hunter noticed the imperceptible changes in the room around him, the background noises seemed muffled and the shadows thickened.

"Excellent." Hunter stated, desperate to hurry this up, they were definitely out of time. "Then let's go, altogether, right now."

Hunter held out his hand to Mel, who looked completely confused by his haste, but obediently slid her delicate little hand into his, her cool fingers curling firmly around his. In his other hand, Hunter grasped the papers Fraulein Kuhn had given him, and held out his arm so Kristen could grip his wrist. Hunter nodded to Mel, who looked at him strangely for a moment, her blue eyes hypnotic.

Then she let go of his hand and Hunter blinked, the atmosphere had changed, the air was cooler and fresher. He finally dragged his eyes from Mel's and looked around, noticing the change of scene, the shelves of books that covered the walls, the old cushioned chairs arranged informally in the middle.

From one of these chairs, a man rose. A man with silver-grey hair and loose robes. A man that Hunter recognised in a way that suddenly calmed him.

"Padre!" Hunter strode over to him, taking his hand as an old friend.

"Signor Astley? But how?" The Abate looked thoroughly puzzled by the sudden appearance of his old pupil, especially in the heart of the Abbazia which was protected from such magical entrances. But his sharp grey eyes moved over Hunter's companions, and when they settled on Mel, he took a sharp intake of breath. "Begone demon, you are not welcome here."

Hunter frowned at the fierceness of this good Abate and glanced between the old man and Mel.

"Padre?" Hunter squeezed the Abate's hand, hoping to stimulate a response, but when none was gained, he dropped his grip and stood there helplessly. In the silence, the need to be an English gentleman reasserted itself. "Padre, may I introduce Miss Kristen Davies, a 6th gen witch-hunter. And Miss Mythanwy Elspeth Lughnasa, who, well, rescued me not a minute ago."

Hunter finished speaking and continued to watch the Abate. He had never seen such disgust on the old man's face.

"Better to die than be in debt to a thing like that. Make her leave, she is not welcome in these walls." The Abate seethed.

And Mel, who was being spoken of so ill, paid the old man no attention, she was far too preoccupied playing with Kristen's ponytail, seeing how her golden hair played in the light in comparison to Mel's. Poor Kristen, who had never had the pleasure of meeting Mel and had only heard about her, merely shrugged at one more bizarre chapter today, and stood patiently.

"Padre, please." Hunter began but trailed off. He could see the stubbornness of the Abate's stance and knew they would have to do as directed. "Ok, we're going."

Hunter gestured to the girls to follow and made his way to the study door.

"You may return, once she is gone." The Abate added in a choked voice.

Hunter barely acknowledged his words and walked out with Kristen and Mel trailing after him.

"What was that about?" Kristen hissed as they walked out into the courtyard towards the main gate.

Hunter shook his head. "I don't know. I'll try and find out." He said, truly worried over his old mentor's reaction.

Hunter stopped as they stepped out of the Abbazia. The rest of the Donili village lay out before them, beautiful and peaceful in the early afternoon sun. Hunter quickly decided on a plan of action and led the two girls down to the village until they came to a small and newly-built cottage, the light wood barely touched by weather. Hunter rapped on the door and waited for an answer.

After only a minute the front door opened and a young man with a head of thick black hair looked out. His eyes lit up the moment they landed on Hunter, and with a loud laugh he flung the door open and hugged his friend without reserve.

"Hi Marcus, how's married life?" Hunter gasped at the strength of the hug and forced his friend back to arm's length to get a proper look at him.

"It is good, good, Hunter." Marcus blushed at his polite enquiry, then looked to the two blonde girls. "Would you like to come in?"

Hunter accepted and the trio went into the house. It was small, but it was obvious that Marcus was proud of it, and Hunter praised it accordingly.

Marcus' new wife came through at the sound of visitors to see if anyone cared for a drink.

"Ah Marissa, you are more beautiful than ever." Hunter greeted, happy at Marcus and Marissa's blissful little life. And a little envious too.

"Marcus, I have a meeting with the Abate. Would it be ok if my friends stayed here until I return?" Hunter asked.

"Of course." Marcus replied without question.

Hunter smiled and pulled Kristen aside in the small room. "Can you keep an eye on Mel? And here, look after these, see if you can find anything."

Hunter held out the folder they had gone through so much for, and Kristen took it with a determined little nod.

"I won't be long." He said, then ducked out of the room.

Back at the Abbazia, Hunter knocked on the study and, not waiting for an answer, entered. The Abate was seated in his chair once more, and looked up expectantly as Hunter walked in.

Hunter looked at his old mentor with a certain disbelief. How could this man have reacted so rudely to one that Hunter considered a friend?

"Hunter, it is good to see you. You look well." The Abate suddenly said, his voice hollow as he knew what would come from his predictable, rebellious student.

"No. No niceties. Why were you so rude to Mel?" Hunter demanded.

"A creature such as she is not welcome in this Abbazia." The Abate repeated slowly and quietly. "Do you not know what manner of abomination it is?"

Hunter paused, having no idea where this was going. He barely knew Mel, and he definitely didn't understand her. But whatever she was, she was here to help. "I realise that she is far from a normal human being, but surely you of all people can accept her, padre. Or were your lectures on leniency and acceptance so narrow-mindedly reserved for witches?"

"And I will not understand how you can vehemently hate witches and defend her!" The Abate snapped, showing his first flare of temper. The old man took a breath and calmed himself. "But you do not know what she is. And I will not be the one to enlighten you. Just be aware Hunter, do not trust her."

Hunter turned away, bloody frustrated. This was the second time he had been warned not to trust Mel, but what was so bad about her?

"Forgive me padre, but I will trust her and anyone else who helps me against the witches."

The Abate froze at this. He opened his mouth to speak, but it was long moments before the words managed to come out. "She… is helping against the witches?"

Hunter looked at the Abate, wondering what caused him such surprise. "Of course."

The Abate stood up and walked over to a bookshelf and raised his hand to take a book, before hesitating and pulling back.

"No, no, I should consult the others." He muttered in the Donili dialect, then looked up, remembering Hunter's presence. "Well? Go, back to your friends, back to England or wherever you're needed."

Hunter frowned at the bluntness of the Abate, but as the older man remained flustered and worried, Hunter backed away, having no answers and more confused than ever.

Hunter walked slowly down the hill, back towards Marcus' house. His thoughts were heavy. How could an innocent little thing like Mel possibly worry the trained and skilled Donili monks?

Hunter reached the house and let himself in. The young couple, Marcus and Marissa, sat in the main room, awkwardly shy hosts. Kristen sat silently; the papers still clasped firmly in both hands. And Mel? Mel sat with a vague smile, softly humming.

"Hunter!" Marcus jumped up at the return of his friend. "How was the Abate? Your friend Kristen explained his unusual behaviour."

Hunter shrugged, not quite sure how to start explaining what was going on.

Marcus saw his hesitation and confusion and quickly spoke again to cover it. "You will stay for dinner, yes? And you can tell me everything then."

Hunter smiled and accepted, although a part of him was ready to leave this peaceful place and return to the stress of the warren. And return to his son. But there was a pressing matter that had to be dealt with now, his brown eyes returned to Mel, and he inwardly sighed.

"Mel, may I have a word please? In private?"

"Of course, George!" Mel replied gaily, immediately springing to her feet. The blonde girl followed Hunter outside with the eagerness and affection of a puppy.

In the quiet sprawling village of Donili, Hunter took Mel's hand and they strolled in the pleasant afternoon sun.

"Mel… who sent you?" Hunter asked.

"Adam did." Mel replied, frowning that she had to repeat herself. "He was worried about you."

"No, I don't mean today. I mean, who sent you to the witch-hunters?" Hunter persisted.

"You… you don't want me? Will you send me away?" Mel asked, her voice cracking with pain.

"No, of course I won't send you away Mel. But I need to know who sent you." Hunter pressed.

But Mel was shaking her head and biting her lip. "We wanted to help. I want to help. Everyone is so nice, and I have so many friends."

"Who is 'we'?" Hunter asked gently.

Mel's wide blue eyes caught him again. "The one who sends me and waits for you to ask for help."

"And who might that be?"

Mel let go of Hunter's hand and started humming and swaying to her own tune.

"Mel, please tell me." Hunter continued softly, knowing that one firm word could have her crying again.

And little Mel turned back to him with a dazzling smile, and started to recite:

"Lucy, satan sataniel,

Fall to earth my fallen angel;

Little fire and little light,

Morning star no longer bright."

The world stilled as she spoke, a cloud passing over the sun, causing everything to be a little duller. No birds could be heard and even the wind dropped. Hunter shivered with a sudden chill.

Then the moment passed, and Hunter's senses returned to the world that still went on regardless. And dear Mel was still smiling so openly at him.

"Right." Hunter said, needing to break the silence with something. "And he wants to help me?"

Mel nodded. "Yes, but you need to ask him for help, otherwise he cannot interfere."

Hunter frowned, hoping that this was one of the times Mel was being cryptic. She couldn't mean what he thought she meant. "Cannot interfere? Except from sending you, of course."

"No silly, I wasn't meant to help." Mel chided him. "But everyone was so nice, I wanted to."

Hunter took a deep breath, completely lost at this point. Were they really having a nice chat about the Devil? Satan, Lucifer, whatever you wanted to call him.

Years of studying the occult – both MMC sources, and the woefully misled public information – and in many witches went hand in hand with the Devil. Literally. In the older texts they were said to invoke him, allow him passage into our world. They were said to fornicate with him and suckle his familiars. Of course, such reports died away over time, as the world became less superstitious and more cynical. Even in the MMC reports and lectures, over time the focus had shifted from the religious implications to the purely physical and scientific. Oh, how they had all moved on, and progressed, and yet here Hunter stood, discussing Lucifer.

"Ahm, Mel, isn't he generally on the witches' side?" Hunter asked hesitantly, not really wanting to encourage this vein of madness.

Mel shook her head, her blonde ponytail flicking wildly. "He made them, representatives of the Devil on earth, and asked only for their lifelong worship. But the naughty witches neglect him. He is forgotten in the shadows, and his familiars starve and perish. Poor Lucy."

Hunter shook his head, unable to think at this point.

Mel smiled sympathetically and slipped her small hand back into his. "Shall we go back? I am sure dinner is nearly ready, and we must help set the table."

**Chapter Twenty-one**

Returning to Marcus' house, there was the smell of rich stew and fresh bread. Mel hurried ahead, as eager and carefree as ever. Hunter walked slowly, more than a little dazed by their conversation.

Kristen frowned at his expression and pressed him for an explanation. But Hunter shook his head, he didn't want to speak of it at all, and would never bring mention of the Devil inside his friend's house. Instead Hunter turned his attention to the folder that Kristen still clung to defensively.

"Did you find anything?" Hunter asked.

"Nothing new. A lot of it didn't make sense. And quite a bit is in German." Kristen replied, readily relinquishing the folder to someone that might make more out of it.

Hunter took it and sat down, flicking through the first few pages. Kristen hovered over his shoulder, leaning in uncomfortably close, hoping to learn something.

"This is just a letter from the 40's from a scientist, Herr Braun." Hunter muttered, moving it aside. He'd already seen a copy of the letter years ago – an experiment involving witches, hunters and the Nazi party. To create a Shadow Witch.

But beneath it, there was a report he'd not seen. It followed the initial trials and reported a more successful attempt at cracking the ancient spell that bound the Shadow Witch's powers. The scientists and gathered witches had followed an old ritual and mass sacrifice, which resulted in the artefact giving off a wave of energy. But unfortunately, they were at a loss where in the world the Shadow Witch had awoken. Ah, Hunter knew the answer to that. He wondered what it must have been like for Sara Murray, in the middle of England, to wake up suddenly imbued with limitless powers and no explanation, and no help.

"Are you staying the night?" Marcus asked after dinner. He was ever the kind host but was uncomfortably aware of how cramped his little house would be with so many guests.

Hunter hesitated. It was so tempting to stay just one evening in this sanctuary and put off the danger and drama that was to come. But he shook his head. "I need to get back."

One bright-eyed little boy came fiercely to the front of all thoughts. Adam would not forgive him for lingering.

Deciding there was nothing to be gained by waiting any longer, Hunter led his two companions outside (he considered it rude to just disappear from Marcus' living room), and with a wistful look up the hill at the Abbazia, they vanished.

Back in the warren, Hunter went immediately to Toby's room. The Council could wait for their report until after Hunter had seen his son.

He knocked on the door and waited. It was wrenched open by a pale looking Toby, who gazed at Hunter with such worried eyes, that Hunter felt his blood freeze.

"What's happened?" Hunter demanded, pushing his way into the room, desperate to see his son safe and well.

But there was nothing to fear, Adam was sitting on the bed, surrounded by toy ponies, playing with a girl of about five or six, that Hunter immediately took to be Molly, Toby's daughter.

"Daddy!" Adam squealed, propelling himself into Hunter's arms.

Returning the hug, Hunter looked enquiringly at Toby, who still hovered by the door, wearing a worried expression.

"It's – it's the witch, Beverley." Toby started. "The Council took her; I don't know where."

"What?" Hunter snapped.

"They tried to take Adam too." Toby now hurried to say before Hunter blew up. "But we refused to hand him over. But Bev – there was nothing I could do to stop them."

Hunter stood dazed, overwhelmed with gratitude to his old friend for keeping his son safe; and predictably furious with the Council.

"Christ, Hunter, be honest with me. Bev is *her* mother, isn't she?" Toby suddenly said, breaking through Hunter's thoughts.

Hunter frowned, sure that they'd been careful with that particular secret. "How…?"

"Well… your familiarity with her. And they look alike. Also, it made sense to send the boy's family to retrieve him."

Hunter was amazed. "You're not bad at piecing these things together."

Toby shrugged, very much aware of his ability to read between the lines.

Hunter stood still for only a moment longer, then turned and stormed out of the room.

"Watch Adam." He shouted back at Toby.

"Don't do anything rash, Hunter." Toby shouted down the corridor, then sighed, knowing it was futile.

Hunter marched down to the Council rooms, banging his fist against the door. Without waiting for a response, he threw the doors open and barged in.

There were only three Council members there. General Dawkins, Theresa, and Reynolds. They all sat sociably at the table, nursing cups of tea, talking of insignificant things. And they all looked up at the unannounced intrusion of the witch-hunter.

"Mr Astley, you're back." Theresa said, looking impressed at his swift return. "Did you find anything?"

"Where is Bev? Where is the witch?" He demanded, ignoring Theresa's question.

The Council members exchanged a glance and Hunter felt the atmosphere cool.

"That is no business of yours." General Dawkins replied without looking at him.

"Don't start that shit." Hunter warned. "Tell me what you've done, or I'll…"

Dawkins stood up suddenly, squaring up to Hunter in an attempt at intimidation that Hunter was far from impressed by.

"Or you'll do what, Astley? Defy us, again?"

Hunter exhaled slowly, his eyes never flinching from Dawkin's gaze. He eventually replied, his voice low and all the more threatening. "Maybe I will. Maybe I will take what I learnt in Berlin and leave you with nothing. Maybe I'll take Kristen and Toby with me, and let you fight this with just your 1st gens. Or maybe I'll see how many of them want to join me too."

Hunter saw doubt creep into Dawkin's eyes. Oh, the General knew well enough the power and influence Hunter had over other witch-hunters. Hadn't he seen for himself how the warren had become excited by their hero's return. But then his gaze hardened again.

"You wouldn't dare." He snarled. "We all know that's not your style – you'd rather run away alone than take on the responsibility of others. After all, didn't your actions kill your last team!"

Just as Hunter was about to snap, Theresa stood up.

"Gentlemen, enough! General Dawkins sit back down. And Mr Astley, please calm down." Theresa kept a solid gaze on them until they both did as they were told, then turned to Hunter.

"The witch had nothing more to offer us, so she has been taken to a secure location."

Hunter hesitated, processing this. "A secure location? Where is more secure than the warren?"

"The warren is designed to be a base, a home for witch-hunters. We do not have the facilities to keep that sort of prisoner here."

Hunter snorted at the idea, these rooms were solid, the doors and bolts heavy duty, and the corridors filled with trained men and women. What threat could a bound witch pose.

"Fine. Then where is she?" He demanded.

"As I said, it is none of your business." Dawkins said snidely from the table.

"Hunter." Theresa stepped between them again before anything happened. "We cannot tell you; I wish we could. But you are a front-line fighter and we cannot risk you being captured with that sort of information in your head."

Theresa reached out awkwardly to grasp his arm in some sort of sympathetic hold. "I'm sorry…"

Hunter shrugged away from her and backed towards the door.

There was a cough from the forgotten Reynolds, who sat uncomfortably watching the scene. "What about your find in Berlin?"

Hunter glanced at him, looking slightly dazed by the change of topic. "Um, Kristen has it all, she'll bring it by."

And then he left, with the unsettling thought that the Council had almost taken his son – and would equally refuse to tell him anything.

## Chapter Twenty-two

*Hunter walked into the familiar cottage with a feeling of trepidation. Everything was as it should be, except for Sophie. She stood, awaiting him in the living room, a look of despair about her.*

*Hunter moved towards her, only for Sophie to step back.*

*"Don't." He pleaded softly, holding out a hand to her tense, half-wild form.*

*"I can't." She stressed, twisting, almost writhing against the rigid pose she dictated for herself. "I can't do it anymore. This is just a fantasy in which I've allowed myself to be human – to allow myself to believe I am human."*

*"I don't know what this is, but it's not a fantasy that I love you, and if I could choose any life it would be this." Hunter continued in soft tones, taking a careful step towards his Sophie.*

*But she staggered back again, shaking her head, her eyes dark with pain. "Yesterday... was so close. I was relieved that you escaped. But these chances have run out. The next time we* will *meet, and I cannot be restrained by love, or desire for a life that was never ours."*

*Sophie finally moved towards Hunter; her hand outstretched. Hunter blinked and looked down as she dropped a small object into his hand. He took a deep shuddering breath as he saw her gold wedding band in his palm.*

*Hunter opened his eyes to the dark room in which he lay. A single tear rolled down his face and fell onto his pillow.*

*The war was swiftly coming back in their direction, he knew it. Their little respite, if that was what it could be called, was over. And he wasn't looking forward to what was coming.*

*He'd been into battle before, many times. He knew he wasn't a coward, he did not fear for his own life, but he dreaded the loss of others, people he had started to grow fond of and felt responsible for.*

It was around 7am, and Hunter had only been awake for half an hour, but still lay in bed, too miserable to move. There was the sudden unwelcome sound of someone kicking the door open. Hunter watched with one lazy eye as Kristen walked in, precariously balancing a tray with what looked suspiciously like breakfast.

Hunter noticed Adam sit bolt upright in the small bed on the other side of the room.

"Hey kiddo, I got orange juice and toast." Kristen greeted the little boy, setting the tray down on the only table in the room.

Adam hesitated, tempted by the breakfast, but wary of the strange lady. The little boy looked over at his father for permission.

Hunter could only groan. "What are you doing, Kristen?"

"Bringing breakfast." She replied innocently. "Think of it as thanks for saving my life."

Hunter sat up in bed, looking his usual ruffled morning mess, with extra dark circles under the eyes today. "Technically, I didn't save your life, Mel did."

"Ok, then think of it as punishment for putting my life at risk." Kristen shrugged, and helped herself to a piece of toast. "It's all a ruse, anyway."

The girl then proceeded to sit on the foot of Hunter's bed. Hunter immediately pulled his feet back and got out of bed, wary of where this might go, and what the forward Miss Davies might do, even with Adam in the room. He walked over to the tray and helped himself to what was supposed to be coffee, but it was the best they had in this time of war. Hunter took one sip and grimaced at the bitter taste, then handed a cup of orange juice to Adam before finally returning his attention to Kristen.

"Ok, what do you want?"

Kristen played with her toast, in no rush to answer. "To clear one or two things up. I heard some stuff since we got back."

Hunter froze, wondering what "stuff" she might have uncovered. But he stayed silent as the girl finished her toast and continued without further prompting.

"Psycho ex, huh? Understatement." Kristen said with a smile that was caught between cruel and disbelieving. "Now that really is the actual cliché of sleeping with the enemy."

Hunter glanced sharply towards Adam, feeling very protective of the innocent little boy, that didn't deserve to hear people slander his mother.

"Kristen, outside." Hunter ordered with a curt nod of his head. Without waiting for her, he marched out into the cold corridor. Hunter frowned, he wished he'd put some shoes on, his feet were bloody freezing.

"Say whatever you want to me, but I would appreciate it if you watch your tongue around my son." Hunter said as Kristen came to join him, more than a hint of a threat in his voice. He leaned past her to pull the door shut, leaving Adam to have his breakfast in peace.

Kristen's blue eyes darted back in the direction of the room. "Then it's true? He's really her son? I thought, and kinda hoped it was just a rumour."

Hunter stood silently, he'd quickly become used to such shock and disgust from the witch-hunters, ever since they had found out.

"How?" Kristen asked, then blushed. "I mean, I know *how*, but how could you?"

Hunter shrugged; it was nearly impossible to explain to these people that were already so biased.

"For a year before the Shadow Witch emerged, we knew her as Sophie Murphy. She was a friend, a colleague, and yes, for a while a lover. Long enough for Adam to be conceived. There was no reason to suspect her of being a witch."

"Is it true you used some bullshit about the boy being a possible offensive weapon to get the Council to agree with kidnapping him, rather than tell them the truth?" Kristen asked, hardly convinced, but jumping to her next train of thought anyway.

Hunter smiled bitterly at the recent memory. "Yes. They would never have understood. Half of them still don't. Besides, it could still be true, I have no way of predicting what Adam might become. But it would involve waiting for him to reach puberty before we get a clue. Although if I'm honest, I don't think we have that long."

Kristen narrowed her eyes at his final comment. "Is it really that bad?"

"It's starting to feel just like it did before Salisbury Plain." Hunter sighed, referring back to the last decisive battle; when almost all the witch-hunters and their supporters were wiped out.

Kristen wrapped her arms about herself, suddenly cold. "Well, what are you going to do?" She asked, her eyes fixing his again.

Hunter hesitated. "I'm going to fight alongside the witch-hunters…"

"No, I mean, what are *you* going to do? You have-" Kristen broke off, glancing down the corridor before continuing in a much quieter voice. "You have powers no one else can dream of; a half-witch, half-eighth gen son; a blonde demon; and an army of magic monks."

Hunter looked at her, utter shock robbing him of his ability to speak. How did she know?

Kristen shrugged, seemingly reading his mind. "I had a nice chat with Mel and Marcus, just to find out where they sided in this whole thing. You've got a lot of powerful friends, Hunter. And y'know, it makes me wonder why you're content to be just a number on the battlefield, when you have all that behind you."

Hunter sighed. "I don't have any miracles up my sleeve." He replied weakly. But he recognised a kick up the arse when he saw one.

"Fine. Can you get your hands on the Berlin papers?" He asked, waiting for her to nod. "Then meet me here when you have them. Bring Mel if you see her before I do."

Kristen nodded, and without another word sauntered off down the corridor. Hunter watched her go, then returned to his room. Adam had finished his breakfast and was currently hiding under his father's bed – the giggling gave him away. Hunter smiled, and played along for a minute, loudly exclaiming that his son had vanished. All the while he pulled on his day clothes. Once he was fully dressed, he bobbed down, and pulled his screaming and kicking son from under the bed.

"Found you! Now get dressed Adam." Hunter said, pulling clothes out of the drawers and helping his son into them. "We're going to visit Uncle Toby-"

"And Molly!" Adam interjected; his voice muffled beneath his jumper.

"And Molly." Hunter agreed. "Then we're going to a very special place."

Hunter took Adam's hand and led the way down the corridor to Toby's room and knocked. He figured it was unnecessary to drag his son along for this part of business, but after the Council had nearly taken him, he was loathe to let the little boy out of his sight.

Toby answered the door within a couple of minutes, still looking quite groggy at this time of the morning.

"Hunter? What-"

Hunter smiled and, taking that as an invitation, let himself in. Adam immediately let go of his hand and took the opportunity to run and jump onto the still sleeping Molly's bed.

"Hi Toby, sorry to bother you so early, but I've just come to let you know I'm leaving." Hunter said, getting straight to the point.

Toby stood there speechless. "What? You – you're leaving? Why? What's the plan?"

"There's no established plan yet. I've just got to go and do what I can to bring the Shadow down. I'll be taking Adam with me. Oh, and Kristen too." Hunter explained, realising it didn't contain much of an explanation

Toby frowned, his mind obviously a little sluggish this morning, and hurrying to catch up. "Fine. Give me an hour to sort things out here, and I'll come."

Hunter knew he'd say something like that. He sighed at the reckless loyalty he seemed to gain from so many good men and women.

"You can't come." Hunter replied firmly.

Toby paused, for once in his life looking angry. "You're taking Kristen. Perhaps you find the girl you've known ten minutes more useful than me. Well tough shit Hunter, I'm not getting left behind this time."

Hunter hesitated, truthfully as an able-bodied 6th gen, Kristen was likely to prove more useful on whatever this mission was, rather than a crippled 3rd gen. But Hunter would rather die than admit this to Toby.

"You can't come." Hunter repeated gently. "I need someone I can trust to represent me here. Due to my unfortunate little clash with Dawkins, more than a few people will assume that I'm a coward and doing a runner, or that I am fracturing the MMC and rebelling. They need to know that I'm doing this for them, and that I'll be with them on the front line when it comes to the fight."

Toby still looked stubbornly furious, but his shoulders started to sag as his resolve wavered. "I don't like it."

"I know. Thanks Toby." Hunter replied, motioning to Adam that it was time to go. "Trust me, when it comes to that big fight, you're the guy I'll want next to me."

"What, so you can spend more time protecting me?" Toby retorted as Hunter and Adam left.

Upon returning to their room, they packed all of their meagre belongings into a couple of bags.

"Dad, can I take Incy?" Adam asked, having finished collecting the few toys and books that Molly had grown bored with and donated to the younger boy.

Hunter winced at the mention of the spider but conceded. If Adam could find him.

There was a knock at the door, and before Hunter had a chance to answer it, his visitors let themselves in. He was suddenly joined by his two blonde accomplices. Mel drifted in, beaming at her young friend Adam, and obviously delighted at the idea of a little trip. Kristen walked in behind her, smiling knowingly. She waved a thick folder at Hunter, who looked impressed.

"Already? That was quick work."

Kristen shrugged. "Pretty minimal security, they trust everyone in the warren."

Hunter looked around. Everything seemed ready. There was no time like the present.

"Hold hands." He instructed, slinging his bag over his shoulder, and taking his son's hand.

Mel held onto Adam, Kristen held onto Mel, and nodded to Hunter.

Hunter took a deep breath and closed his eyes, thinking firmly of his destination, an image so strong in his mind that he knew he was there before he opened his eyes. It was a beautiful summer morning, to be stood in the English countryside, in front of one of the grandest houses in the county. Hunter looked up at the old building and squeezed Adam's hand.

"This is Astley Manor, where I grew up. And one day, it will be your house." Hunter explained, introducing his young son to the family estate.

"Wow, so this is the famous Astley Manor?" Kristen said, apparently in awe of the place she had obviously heard about. "So, this means you're like, a Lord or something?"

Hunter gave her a withering glare. "Why don't you all come in?"

Hunter led the way up to the main door and on into the entrance hall. "I'll give you the full tour later. But for now, let's just say that Astley Manor was built in the last half of the nineteenth century by George Astley II. It has many witch-repellent spells and devices built into the very foundations – no witch can enter without being stripped of their powers. It is also the home of the most extensive witch-related library in the world – which we will be taking full advantage of."

Just as Hunter finished speaking, two men appeared behind him, their guns held steadily towards them. Hunter turned around, unsurprised by their presence.

"Ah, Jack, Shaun, how good to see you both again. Don't worry, these people are guests of my house."

The two men stood silently, sharing a glance as they tried to work out what to do next. The Council didn't have protocol for this.

"Now, you're probably wondering what to do." Hunter added helpfully. "To be honest, you're probably best reporting this to headquarters and awaiting orders. Or you could help us find what we're looking for, so we can defeat the witches."

The two men, still suspicious, lowered their guns.

"Sir," Jack began, hesitantly. "There is something you should be aware of…"

Before Jack had a chance to explain, the something, or rather someone, became apparent.

"All this noise, this early in a morning is uncalled for. On a Sunday too! Why, if you had any shame-" The arrogant female voice stopped suddenly, as the person came down the stairs and saw who had blustered in.

'Oh no.' Hunter thought. He'd much rather face demons and witches. He watched warily as the petite figure made her way down the stairs. Dressed in black, with her make-up flawless as ever, looking as though the war had not touched her.

"George?" Even her monosyllable enquiry sounded harsh. "So, you came back then."

Her cold grey eyes swept over the small group, assessing the visitors unforgivingly.

"Mother, it's good to see you, no one would tell me where you were." Hunter replied, suddenly guilty that he hadn't done more to find her sooner.

"Well." Mrs Astley began huffily. "Your witch-hunter rebels came and claimed Astley Manor for 'the cause' in your absence. They stuck me in some poky community building."

She exhaled her displeasure. "But I heard you had returned, and there was no longer any legal reason they had to hold me.

But to think that I have no right to live in my own home without my son's approval is appalling."

"I'm sorry you had to go through that, mother." Hunter replied, his guilt increasing. "I had no idea that would happen when I left."

"Well, you did leave. Gallivanting off and having a fine old time, just like your father, I'm sure. While I stay behind and try to make the best of the neglect." Mrs Astley paused, finally acknowledging the rest of the group. "And you bring a party back as always. You seem incapable of acting alone George."

Hunter looked to his small group of friends, feeling regret again that he should drag them into his misfortunes. "Mother, may I present Miss Kristen Davies and Miss Mythanwy Elspeth Lughnasa."

"Pleased to meet you, ma'am." Kristen said, more polite than Hunter had ever known her, obviously wary of the petite battle-axe before her.

Kristen held out her hand, but Mrs Astley just let it hang there, looking with disdain at the girl. "Oh no, George, not an American. Too gaudy and pretty, and nowhere near as elegant as the last one. And your other friend keeps rather quiet. Modesty is a virtue, but extreme shyness a curse. And look at her, one can hardly tell her age she dresses such a lamb!"

Kristen's mouth was agape at the criticisms that were thrown her way, and poor little Mel pressed closer to Hunter.

"She scares me." Mel breathed, making Hunter smile that an accomplice of Lucifer should fear his mother.

"And who is the boy?" Mrs Astley demanded, speeding along the introductions.

Hunter gave Adam's hand a reassuring squeeze before replying. "Mother, this is Adam – your grandson."

And finally, Hunter got to witness his mother being shocked into silence. Mrs Astley stood there, her normally pale cheeks fading to white and her thin lips opening and closing as she tried to comprehend this.

"No, but… how is this?" The normally articulate Mrs Astley was at a loss.

"He's mine and Sophie's son." Hunter answered softly. Then he looked down at Adam. "Say hello to your Grandmother Astley."

But the little boy clammed up, and faced with his daunting grandmother, he squeezed harder on his father's hand and shuffled to hide behind Hunter.

Mrs Astley pressed her fingers to her lips, looking quite choked up. "Finally, a grandchild. One I can help raise right this time."

Hunter frowned at this; he knew that his mother had long craved a grandchild – she had been less than subtle in her hints for years. But there was no way he was letting that poisonous woman near Adam – with his contradicting parentage the boy already had enough issues.

"Sir?" A male voice cut in, and Hunter turned to Jack as he spoke up, looking both nervous and amused by the exchange. "Sorry to interrupt, but you said you were here looking for something."

Hunter blinked, oh yes, back to business. It was almost a relief to turn his attention from his mother, back to the imminent witch threat.

"Right, I need to finish translating a few newly acquired papers. Kristen, I'll show you to the archives, bring up everything you can find from Old George, my grandfather, especially pertaining to the 1940s. Mel, can you go to my family's collection of artefacts – see if there's anything you recognise as useful that we might have mislabelled."

Hunter looked up to Jack and Shaun. "Gentlemen, if you wouldn't mind aiding the ladies."

Shaun stepped forward, introducing himself to Kristen and Mel and offering to show them the way. Jack gave Hunter one last look, then followed the trio towards the library.

And so, Hunter was left alone with his son, and his mother. Mrs Astley stood quietly; her eyes fixed on her grandson. Then suddenly she clapped her hands together.

"Well, I suppose I should start with tea and coffee for everyone while they work."

Hunter looked at her warily. Mrs Astley was infamous for being a cold hostess, and this out of character offer made Hunter start. "Mother..." He began but was quickly cut off.

"With Charles gone, we can hardly offer hospitality as we once did, but it will have to suffice." Mrs Astley mused aloud, then feeling quite determined, she headed off in the direction of the kitchen.

For a few minutes, Hunter was left alone with his son in the entrance hall of his old home. He stood and breathed in deeply, taking in the familiarity of this house that seemed to awaken, as Hunter's party began to move through it, and the cheerful atmosphere recognised the return of the master of the house, and the young heir.

**Chapter Twenty-three**

Hunter had been sitting in the study for a couple of hours, poking over the Berlin papers. He was slowly beginning to piece together what Laura Kuhn had found so important. But it was hard to concentrate while his mother hovered in the room.

Oh, she was silent, Hunter had never known her to be so quiet; Mrs Astley was rapt with delight with Adam's existence. Well, at least she did not seem disturbed by the fact that his mother was a witch, which was a refreshing change. No, for once it was the other way around, with Adam feeling quite unsettled by her unwavering attention.

As Mrs Astley sighed contentedly once more, Hunter snapped, slamming his pencil on the desk.

"Mother, perhaps another round of coffee is in order. And you should probably assign our guests rooms for later." He suggested, hinting heavily that she should make herself busy.

Mrs Astley looked towards him; her gaze steely again, now that it had been torn from her grandson.

"If you wish to be alone, you only had to say, George. I do not know why you insist on treating me like an idiot." Mrs Astley stood up and brushed her black skirt into neat lines. "I shall see to lunch, as I doubt anyone else has cared to plan it."

Hunter looked at her sceptically. "But you can't cook, mother."

Mrs Astley raised a neatly plucked eyebrow at his comment. "You would be surprised, my son, what I have had to learn these past few years." Mrs Astley said without modesty.

Hunter stared down at the book in front of him, taking in none of the words as his mind ticked over. "Where is Charles?"

Mrs Astley didn't reply immediately, but took the time to straighten the cuffs on her blouse. "He died. Last autumn. Not that you care, of course. You did such a good job of abandoning us."

"Mother, I-" Hunter stopped, aware that he had no excuse for his past choices. Charles had been a loyal part of the household for as long as Hunter could remember and had been a source of company for his unpopular mother. "I'm sorry, I thought you were safer without me. How did they get to him?"

Mrs Astley blinked in surprise. "Not everything comes down to witches, George. Charles had lung cancer. I thought he had pneumonia that would not shift. He only told me the doctors had diagnosed him with cancer months later, near the end. He said that he did not want to cause any unnecessary hurt or fuss." Mrs Astley gave a wistful smile.

Hunter sat silently, noting his own pang of grief and, shockingly, sympathy for his mother. Mrs Astley had depended on Charles for years, and Hunter had often wondered about their friendship.

Mrs Astley took a single glance in her son's direction and tutted at the emotions that he was daring to feel. "I do hope that isn't pity your feeling, George."

Content that she had made her point, Hunter's mother picked up their empty mugs and made her way out of the study.

Hunter shook his head, while he waited for the stuffy feeling to leave the room. When it didn't seem keen to clear, he decided he needed to stretch his legs. With a sigh, and a creak of the antique chair, he got to his feet. Hunter held his hand out to his son, and together they headed to the library.

Inside, Kristen and Shaun were ensconced at a desk, their heads close together over a stack of papers. Before Hunter had a chance to ask what had them so riveted, the opposite door opened and Mel danced through from the cellar, Jack following more calmly, carrying a few bits and pieces from the famous Astley collection.

Jack looked sheepishly up at Hunter, the older man excited to be able to handle the artefacts they had previously guarded and treated with near reverence.

"Did you find something?" Hunter asked hopefully.

Mel smiled brightly, her blue eyes shining. "So many pretty somethings, some we thought lost long ago!"

"But anything useful, Mel?" Hunter tried again, focusing his question.

"Oh, nothing as useful as that." Mel answered, pointing vaguely towards Hunter. "But some of these will protect against strong magic."

Hunter nodded, then paused and rewound over what she had just said. "Wait, you mean they're not as useful as me?"

That was interesting; both exciting and frightening that a demon should value his ability to shield others above these amulets and trinkets he'd been taught to respect.

But that wasn't what Mel had in mind. She giggled, and playfully smacked his arm.

"No, silly. That." Mel reached up and pulled at the dog tags Hunter perpetually wore, until they slipped out of his shirt and were visible for all to see.

Hunter wrapped his hand around the familiar piece and raised it for inspection. Nope, they looked the same as they always had; a soldier's old dog tags that Hunter had worn for as long as he could remember. "Why do you say that Mel?"

Mel's eyes narrowed as she tried to work out why her friend George didn't understand his own history. "They belonged to your grandfather, when he was a young man, fighting a world war."

"Really?" Hunter mumbled. He wondered how it could be that he had never known this; had never asked. He had always assumed that it was just one of many protective amulets owned by the Astleys.

"Uh-huh, and then his witchy lover put her super-strong spell on it. She was super-strong, after all, sweet little Sara."

When Mel stopped speaking, Hunter was aware how deathly quiet it was in the library. No one spoke and no one moved.

Hunter coughed, trying to find his voice. "Sara? As in Sara Murray?"

Mel brightened up at his recognition. "Oh, so you know her? She is lovely. We tried to send her a familiar, but she'd popped her clogs before she had chance to meet it."

Hunter stood silently, staring out unseeingly. Then he snapped back to attention and shook his head.

"That's crazy." He snapped.

Feeling a familiar wave of anger and frustration threaten to rise up, Hunter turned and left the room. Everyone else was left in awkwardness, sharing embarrassed glances with one another that they should have witnessed this.

Without a real destination in mind, Hunter ended up on the first-floor corridor. He paced up and down it a couple of times, the familiar portraits of his ancestors silent in the background.

Eventually he stopped at his grandfather's. It was the second to last, with the final one belonging to Hunter's father, "Young" George Astley. Beyond that was a space that always hinted that a portrait of Hunter would join the others, but he had always put it off.

He took a deep breath and looked up at his grandfather's likeness. Hunter hardly remembered him from real life, he'd died when Hunter was a young boy. But from what Hunter gathered, Old George was an unremarkably average man (when one ignored the witch-hunting occupation). People liked him, although he wasn't exceptionally outgoing. He was giving and charitable, without being overly kind. Old George had not married until he was in his forties; and by all accounts it was a pleasant marriage, with the production of a single son.

In fact, as far as Hunter could work out, the only remarkable thing that Old George did was to defeat a Shadow Witch. And now thanks to Mel, even that was in question.

Hunter sighed, his right hand moving instinctively to the dog tags at his chest. Had they really belonged to his grandfather? He looked up at the portrait of Old George. There was something at his neck, but it was hard to tell at this angle.

Hunter glanced guiltily down the corridor, then reached up and unhooked the painting, lifting it down from the wall. On closer inspection, the brush strokes only revealed a hint of grey tucked into Old George's shirt. It could be anything, and Hunter knew it was only his desire to see his dog tags that made his eyes depict and translate the image. He moved to return the painting, when something else caught his eye.

Hunter frowned. Now that the painting was no longer on the wall, he could see a rectangular shape carved into the plaster. Hunter put his grandfather's portrait down gently. Then he reached up and traced the groove,

Hunter shook his head and sighed. It couldn't be this obvious, could it?

He searched his pockets and pulled out his battered old pocketknife. He ran the blade through the groove and felt little resistance; then he twisted it until the small panel shifted and fell obediently into his hand.

Hunter looked down at the wedge of wood and plaster, then turned his attention back to the wall. Someone had made a nice little hidey-hole, only big enough for the book that was nestled within.

Hunter pulled it out; it was a notebook, looking very unimpressive with its unadorned navy cover. Hunter flicked through the pages that were filled with tight black handwriting that looked very familiar.

Hunter finally settled on the first page. It was clearly dated November 1948 in the top right corner.

"By the hand of George Astley V.

"It is three years since the death of the Shadow Witch, and I am finally fulfilling my promise to write down all of my dealings with Ms Sara Murray."

Hunter's heart beat faster. It was here. How long had he been looking for his grandfather's account of the 1940's Shadow, and mad Old George had hidden it in the bloody wall!

Hunter looked down the corridor, but all remained silent, no one had followed him here. He looked about for a nearby chair; and seeing none he sat down on the floor, his back against the wall and his knees propped up in front of him. Hunter opened the seventy-year-old notebook again.

## Chapter Twenty-four

*In the summer of 1939, I was seventeen years old, and the only son and heir of George Astley IV, the famed witch-hunter. My older sister Elizabeth is married and living a life away from the witch-hunting madness. She always was the sensible one. I felt that my life was always planned before me – I would follow my father, of course, and look after the Manor when my time came.*

*But that year was to upset everything. In summer, I met the most beautiful girl I had ever known. Although, perhaps less girl, and more grown woman. Sara Murray was twenty-one years of age, and the mother of a two-year-old daughter. She came to Little Hanting to stay with her uncle's family. 'So, the countryside could improve her health,' was the official story. But the village is small, and secrets are not easily kept, and shortly after her arrival it was widely known that she had been sent because her parents could no longer bear the shame of a child born out of wedlock.*

*As you can imagine, my own parents discouraged all association with her, and forbade any romantic inclinations I might feel. Stuffy, antiquated pair that they are. Of course, it did not put me off from seeking her company. Over that summer we became good friends, and I discovered that Sara was not only beautiful, with her bright green eyes and rich brown hair; she was also smart and sweet and funny.*

*I confess that I was quite in love with her within a month of knowing her. For who could not love such a kind and honest lady. Indeed, several of the young men in the village sought to court her, despite her sins of the past. But she declined them gently, wishing for nothing more than friendship. And friendship I readily gave, rather than be cast out of her acquaintance.*

*Sara was always a very sensitive person, she became uneasy when foul weather arose, and would shake with fear at bad premonitions. She had an uncanny ability to see future events, although the visions often didn't make sense until it actually came to pass. I attributed it to mundane wiccan skills, because I could never sense a hint of magic around her.*

*That autumn she became worried to the point of being ill, but so did the rest of the country. It was no surprise when we fell back into war with Germany, tensions had been building for so long that it had been a question of 'when', not 'if'. It didn't alter life much in Little Hanting; we were too far from any city or place of interest.*

*Personally, I was itching to help, but had to wait until the following summer to be old enough to volunteer. Sara begged me to wait another year, but she seemed resigned to the fact that I would go immediately. Her objections were so mild, that it was actually comforting – I was becoming so used to trusting her future sight – had she seen my death she would have tried harder.*

*I will not go into my time at war, this account is on one focus only, and I do not need to raise any more painful ghosts. It was a year until I returned home, and I arrived to find Little Hanting showing signs of war. Many homes had taken in children from London, and many of the women had joined together to manufacture uniforms on top of their daily chores.*

*When I met Sara, there was a little awkwardness after twelve months apart; but that soon melted, and we were close friends once more. I could tell that something was upsetting her, and after many attempts to distract me, pleading that it was trivial, Sara finally confessed that she felt something was coming. And it was coming for her. When I pressed for more information, she shook her head, swearing that was all she knew.*

*I only had a month's leave and was due to re-join my squadron. When I went to the train station, Sara came to say goodbye, her daughter Beth walking confidently next to her now. I made a big fuss of Beth, as always, and promised to bring something back for her. And to Sara, I wanted so desperately to tell her that I loved her, that I would come back to her. But her eyes willed me silent, we both already knew. I had to suffice with a polite kiss to her hand, and then boarded the train and was away.*

*I would be away longer this time. I spent a lot of time in Africa in 1942. Summer flew by without a break, as did autumn. Hallowe'en came around, not that the army celebrate such a random festival, but as a witch-hunter I always acknowledged it. I wondered if my father and other witch-hunters were kept busy back in Britain. The war had disrupted so much, even the witches were quiet this time last year. And of course, thinking of home always made me think of Sara, and little Beth. I had decided now that they would be my family, regardless of any scandal that might arise. The next time I was home I would ask Sara to be my wife.*

*And then I heard her voice. At first, I thought it just a fragment of a memory as I thought of her, but then it came again.*

*'George, help me.'* It was as clear as though she were standing beside me. I looked about the tent to see if anyone else had heard a female voice, but only I was alert, no one moved from their books or broke their low conversations.

"I thought I must be going mad, but I heard her again, her voice worried and pleading, and somehow I knew it was real and that I had to get home immediately. Thankfully my superior is a member of the Malleus Maleficarum Council (senior in army rank, though from a lesser family of witch-hunters) and he readily accepted that urgent matters of witchcraft called me home – and oh how I would curse that my little lie would become true.

The five days it took me to get home were the longest of my life. I took connecting cargo flights, followed by a bus to London, before finally a train that would take me within five miles of Little Hanting. I don't think I spoke one more word than necessary on the whole trip, only fretted over what I might find.

I arrived in early evening and went directly to Sara's house. It seemed deserted and lacking all life, but a couple of minutes after I knocked, the door opened to reveal a very pale Sara. Her green eyes locked onto me, the panic in them clear. She led me into the lounge, where Beth sat by the fire, quietly reading a new picture book.

As soon as we sat down, Sara's emotions overcame her, and tears fell as she retold all that had happened of late. On Hallowe'en, she had been in the house alone with Beth, making up scary stories, and fashioning a witch's cloak for her daughter from spare clothes, nothing unusual at all. And then she was suddenly speared by pain and ambushed by deafening voices chanting. Sara collapsed, and when she came to, she was aware of Beth sitting next to her, sobbing. Sara comforted her child, reassuring her daughter that she was fine, when *she noticed that the fire and the lights had gone out. But even as she thought of relighting them, the fire in the grate burst into life.*

*Sara was always so logical; I can well believe she tried to find other reasons and causes. But the truth made itself clear when she merely thought of changing the blown lightbulb, and she found herself in the kitchen. Beth's scream at the mother's disappearance drew Sara's attention back to the living room, and with her attention her physical self followed. In a moment she was kneeling, cuddling and reassuring her daughter once more.*

*And then she called for me, sent her fear across continents, and bade me return. Which I did dutifully.*

*After telling her story, she began to shake, and I held her until the panic left her. We both knew what she had become – I could almost see the magic roll off her; and Sara had heard enough of my tales of witches to be beyond any doubt herself. The big question was how this had occurred, and more importantly what we were going to do about it.*

*Thankfully my parents were in Scotland, making an annual visit to family there; with my father out of the way there was not another witch-hunter for miles around, so Sara was safe from the immediate threat of detection. Long-term solutions evaded me. I mentioned that we could bind her powers, like any other witch. Sara readily agreed, but when I placed the amulet on her skin it swelled with her energy and shattered. I had never seen such power before. And I had a feeling that we would not be able to contain it 'til we knew how it had formed.*

*I interrogated Sara over her history, her family. I broke down every tiny detail of what had happened lately and found nothing. There was nothing to explain what had happened to her. We spent hours trawling through my family's library – set up by my grandfather, it is considered the vastest in the country. It was here that one term kept cropping up when we researched powerful witches - the Shadow Witch.*

*Magic without limits. It had been over five hundred years since the last one, for all we knew Sara was her descendent. But we were no closer to knowing why it had suddenly awoken now.*

*And then one day we had company. A small coven of three witches had felt Sara's simmering power from across the county and had come to Astley Manor to seek it. They came right up to the door, and I could feel their magic railing against the protective amulets there. But no defence is impenetrable, and I knew it was only a matter of time before they broke through. I ordered Sara to stay hidden and went out to meet them.*

*They did not back down when confronted with a witch-hunter, and swiftly one died at my hand. But the other two bore down on me fiercely, when suddenly they were blown back by a wave of power I was beginning to recognise. Shaking, I turned to see Sara standing at the open door, an unfamiliar and furious look on her face. But she snapped out of her trance and was nervous and worried once more; and guilt entered her green eyes as I checked the witches and found them dead. One had a broken neck from their fall, the other looked as though a heart attack had claimed them.*

*Sara was highly distressed that she had brought danger to my home, and swore that no witch would ever set foot on my land again. I felt her power rise up and ripple out, although it would not be until much later that I would understand what she had done.*

*Sara became very unsettled and insisted on leaving Little Hanting. I tried to talk her into staying, even moving into Astley Manor. I tried to persuade her that I could talk my father round to trusting her, but even as I said it, I knew I would struggle, my father was very much of the old code of witch-hunters. Perhaps it was wise she left, that we kept this secret between the two of us only. I found her a cottage in the unspoilt countryside to the North, out of range of any witch-hunter.*

*While she settled into her new home, my research was going nowhere, and in the end, I had to approach the MMC and use their connections to dig further on what might have caused this change in Sara. It was more rumour than fact that the Nazis had been experimenting with the occult. It was so slight, but the only lead I had. Germany was probably the least safe place to be right now, but if I waited, I feared the trail would go cold, or be destroyed completely by this terrible war.*

*I went to visit Sara before I left for the continent. She was less than happy about the danger I was putting myself in for her. While I was there, she begged to be able to do one small thing – she took my dog tags, and I could feel the familiar build of her magic. The dog tags glowed for a moment, before returning to their unimpressive state. She gave them back to me, explaining that they would protect me. I was not fully convinced, but I would accept anything from her.*

*I returned to my post in North Africa. I started my journey from there, a journey that would take over a year. It was a frustratingly slow process, but they were dangerous and difficult times. Eventually in the summer of 1944 I arrived in Berlin. We had been told that we had won the battle, but all I saw when I arrived was destruction. Berlin echoed London in the Blitz, the survivors moving around quietly, their faces drawn. Apart from the children, somehow children can find joy, however slight.*

*I cautiously approached the German MMC under the guise of a German soldier that wished to join them as a 1st gen. The MMC is an establishment over five hundred years old and has withstood more wars and disasters than I'd care to mention but has always maintained a detachment and its own strict code. But I was not going to risk revealing who I really was – I might put my trust in the MMC, but I could not forget the years our countries had spent fighting.*

*They accepted me with relative ease – I believe they were struggling to recruit young men with the cost of war to young lives. The British MMC had even started to accept women (as long as they were the daughter of a witch-hunter and naturally gifted) to swell their ranks, something previously rare and strongly dissuaded.*

*The German MMC put me with a 3rd gen, Herr Magnus Becholsteim, who was ten years my senior. Magnus was a good enough man, and under other circumstances I believe we could have been friends. He was very proud of his skills and for the month I was with him I had to force myself to be slow and clumsy in everything I did, knowing as I did so that I could easily outmatch him and most of the witch-hunters Germany had to offer. By day we would 'train' and revise over old cases; by night we would relax and over a few drinks Magnus would regale me with stories of his great and daring deeds. I took them with a pinch of salt, but it was during these quiet evenings that I finally learnt a little more.*

*Magnus was telling me about his time training when he was younger, at the feet of the Herr Ancles (who I will confirm was known worldwide as one of the best in our era), and Magnus spoke of a fellow apprentice Herr Hartmann, a 2nd gen that Magnus took great joy in teasing with his own, greater inborn skills. I asked out of politeness rather than true interest, if they still kept in touch, but Magnus' reply intrigued me.*

*He initially shrugged and said that Hartmann ended up transferring his loyalties from the MMC to the Nazi Party and fell in with a bad crowd. Sensing that he had my interest in this bit of scandal he smirked over his brandy glass and gave me the whole story. I shall not waste time and paper with his possibly exaggerated tale, but give a brief account:*

*After joining the Nazi Party, Hartmann became convinced that the MMC could contribute more, their knowledge and their artefacts. The MMC was not going to be persuaded to take sides in a war, but Hartmann ended up being poached by a Herr Richter to join a faction that experimented with the occult. Magnus couldn't confirm what Hartmann might have achieved, but there were strong rumours of mass sacrifices and the co-operation of a certain witch (later caught and executed – Herr Brawn).*

*Magnus was vague about having any idea where Hartmann was at present, but I was convinced that the German MMC was as stringent as we were about keeping track of potential witch-hunters, regardless of whether they'd turned their back on the MMC, or not.*

*It took two more weeks of snooping through the MMC's files, while pretending I was doing the dull background and paperwork for my trainer, but I finally found the last known location of Hartmann. I told Magnus that my mother had fallen ill, and that I needed to return home, giving me a week at least before anyone became suspicious enough to track me.*

*I set off to the North of Germany, to find Hartmann where he worked in a secure compound. I followed him one evening to his civilian home and I waited for morning, and when he left for work, I broke into his house. I spent that day meticulously going through everything.*

*I found a few letters in his desk from Braun and Richter, pertaining to past and present experiments. I found a drawer marked 'Failures', which held several artefacts. But no clear answer. So, I waited for Hartmann to return home.*

*As soon as he walked through the door, I grappled with him. I am not proud to say that the man had to be beat into submission. I questioned him over the mass sacrifices and his work around*

*Hallowe'en 1942. He wasn't very forthcoming with words, but his eyes moved to the drawer I had searched earlier. With a little more persuasion, he confessed about the dagger, which he had smuggled from the MMC in Berlin, that his colleague Braun swore held immeasurable power. They just had to find the right witch and the correct volume of sacrifices. He told me that at one Hallowe'en it changed. They broke the spell binding the dagger, and nothing happened. They were just left with an old, blunt dagger with no special qualities. He claimed that despite the disappointment, it was not unusual for their experiments to fail, and he always took his failures home as a memento and reminder.*

*I took the dagger, and a handful of his letters. For a moment I thought that I should kill him, but he was an outcast of the MMC, and knew nothing of my identity; and I had seen enough death to last a lifetime. I knocked him unconscious and left immediately.*

*My journey back to England was frustratingly slow, when I knew I had completed my goal and longed to see Sara again. I returned by Christmas 1944, and went straight to Sara's cottage. With her uncanny foresight she knew that I was coming and had dinner almost done by the time I arrived.*

*I slept for a day, exhausted and finally safe enough to relax for the first time in nearly two years. When I was conscious and finally refreshed, I took about a week to relay everything I had seen and done. There was a lot to tell, and my story had to wait for when Beth was at school or asleep. She had grown so much since I last saw her, but Beth was still excited to see me and seldom left my side.*

*I stayed with them for Christmas and the New Year, then finally started to plan to head back to Astley Manor to further research the dagger. Sara came to my room to help me pack, and curiously picked the dagger up. I remember her face as she looked at it – confusion and contemplation written across her pretty features.*

*"You realise there's writing here." She said, wondering why I had not mentioned it to her before, I looked over at the blade that I had carried for months, but saw the same dull, plain metal with no inscriptions. But Sara went on to insist there was 'By Her Hand Only' written there.*

*I went home, this thought plaguing me. I ignored the fuss my parents made at my return and went right back to researching answers. The only thing I found was an old and questionable bit of information that I was not willing to share. But in the end, I didn't have to. Sara sent me a message to see her immediately.*

*I dutifully set off for her cottage once more and had scarcely entered the door when she revealed that she had been having vivid dreams ever since touching the dagger. She started to tell me about them, and my heart dropped, they echoed precisely what I had learnt. That the last Shadow Witch had been infatuated with a mortal man, who was killed by her fellow witches. She had grown so distressed over what she had created that she had killed herself rather than subject the world to her power any longer.*

*Sara swore that she would do the same. That was the first and only time we ever argued, voices raised and Sara looking fiercely angry. She, trying to destroy her life, and I trying to save it. Sara tried to make me understand how tense and frightening her life was, trying to hide from witches and hunters alike. How even Beth was afraid of her when strange things happened. And I- I could not give up on the woman I loved when I had been to hell and back to save her.*

*I stormed out that day, furious that she should take the easy way out. And how I regret that was the last time I saw her.*

*A couple of days later, the dagger was missing from its drawer, and in its place a note.*

*'Dear George,*

*By the time you read this, it shall be too late to stop me, I know what has to be done.*

*Please know that I have always loved you, and I don't know how I would have gotten through these last few years without you. How I wish things were different and the curse had fallen on any but me. But it has, and I can't let the temptation of the power I could wield push this damaged world any closer to destruction.*

*As for Beth, I hope she remembers that I love her, but my last use of magic will be that she and her children will be bound from powers themselves. I would not wish them to be persecuted by the MMC.*

*I am sorry to rip her from your life also, but I think she is safer where none know her, or me. A distant cousin with whom I am friendly is to adopt her. There are so many parentless children after this war, it will not be suspicious.*

*There is one thing I ask: something tells me that the Shadow will rise again, and I see it involving the Astley family once more. They will need to know the truth, when the time is right – will you write an honest account of all that has occurred?*

*With all my heart,*

*Sara*

**Chapter Twenty-five**

Hunter held the original letter that had been folded and inserted in the pages of the small notebook. The writing was delicate and very different to the hand that had gone before it. He looked back at the book and flicked through the rest of the pages but found nothing.

Old George must have considered his story told, either that or he didn't have the will to go on. It put his life in a different perspective. Hunter had thought him relatively dull, except for his one shining achievement of killing a Shadow Witch. An achievement that was now overturned. No wonder he hadn't liked talking about it; Hunter had thought he was just being modest.

Hunter closed the book and turned it over in his hands, brushing off the last of the dust from the navy covers.

"Hunter?"

Hunter sighed as he heard his name in that cautious tone everyone seemed to adopt around him.

"Hunter, we were worried where you got to." Kristen said, walking up to him. "Well, we were all worried, but then Mel started teaching Adam Gaelic or something, so they're happy."

Hunter looked up at Kristen, dragging himself firmly back into the present.

"Did you find something?" Kristen asked, looking at the notebook she was sure Hunter did not have before.

Hunter held up the offending article.

Kristen nodded, her eyes narrowing at the very plain little book in his hands, wondering if that was the source of Hunter's current weirdness.

"And?" She prompted.

Hunter took a deep breath as he thought over what he had learnt, of Old George and everything he had gone through for the woman he loved, he thought of the history and connection that had been hidden…

"It tells of how to kill a Shadow Witch." Hunter finally replied in a low voice. He eventually pushed himself up off the floor and stood on numb legs. He looked at the offending item in his hands, weighing his options. He didn't want to share what he'd read, it felt personal; but he also didn't want to seem like he was keeping secrets from the people that were risking everything to follow him. With a sigh, Hunter handed Kristen the book, then without a word he started to walk back down the corridor.

Kristen looked at him, her blue eyes wide with curiosity. She looked down at the book that had been shoved into her hands, and then flicked through a few of the pages, scanning what was written.

"Hunter, wait!" She called, jogging to catch up with him, wanting to keep him on his own for a little longer. She grabbed his arm, yanking to insist that he stay. "So... Mel was telling the truth? About your grandfather and the witch?"

Hunter stopped, reluctant to meet Kristen's eye, he shrugged. "Isn't she always telling the truth?"

Kristen paused for a moment. "Good point."

Hunter used her hesitation to pull away again.

"Hunter... do you want to talk about it?" Kristen asked, uncertain.

Hunter stood still, hovering between what he wanted to say, and what was polite to say. He took a deep breath and turned back to Kristen, a half-attempt of a bitter smile on his lips. "Talk about what? That it's in my genes to fall in love with a Shadow Witch? Or that my whole family's history is a lie; and our right to persecute witches suddenly questionable? No, I don't want to talk."

Kristen blushed at Hunter's little outburst, feeling embarrassed on his behalf. And feeling uncomfortable at the prospect of bringing up a certain something. "So, if they were lovers, does that mean you're related to... um, Sophie?"

Hunter looked at her sharply, surprised to hear anyone use Sophie's name; and also, a little disgusted at the insinuation.

"No!" He snapped. "Old George loved Sara, but they were nothing more than friends. Sara had a daughter with another man before they met."

"Alright." Kristen replied calmly, tapping her long nails against the hard cover of the notebook, trying to think of a polite way out. "I'll... um, add this to the rest of our sources."

Kristen pushed past Hunter and hurried away, back to the library.

## Chapter Twenty-six

Later that evening, when everyone else had retired to their rooms, Hunter sat alone in the drawing room. Despite it being summer, a fire crackled in the grate, for extra light and to try and push back the interminable chill of this big old house. Hunter nursed a glass tumbler of whisky – he couldn't remember the last time he'd had whisky, being on the run had left no time for a drink, and the Donili had favoured wine only. To be honest, he was surprised that his personal stock hadn't been raided in his absence.

He took a sip of the amber liquid and gazed into the flames of the fire. He thought again over what he had learnt today, and his mood didn't improve. He felt like his grandfather had lied to him, betrayed him. Old George had led Hunter and everyone else to believe that he had killed a serious threat. The truth was just depressing.

Hunter sighed and silently cursed Old George and Sara. By the sounds of it, they were doing what was right at the time. But surely this was not the outcome they had wanted. For such a smart woman with allegedly accurate foresight, Sara Murray had done a shite job in saving the world from the power of a Shadow. She'd only managed to postpone it for seventy years. And she'd foolishly allowed her death to spark a fierce desire for revenge in her great-granddaughter.

Hunter wondered what Sophie would make of all this. She would probably think that he was making it all up for some hidden reason.

Hunter heard the soft pad of bare feet in the hallway. He glanced up briefly to see Kristen opening the door, then returned to his comfortable haze of whisky and thoughts.

"Is this for anyone?" Kristen asked, nodding to the bottle on the table next to him. Not waiting for an answer, she poured herself a generous portion.

Kristen tried a couple of times to strike up light conversation – on the history of the house, or Mel's newest piece of randomness. But Hunter was proving an unwilling companion, his answers short and uninterested. Eventually things dissolved into silence, both of them drinking wordlessly.

The small carriage clock on the mantelpiece chimed eleven times, claiming Kristen's attention.

"Well, I suppose I better head upstairs." She announced, and then knocked back the rest of her whisky. Kristen looked at Hunter, her eyes bright. "Care to join me?"

Hunter looked up at Kristen. Her proposition came as no surprise. And of course, he would politely turn her down. He should turn her down.

Hunter didn't reply immediately, instead his eyes lingered on the young woman in front of him. He couldn't deny that she was attractive, her features delicate, but far from weak; her blonde hair falling in soft waves past her shoulders. His eyes travelled down, appreciating the simple t-shirt and jeans that showed off her womanly curves and narrow waist.

Noticing Hunter's new focus, Kristen opened her mouth to come out with some witty barb, but then she thought better of it. She set down her empty glass, then removed Hunter's from his hand. The faint chink of the glass being set down on the table was the only sound.

Kristen felt a familiar lick of desire, along with an unfamiliar tension that rose through her as she moved closer and wordlessly straddled Hunter's lap.

Hunter watched her careful and precise movements. He breathed deep as her scent enveloped him, and his hand came up to catch the back of her neck and pull her into a desperate kiss. Kristen's heart began to race, as she tasted the whisky on his warm mouth. She kissed back hungrily, her teeth grazing against his lower lip.

When they eventually pulled apart, their eyes met, equally dilated with passion. Hunter felt his own pulse demanding more, and he watched Kristen as she gave a mischievous half-smile.

Kristen pulled her t-shirt up and over her head, revealing the pale, toned body that Hunter had occasionally speculated about. A black bra stood out against her milky skin, and her curves were emphasised. Her breasts rose and fell with her quick, shallow breathing. Kristen leant down and caught his lips again, moaning into the kiss as Hunter's hands dug firmly into her thighs, pulling her closer.

"Wait." Hunter breathed, then spoke stronger. "Stop."

Kristen froze. That hadn't been what she had been waiting to hear. She caught Hunter's eye. "Seriously?"

"We shouldn't do this. It's neither the time nor place." Hunter muttered, pushing the semi-naked girl off his lap so he could stand up.

"This is exactly the time and place – we live in dangerous times; can you promise we'll still be safe tomorrow? And you can't go back to pretending you don't want me." Kristen snapped.

Seeing that Hunter wasn't going to reply, and even less likely to reignite the mood, Kristen silently swore and reached for her discarded top. She pulled it back on, embarrassed that she had to do so in this manner.

Her eyes flashed dangerously in Hunter's direction. "Did you forget how to use your dick in that monastery? Or is it still her? You know it's pretty twisted if you're still in love with her."

Hunter took a deep breath, and tried to argue, to deny it, but the words died in his throat.

"That's it, isn't it?" Kristen asked, her voice and her sweet blue eyes filling with pain. "She should mean nothing to you. You had what – a fling for a few months, *years* ago. Get over it."

"I wouldn't expect you to understand." Hunter replied, smoothing down his appearance, and careful not to catch her eye.

But Kristen was determined to get his attention one last time. She walked straight up to him, her fierce gaze meeting his.

"Just remember Hunter, that whatever you *think* you feel for her, we will fight, and we will kill her. Just as she will strive to kill you." And with that, she turned on her heel and left.

Hunter watched her go and continued to stand silently while he listened to her light steps up the staircase and across the landing. When he was confident that Kristen was in her room, he finally moved.

Hunter only thought of his warm bed now but made a stop by Adam's room. It was the first time the boy had slept alone since he had been kidnapped. Having always shared a room with either Hunter, or Molly.

Hunter paused at Adam's door. Upon hearing nothing, he quietly opened it, letting in a stream of faint light. Hunter felt a vibration, similar to magic, but too faint to make out. He frowned but was suddenly distracted by his stirring son.

Adam rolled over, and seeing someone in his doorway, he sat bolt upright. "Daddy?"

"Yes, it's me." Hunter replied gently. "Were you having a bad dream?"

Adam rubbed his eyes and didn't even try to hide his yawn. "No. You woke Incy." His little voice sounded surprisingly accusing.

"Sorry, I'll not do it again." Hunter replied, confused by the random comment, and thinking that he should perhaps limit Mel's influence. "Go back to sleep, Adam."

Hunter watched as his young son obediently lay down, cuddling close an old bear Mrs Astley had dug out. Hunter smiled briefly, recognising the teddy from his own childhood. Trying not to make a sound, Hunter gently closed the door, and made his way to his own bed.

**Chapter Twenty-seven**

The next morning Hunter woke up disorientated. He lay still, his eyes flicking from the high ceiling, to the long dark drapes, and the antique furniture. He'd not slept in this room for years, but it hadn't changed. It all echoed back to a time when things had been normal – well, more normal.

Hunter wished he could freeze things now, something telling him that from here on, things would only get worse. But he could already hear the rest of the house stirring, and reluctantly got up. Hunter winced at the whisky hangover that casually reminded him that his body was out of practice imbibing his old levels of alcohol.

When he made his way downstairs, the smell of fresh coffee was already wafting out of the kitchen – and thankfully Jack had gotten to the task of producing drinkable coffee, before Mrs Astley could delight them with another pot of tar.

Hunter didn't say much to the motley bunch that crowded into the kitchen. Discussing their next step over breakfast, while still half asleep was not the best plan. But finally, after his second cup of coffee, Hunter called for his team's attention. His team – it felt strange ever acknowledging it again. He took a deep breath and pushed back the memories of sitting in this kitchen with James, Maria, Ian and Alannah. Even Sophie once upon a time. Now was not the time for emotions or weakness.

"We've got a lot of work to do. We know how to kill the Shadow Witch, which is a big step in the right direction, but it won't win us this war. The whole world is at war with the witchkind. Oh, I know Britain will bear the brunt of it, being the home of the Shadow Witch and her Council, and they may crumble without her. But we have the rest of the world to contend with.

"We need to co-ordinate with our foreign allies, with other witch-hunters, and even witches like Laura Kuhn, if any exist." Hunter broke off, hardly believing what he was suggesting: an alliance with witches. Padre would be so proud that this stubborn Astley was finally opening his mind to the possibility of good witches. "So, we need to get Marcus, and any other Donili I can persuade to help with transport.

"And... we're going to America. Five years ago, the witches used a machine to bring down civilisation. Let's see if we can restore it." Hunter tried to sound more convincing than he felt, and his gaze finally drifted to Miss Davies.

Kristen looked a little nonplussed at his attention. "I hope you're not waiting for me to drop critical information here, Hunter. I'm from New York; I only ever went to D.C. on a school trip in eighth grade. And I was never part of their MMC."

Hunter waited for her to finish, then shrugged. "Ok... does that mean that you don't want to go?"

Kristen opened her mouth to retort, then closed it again, her eyes narrowing at him in a silent warning instead.

"Thought as much." Hunter muttered, choosing to ignore her look.

Jack glanced between the two witch-hunters, suspicious at their sudden hostility.

Hunter sighed and suggested that they should inventory and pack everything they had found, so they could take it back to the MMC at a moment's notice. He also asked that they start making a list of potential allies while Hunter sought the Donili.

The chairs scraped back as everyone rose, ready to leave their impromptu meeting in the kitchen. Poor Shaun was nominated to clean up, and everybody else made a quick exit.

Jack stood in the hallway beside Hunter. The older man looked questioningly to his 'leader'. "What if the Abate refuses to help - are you willing to fracture the Donili?"

Hunter shrugged, not the most persuasive argument. It had already crossed his mind many times over the last two years that, if he asked for help and the Abate denied him, what path was there for him to take? Could he betray the man that had trained him; to whom he had sworn not to force his views on others? There was no satisfactory outcome, and Hunter felt a knot of anxiety that the time had come to find out.

"I only give the monks the option to help us. It is on them to take it." Hunter finally said, not entirely convinced himself.

"And, ah, what's happening with you and Kristen?" Jack asked, nodding towards the library where Miss Davies had disappeared. "Things looked a little tense."

Hunter grimaced. He hardly knew Jack and wasn't about to unload his personal grievances on him. But he must have looked somewhat embarrassed because Jack suddenly smirked.

"Look Jack, it's…" Hunter began, but trailed off, having no idea what he was going to say.

Jack put his hands up defensively. "Hey, forget I said anything." He gave a small chuckle and walked away.

## Chapter Twenty-eight

It was still morning when Hunter and Adam suddenly materialised in the Donili Village. The villagers barely spared them a glance, so used were they to the monks appearing.

Hunter walked up to the abbazia, Adam holding his hand tightly, looking around in wonder. Adam had wanted to come with his daddy and, as the trip was perfectly safe, Hunter had agreed immediately. To be honest, he didn't like the idea of leaving his son in his mother's care; and he was wary of encouraging any further influence from Mel.

The Italian sun was already hot on their backs as they walked up the hill to the Abbazia di Donili.

Hunter and Adam were unhindered as they entered the large gate and headed towards the Abate's rooms. A few of the monks watched them curiously as they passed, but then returned to their daily tasks.

"Si, entrare." The Abate called after Hunter knocked.

Hunter smiled encouragingly at his son, then pushed the heavy door open.

The Abate was sat in the window seat, a heavy tome on his lap, and the window open to encourage the morning breeze.

"Ah, Signor Astley, another visit so soon, I am honoured." The old man said politely, though his blue eyes carried his questions.

"The honour is mine, padre." Hunter replied formally. "Things have, ah, progressed quickly since last we spoke."

The Abate gently closed his book and placed his hands upon it. "Go on."

"The witches are stirring and preparing for war. I can feel it; the fragile peace vibrates and is ready to splinter."

"Very poetic. Perhaps you have missed a calling in life." The Abate replied drily. "And what is your purpose in coming here?"

Hunter took a deep breath. "To ask what I once asked before: for help. I know that you will not fight or defend, but I beg you to consider helping us reach out to our allies. We have no way of communicating quickly with them – I can't be everywhere at once."

The Abate sat, silently considering this request, then finally nodded. "I will bring this up with the other monks in a meeting this afternoon. You may attend it, but you will not have permission to speak. Is there anything else you wish to tell me?"

Hunter hesitates, thinking over the discovery of his grandfather's notebook. He weighed up getting the Donili's help regarding the knife, but the cost of sharing Old George's attachment to the old Shadow Witch.

"There's a dagger we need to locate. It is from the time of the original Shadow Witch and has the engraving 'By Her Hand Only' on the blade." Hunter finally admitted, carefully leaving out the how and why they came to this information. "We believe it can bind the power of a Shadow. And kill one."

The Abate looked a little worried at the mention of a weapon against their enemy. One with the strength to bind her? Why did the old man suspect that Hunter was more likely to take the kill option?

"I vaguely recall a mention of this dagger in our historical archives… I shall have to find the particular parchment before I start misquoting it." The Abate replied. "Now, let me account you with all that we have discovered since you were last here."

The Abate glanced down to Adam, hesitating. "This is your son, I take it. Does he understand Italian?"

"Yes, this is Adam, padre. And he does not know Italian. Just English. And some German… and Celtic – it's a long story."

The Abate nodded. "Then I may speak freely without upsetting him. Biagio has been trawling through the libraries, day and night, in the hope to find some obscure information that may help you. There was a child mentioned, one from two enemies – and he shall become a leader in a united world."

Hunter tightened his grip on Adam's hand. He had previously voiced that Adam could prove important, but that had been to appease the Council so that he could keep his son safe. Hunter wasn't sure if he liked his speculations being confirmed. He'd much rather let Adam be normal and lead a safe and happy life.

"You never made mention of this before." Hunter said accusingly. He had never kept his son a secret from the monks, and it struck him as odd that they had never brought it up in the year and a half that he had lived here.

The Abate gave an understanding smile. "It is written in the scriptures of San Fiedro, who was known to see portents and futures with persuasive accuracy. But the Donili do not hold with the questionable prophecies and such. It was only Biagio who thought to look through the dusty, unpopular parchments."

Hunter gave a brief smile and felt a little relieved. He was not one to believe in prophecies, but he thought of his young son at his side. Young being the important word. How could a four-year-old boy become a leader? How would the years play out until he was old enough?

"He's just a kid. Does it say how?" Hunter asked weakly.

The Abate made a non-committal gesture. "It is vague. You may read the original source; they have been set aside for you."

Hunter looked down at Adam, who appeared bored by these two grown-ups who talked in unknown words. He didn't want his son in danger – he would make this a safer world for him first.

"Thank you, padre. We will head to the library now."

The Abate held up a hand to stop him. "There is something else."

Hunter looked to the old monk, the Abate's usually serene expression betrayed his concern.

"Something worse?" Hunter asked warily.

"Perhaps worse, but definitely more solid." The Abate glanced over to Adam, before looking to Hunter again. "It is about the demon you brought here…"

Hunter suddenly bristled at how the leader of the Donili was so prejudiced against Mel. "I told you before, she is here to help, and I am happy to accept it."

A rush of breath hissed through the Abate's clenched teeth. "Be careful how you say that. There are some powers that will twist an oath and hold it against you. But Signor Astley, do you know why she helps you?"

Hunter shook his head. "Mel is free to do as she pleases. From the sound of it, her boss wants more balance between the witches and the rest of the world, to reassert his control."

"And you believe that?" The Abate asked, then ploughed on without waiting for an answer. "I must ask, Signor, does she show interest in your son?"

"Well she..." Hunter broke off, thinking of the past few weeks. Mel had been spending time with him, Hunter. But he could not deny that the blonde girl was fascinated by Adam. Surely that was natural and innocent, as she seemed half a child herself. "She... why?"

The Abate sighed, relieved that his former pupil wasn't defending the demon blindly. When it came to this mysterious Mel, even the Donili were unsure what she was capable of.

"I have discussed her with the other elders, and our strongest theory is that she is here to claim Adam for her master. You say that Lucifer wants balance and control. What better control than to have the loyalty of an exceptionally powerful being from childhood?"

Hunter stood, dazed by what the Abate was proposing. "Mel wouldn't – she couldn't do that." He argued feebly.

"I hope you are right." The Abate replied gently.

Hunter turned down the wrong corridor as he went to the library, and had to turn back, a flash of embarrassment at his mistake. His mind was still firmly fixed on what the Abate had said. Demons, and prophecies, and greatness. It all seemed far-reaching. But then again, if someone had told him five years ago that the world would fall to ruin, and witch-hunters would use magic, he would have thought it equally unlikely.

When they finally made it to the library, Hunter received a warm welcome from Biagio. The young monk seemed as taken with Adam as everyone else, and immediately knelt down to introduce himself to the boy.

"Biagio, the Abate said you had set aside some articles for me." Hunter pressed straight to the point.

A look of concern crossed Biagio's face, but the monk covered it so quickly with his usual smile that Hunter wondered if he had been mistaken.

"Of course, I shall show you to my desk." Biagio replied, then looked back to Adam. "And while your father reads, perhaps you will teach me more English, giovane."

Hunter clapped Biagio on the back. "Teach him Italian instead, he has been learning every other language!"

Hunter was led over to a large table, where there were scrolls and papers as promised. After Adam and Biagio drifted away in the library to give him space, Hunter began to sort through what was before him. He could sense how old some of these scrolls were, and handled them slowly and carefully, despite his desire to pull out what he needed from them.

His head had started to ache from processing the handwriting and translating the various Italian dialects. Then something finally caught his attention – a scroll dictated by San Fiedro – that was the name of the seer that the Abate had mentioned, was it not?

Hunter read through the whole, confusing piece. San Fiedro had been a rambler, and most of this did not apply to Hunter. He went back and re-read the section that seemed related to them. And read it again to make sure that he had translated it correctly.

The information was hard to take in; the Abate had been careful in what he had left out!

Hunter sat there looking very dazed when Biagio returned to tell him it was time for dinner. Upon seeing his friend, Biagio could tell what he had read, and stood there silently, waiting for Hunter to say something.

Hunter forced the words out. "The child shall be an orphan of war." Hunter looked up to Biagio, hoping the monk would correct him. "I'm not supposed to survive this?"

"It could be translated differently. Metaphorically, instead of literally." Biagio translated. "Seers are notoriously misleading, hence why the Donili do not put stock in their words."

Hunter gave a bitter laugh at Biagio's attempt. "And yet the Abate thought it solid enough information for me to read."

Hunter sighed, glancing around the room. "Where is Adam?"

"Playing football with the younger monks." Biagio replied. "They shall meet us in the dinner hall."

Hunter tried to smile at the amusing image of the monks playing football (some of them were rather good) with his small son, but he found it hard to be even remotely happy right now.

Death did not scare him. Long ago he came to terms with the fact that he would die relatively young. It was part of being a witch-hunter. And there had been countless times when he had thought that his time had come, only for a last-minute rescue, or lucky distraction, to allow him one more day. He had proven that he was brave, time and again.

So why was this so hard to take? A random hint from a long-dead stranger?

Hunter sighed and decided to treat it with the same scepticism that the Donili bore it. He re-rolled the parchment and left it on the pile, then followed Biagio to dine with the others.

Dinner was a regular, pleasant affair, and was followed by the migration of the senior monks to the meeting room to the left of the great hall.

After leaving Adam once more in the care of Biagio, Hunter slipped into the back of the room. No one acknowledged his presence as he sat quietly as requested.

The Abate stood at the head of the long table and glanced briefly to Hunter before he began to speak.

"My brothers, we have observed over the last few years the increase of witch infringements, and we have done our duty defending Friuli. But there have been rumblings amongst our ranks that we should take a wider concern.

"There is evidence that the witches are gearing up for another war on those that refuse them. Signor Astley comes again to request our help. Now we must decide whether to break our oaths and restrictions; or sit idly by while many lives are lost."

The Abate looked around the group, meeting each monk's eyes, before settling his gaze on Hunter, with a ghost of a smile.

Hunter near held his breath, and the realisation of the Abate's words sent a shiver through him. The Abate was taking his side! His pulse began to race with the excitement of possibility now. But Hunter forced himself to remain passive on the surface as the rest of the monks had their say.

It was a blur of discussion with gentle debate. A couple of the oldest monks clung to the tradition and what was known, but the majority followed the Abate's lead after a few arguments that seemed more perfunctory than anything else.

The meeting quickly moved onto the practicalities, the Abate laid down the rules of those that could help – only adept students that were of age would be given the option.

After the main point of discussion, the Abate opened the floor to other topics, but the monks were too distracted and eager to get on with rallying their students to be able to think of anything else. Everyone departed, leaving the Abate and Hunter alone.

"Padre... how can I thank you?" Hunter asked, a grin splitting across his features.

The Abate dismissed his thanks with a wave of his hand. "It is necessary, Signor Astley. As much as I have come to care for you, it is not just for you that I do this. There are countless lives at risk – it would lie heavy with me if I stood by and watched and forced the others to stand by me."

The Abate walked down the room and sat closer to Hunter. "So, what are your plans?"

Hunter took a moment to work out the best way to explain. "Five years ago, the witches used a device to knock out technology. I'm going to find it and reverse it, to bring us back out of the dark ages. But it also occurred to me that if this device could cast a global spell, then it might also be used to block magic. If you could spare some Donili, we could experiment with-"

"No." The Abate interrupted. The old monk looked towards Hunter with calm curiosity.

Hunter was surprised how yet again the Abate could so firmly dismiss an idea without consideration. "But padre, just think – we could remove magic forever."

The Abate clasped his hands in front of him, and again thought how to get through to his passionate student.

"You have come to the conclusion that witches can choose to be good, or bad, no? When you win this war, as I believe you will, would you leave all witches defenceless? There will be many desires for revenge that will not end with battle – every man and woman who is called a witch will suffer. You will start a new witch craze. I say, let them keep their magic and allow them to govern themselves. I would also say, do not voice your plan with this device with anyone – others might think it worth the attempt." The Abate gave a knowing smile. "Not that you have ever heeded my advice before, Signor Astley."

Hunter sat quietly, taking this in.

"Now, you shall return home and turn plans into actions." The Abate added.

Hunter stood up to leave but paused. "Padre… I read the San Fiedro papers. Do you think there is any truth in them?"

The Abate smiled a little sadly. "I believe that if I were to prophesise a female pope it would happen. Not in my lifetime, or for a thousand years perhaps. But it will happen; will people say it is because a Donili monk predicted it so? San Fiedro could mean you, Sophie and Adam; or he could be predicting the reunion between North and South Korea. If you want to live a long and happy life with your son – go do that, prove it is nothing to do with you."

Hunter took a deep breath, trying to let the logic of the Abate's words reassure him.

"You are the most stubborn man I know, George." The Abate added with affection. "Personally, I truly believe that you would ignore the grim reaper himself, if it did not suit you. I believe that whatever happens will be your choice."

**Chapter Twenty-nine**

Hunter and Kristen appeared in one of Washington's many parks, startling a young couple from their midnight tryst.

"I think we ruined someone's romantic ambitions." Kristen muttered bitterly.

Hunter ignored her comment, and watched the couple walk away, the guy casting suspicious glances back over his shoulder. But the guy eventually accepted that Hunter and Kristen must have always been there, and he had just been distracted – because people appearing out of nowhere was impossible.

Kristen glanced around their surroundings, as she straightened her cuffs and rechecked her weapons. "Welcome to America."

"I've been before." Hunter admitted, looking guilty. "When I was on the run a couple of years ago, I went everywhere. Which included breaking into Georgetown University."

Kristen looked at him, aghast. "You broke into a uni? Why?"

Hunter shrugged. "To see their research on witches and the Benandanti. Why would anyone else break in?"

"Most people would get a library card and go during opening hours."

Hunter sighed. "What a boring option."

He turned and led in towards the city. Even without lights, the Washington monument held its own, dark against the horizon, allowing Hunter to gain his bearings. He pulled out a DC roadmap, checking their best route from here.

Washington's MMC headquarters had been in the countryside when it had been built a couple of hundred years ago; but was surrounded by the inevitable expansion of suburbs. Hunter and Kristen jogged along, two inconspicuous figures in black.

"Remember the plan?" Hunter asked as they drew closer to their target.

Kristen looked at him sceptically. "'Keep quiet and don't get seen' is not a very professional plan. Did you have anything else to add?"

"We can't get any intel on what to expect, so we need to use the time-honoured technique of improvising. We find the device and destroy it." Hunter replied, thinking aloud.

Despite the dozen questions she wished to ask, Kristen just nodded. Her hands flitted from the protective charm at her neck, to check the knives and guns for the umpteenth time. "Let's get this over with, then."

Hunter stopped in the shadows, a hundred yards from the front gate of the old headquarters. There was a gatehouse, well-lit, with at least one guard. Beyond that, the drive leading to the house was wide and open, with nowhere to hide from any prying eyes.

Hunter wouldn't take that route unless there was no other option. He motioned silently for Kristen to follow him. He kept a safe distance and followed the perimeter round.

The grounds were extensive, and Hunter noticed the stately house disappearing behind the wall. He stopped, listening carefully. He couldn't hear anyone near. This would have to do.

After legging Kristen up, Hunter pulled himself over the wall. He quickly dropped into the darkness on the other side. They kept low as they made their way across the grounds to the big white stone building.

There was the low murmur of voices of the guards on duty. Hunter knelt in the shadow of the doorway and sent his mind out until he felt two others. They hesitated in their chat as they felt the presence of something, but before they could act upon their suspicions, Hunter pushed the desire to sleep deep into their conscious. Within a minute they had already settled into a deep and stable sleep.

"Neat trick." Kristen breathed into his ear.

"Are you impressed, Miss Davies?" Hunter asked as he unlocked the door, to reveal two slumped guards.

Kristen shrugged. "Maybe." She admitted as she pushed past Hunter, stepping over the inert bodies and slowly drew out her knife. The witch-hunter looked about warily.

"A lot of magic in this place. Can you find the right source?" She asked Hunter.

Hunter took a deep breath and concentrated again. He felt the same as Kristen, the oppressive wave of magic from many witches; but as he focussed, he could feel the different patterns, including one that was terribly familiar.

"This way." He murmured, nodding where the corridor led off to the right.

They moved slowly through the house, their senses stretching out as they moved deeper into enemy territory.

Kristen had moved in front but hesitated as she felt magic ahead. Hunter stopped beside her to feel the steady throb of power.

"The machine?" Kristen murmured warily, her blue eyes taking in the darkness before them.

Hunter let his senses range out, then shook his head. "No, a shield." He replied, his eyes following the shape of it.

Kristen looked on more blindly. She rummaged in her pocket to pull out a coin. Before Hunter could stop her, she tossed it down the corridor. The penny flashed as it flew unhindered through the air and clattered against the wooden floor.

"It's not a solid barrier." Kristen commented.

Hunter cast her a warning look. "What if that had set off an alarm?"

"I kinda wish it had – we could spend more time killing witches and less time sneaking around." Kristen checked her gun for the hundredth time, then moved hesitantly forward. She had only gone two steps when she stopped again.

"Hunter, I can't get through." She said, her voice rising slightly as the only hint of her stress. Kristen pressed her hand firmly against an invisible wall, frowning as it didn't shift, then pressed her shoulder against it and shoved with all her weight.

Hunter stepped up beside her, his hand raised. But he felt nothing and was able to step further down the corridor.

Kristen let out a disappointed sound.

"It appears the shield is selective. I'm guessing it blocks anyone without magic – witches can come and go as they please."

"That's great." Kristen snapped. "Can you get the blasted thing down and let me through?"

Hunter looked at the shield from this side; the rhythm of the magic had the same familiarity as that of the machine. "This is the work of the Shadow Witch. It could take hours to find a weakness – if there was even one to be found."

"You can't just leave me here." Kristen hissed.

"We don't have much choice. I'll destroy the machine and be back here before you know it." Hunter promised.

"You better be. I'm giving you fifteen minutes Hunter, then I won't be held responsible for my actions."

Hunter silently swore but seeing how futile it would be getting into an argument with Kristen right now, he set off further into the house. There was the steady thrum of power that led him on. The machine. Hunter and the rest of the British MMC knew so little about it, save that the Americans had been experimenting with what they had commandeered from witches, rather than storing or destroying it.

Hunter followed his senses to the bowels of the house. What had originally been built as extensive cellars had been converted into storage rooms by the American MMC. He moved past the shelves of tempting artefacts, and on towards the source of the pulsing power.

It didn't look impressive, a dark cabinet that came about waist high. Hunter felt along the wooden edges, looking for the opening. His hands spread over the pentagonal top, and prised it lose.

The inside shimmered silver and pearl. There were five mirrors on the inner panels, all reflecting a twisted glass block that hovered in the centre.

It was not quite the 'machine' that Hunter had been expecting. But he could scarce breathe from the thick waves of magic that emanated from such a simple thing. He stepped back to get a better view of it. A part of him had hoped there would simply be a plug to pull, or a switch to flip.

Hunter looked at the glass centre, he could read the rhythm of magic clearly – although the amplification was purely Sophie's work, the basis was someone else's. Something that could be changed, or broken.

Hunter's fingers drummed against the edge of the cabinet. He could change the function of the machine. Standing over it, here and now, he could see how easy it would be for him to alter the basics. It wouldn't be long before it pulsed out with anti-witch power that would leave the witches defenceless.

The thought had barely taken place, but Hunter could already feel the guilt weigh heavy upon him. He couldn't do that to individuals like Laura Kuhn and Bev Murphy. Damn the Donili for messing with his moral compass!

Before he could change his mind, Hunter grasped the glass. It felt surprisingly cold against his skin as he lifted it out of the mirrored case. He threw it to the ground and watched it shatter. The magic in the room immediately shrunk back.

Just as Hunter thought that felt a little too easy, a wave of power exploded out, knocking him off balance. Hunter scrambled back to his feet, his head pounding with the alarm that refused to stop.

Hunter retraced his steps, hurrying back out of the basement level, listening for the sound of alerted witches above the drone of the alarm.

Hunter jogged up the stairs and back along the landing.

"Kristen." He hissed, seeing no sign of the blasted woman.

At that moment a figure turned the corner at the far end of the corridor. The unknown woman froze in shock at the sight of the intruder, then she raised her hand. Hunter could feel offensive magic building up and pulled his shield around him.

Suddenly Kristen jumped out from the shadow of a doorway, her arm wrapping around the witch's neck and tightening. The witch struggled, her hands clawing at Kristen's sleeve, but eventually her eyes fluttered shut.

"You were supposed to keep out of trouble." Hunter snapped.

"Yeah, well you left me in a house overrun with witches." Kristen countered. She bent down to pick the unconscious witch up by the arms. "Help me put her with the other one."

Hunter stooped to pick up the witch's legs, and they lugged her towards the nearest broom closet.

Hunter looked down at the second slumped figure, a young male witch.

"You've been busy."

"I know, as I said-"

"I'm sorry." Hunter interrupted before she could start again. "But let's get out of here before all hell breaks loose."

"You should have thought of that before setting of that blasted alarm." Kristen snapped, but willingly followed Hunter as they made their way through the maze of corridors.

They made it all the way to the back door, when Hunter suddenly stopped, Kristen slamming into the back of him.

Three people blocked the way, one of them kneeling down to check the pulse of the two witches Hunter had knocked out earlier. They immediately locked onto the trespassers; Hunter could feel the build of magic as two of them prepared to cast. The third was apparently human and pulled out a gun instead.

Hunter reached for Kristen's hand, ready to blink them out of here; but the American had other ideas and pushed past him, barrelling towards the new enemy.

Hunter swore beneath his breath, pulling his shield up just in time to catch the opening spells of the witches. He felt the magic dissipate in the air but had no time to work out what game the witches were playing as he went for the gunman. He knocked the gun aside as a shot fired, mercifully wide; then twisted the man's arm until he dropped it.

Hunter looked coldly into the eyes of the weak human, disgusted that any person could choose to serve the witches that were intent of stamping down the world. But he was still human, and Hunter couldn't bring himself to kill him. A swift blow to the temple made the man crumple to the ground, unconscious, but alive.

Hunter turned to see Kristen dispatching the second witch.

"Don't you remember your training – hit the gunman first."

Kristen raised a brow. "Sorry, I was preoccupied."

Before he could make a retort, Kristen stepped away the bodies and out into the cool night air. She darted across the dark lawn, Hunter following close behind her. The house was really beginning to stir, each window quickly becoming lit.

He paused at the wall, listening for any out-lying guards; but everybody seemed to be converging on the house.

Realising that Kristen had already climbed the boundary wall and was ahead of him

Hunter followed Kristen as she ran back to the park, his 7th gen night-sight easily keeping track of her figure in the dark. He felt the adrenaline rush washing over him. It had been a success – one major advantage removed from the witches. Hunter again felt the regret that he couldn't do more to completely overturn it, but he had sworn a promise to the Donili.

Up ahead, Kristin shouted to hurry him up, as she ran on towards a still, silvery surface.

Hunter caught up to her as she reached the partially man-made lake, a lonely pier casting a shadow over it, and a lake house hunkered on its edge.

Kristen jumped up the porch steps and pushed open the door. The place was abandoned, everything of value stripped out long ago. Such a shame for a fine husk of a building.

"Now, why did we have to run all the way out here?" Hunter asked, hovering in the doorway.

"Sorry, adrenaline rush." Kristen said, her blush showing in the dark. "It was either run here, or… ahm. So, a friend told me about this place and I suddenly wanted to come see it."

Kristen pushed a lock of blonde hair behind her ear and looked about the immediate vicinity. "Not quite how he described it."

Hunter stepped into the bare room. "It's not the worst place I've seen."

So much of the world ruined – all manner of thugs and thieves taking advantage of the discord. But also, surprisingly, the same discord had given so many normal people the spark to step up and shine brighter as they defended their home, their neighbourhood, even their country.

Hunter walked up to Kristen, not thinking, only knowing that he had grown accustomed to being comforted by her presence. Perhaps it was because she was a very capable 6th gen – he didn't have to worry about her, she could take care of herself. Or perhaps it was because she was a link to his past, the daughter of his mentor; although he never looked at Brian in the same way.

There was nothing wrong with putting a friendly hand on her shoulder, but Hunter frowned as Kristen winced away from his touch.

"You're hurt?" He voiced. "Why didn't you say?"

Kristen bit her lip. "It's nothing; a scratch. I'll patch it up when we get back."

"Nonsense, come outside so I can see it better." Hunter insisted.

Outside, the full moon was distant in the night sky, its faint light making out the clean shapes.

Hunter walked towards the lake, picking a spot to sit where they were free from shadows. He looked up expectantly to Kristen, then patted the ground beside him. "Sit down, let me see your shoulder."

Kristen hovered next to him, then obediently sat down, with her back to Hunter. She gingerly pulled her jumper over her head, revealing her pale skin and blood-stained tank top. "See, it's nothing."

Hunter tutted, looking over the gash across her shoulder blade. It wasn't deep and most the bleeding has already stopped, but Hunter was sure that didn't make it any less painful.

"Hold still." He murmured. Hunter lightly pressed his fingers about the wound, then closed his eyes and focussed on what the Donili had managed to teach him.

After a minute's silence, Kristen squirmed, trying to see over her shoulder. "What are you doing? I've bandages in my pack if you've forgotten them."

"Shush and sit still." Hunter repeated. "I'm knitting the wound closed."

"One of your tricks?" Kristen asked as she sat straight again.

Hunter sighed. "Yes, one of my tricks." He admitted quietly. Hunter concentrated again on her injury. It was not difficult, even for the relatively unskilled Hunter. He remembered the headaches and sickness he felt when he had tried to heal worse wounds than this. Healing Kristen's gash caused no detrimental effect to himself.

Hunter opened his eyes, happy that the work was done. He went into his pack to find an antiseptic wipe, cleaning away the blood from her shoulder blade. The skin beneath was pink and tender, but no sign of the injury.

"Nifty trick, I'll have to remember it." Kristen said. She sighed with satisfaction and pulled her blonde hair out of the way of Hunter's gentle touch. "If I'd known this was all it would take to get some attention from you, I would have let a witch stab me earlier."

Hunter smiled at her comment, as he leant forward and kissed her bare shoulder, earning a gasp from Miss Davies.

"Y-you're not going to spoil the moment and say we're heading home now?" Kristen asked, a hint of hurt beneath her voice.

"Not just yet." Hunter murmured, pulling her closer.

## Chapter Thirty

"You're back, finally." Jack remarked, not hiding his relief. "How did it go? Were you successful?"

Hunter reluctantly let go of Kristen's hand and moved to sit down in the comfy seats by the fireplace.

"Yes, it worked out better than I could have hoped." Hunter stated, his eyes following Kristen as she sat across from him. A mischievous smirk crossed her lips, but the American didn't say a word.

Jack caught the look and glanced between the two, his suspicions raised.

"Brilliant." Shaun crowed. The young man immediately picked up the house phone. He put the receiver to his ear and his face dropped. "It's still not working."

Hunter shrugged. "Magic will no longer interfere with technology. But we have five years of disuse to contend with. It could take months, or even years to repair the deficit."

Shaun replaced the phone in its cradle and looked to Jack for support. "So, this won't help us in this war?"

Hunter ignored the confused look Kristen was trying to get across to him. "No, it likely will not. Unless the news of it can be used to put the witches off their stride."

"You need to think long-term, Shaun." Jack said in support of Hunter vocally, although he looked far from convinced.

Hunter sighed. "I'm absolutely knackered. I wanted to see my son before I crash. Where is Adam?"

Shaun snapped out of his daze of disappointment. "He and Mel are in Mrs Astley's quarters."

Hunter stopped in his movements. "I'm sorry, Mel is in my mother's rooms?"

"Um, yeah." Shaun confirmed. "Mrs Astley invited her after breakfast. I think she thinks Mel is a nanny."

Hunter swore beneath his breath and got to his feet; there were far too many things wrong in that picture.

Hunter made his way up the main staircase but stopped as he heard footsteps behind him. He turned to see Kristen catch up with him.

"Kristen?"

"Why did we do it, Hunter?" She asked, her blue eyes hard and demanding.

"Can you be a little more specific?"

Kristen blushed, but didn't drop her gaze. "Why did we destroy the witches' device now? Why not just wait for the war to be over?"

Hunter took a step down, coming closer to Kristen. He reached out and gently brushed his fingers against her waist, a crackle of electricity went between them and he wasn't about to deny it.

"You didn't enjoy Washington?" He asked in a low voice.

Kristen leant in closer, her eyes closing and her soft lips parting – but then she snapped out of it and batted Hunter's hand away.

"Don't try and distract me, Hunter. There's something you're not telling us."

"There's plenty I'm not telling you, I'm sure." Hunter replied wearily. "It may take months to start fixing even the basics, but the sooner we get the ball rolling the better."

Not to mention that Hunter couldn't guarantee that he would be around after the war to destroy the machine. The Donili's prophecy hung heavy above him, as much as he tried to logically deny it.

"Now, if you don't mind, I'm off to face my mother." Hunter added, moving up the staircase again. "You're welcome to come."

Hunter saw that doubt cloud Kristen's face from the very idea of being voluntarily in Mrs Astley's presence.

"No, I thought not." Hunter muttered beneath his breath, a little disappointed that he had to deal with his mother by himself.

As Hunter walked along the corridor to his mother's quarters, he could hear piano music drifting out, beautiful in its simplicity.

Hunter pushed the door open to see Mel sitting at his mother's gleaming Bösendorfer piano. Mrs Astley sat on the large leather settee, Adam beside her, a book open on his lap.

Mrs Astley looked calmly up at the interruption. "Oh George, you're back. Only gone for one night, this time?" The woman huffed. "You take after your father, swanning off and returning when it suits. Having a fine old time, I daresay."

Hunter had heard this too many times to let it wind him up. "I told you yesterday, mother, I went to Washington DC to destroy that American machine. We can bring back technology now."

"Why bother." Mrs Astley said dismissively. "The world is better without it."

Hunter didn't know whether to smile or groan. It was too much to expect any sort of praise or concern from his mother.

"Miss Myfanwy plays quite well." Mrs Astley commented, decidedly changing the topic of conversation. "But then, I always find that those with special needs have talent that surpasses the rest of us."

"Mother! Mel does not have special needs. She is…" Hunter broke off. What could he tell his mother, that Mel was a demon, a servant of Satan? And worse, that Mel found Mrs Astley scarier than her master?

"I do wish you would see people for what they are, George. No wonder that Sophie girl duped you." Mrs Astley remarked, glancing down at Adam, her gaze softening. She clearly didn't care what had gone wrong with her son and Sophie, when the outcome had given her a grandson.

Hunter felt distinctly nauseous. "Right I need to get some sleep. Adam, are you ok staying with Grandma Astley?"

Adam scrunched up his face. "But it's only lunch time, daddy!"

"I know, I know, I'm sorry." Hunter said quickly, some amusement slipping through the fatigue. "If you would like, I can ask Shaun to practise football with you again."

Adam sat thinking about it, pulling the big old book close about his chest. Hunter could see the familiar early edition of 'Winnie the Pooh' – obviously Mrs Astley was playing the doting grandmother.

"Later." Adam decided, opening his book again. "Night, dad."

**Chapter Thirty-one**

That night, Hunter was in a deep and dreamless sleep when he was suddenly awoken by a flying five-year-old.

"Dad, dad! A monk is here!" Adam shouted, bouncing erratically on the bed, his bony knee hitting Hunter's stomach and making him groan.

Not happy with how slow his father was reacting, Adam grabbed the spare pillow and hit him as hard as his young arms could manage.

"I'm awake, I'm awake!" Hunter protested, pinning his son's arms down before the boy could take another swing.

"What time is it?" Hunter croaked, glancing at the curtain-covered windows. There was hardly any light coming through the gaps, so he guessed it was ridiculously early.

"Adam, why are you up this early?" Hunter asked, more out of exasperation than any real desire for an answer. "How did you know one of the monks had arrived – you were supposed to be in bed."

"Incy saw him in the living room, he woke me up and told me."

Hunter groaned. He was definitely restricting how much time Adam spent with Mel from now on. Something – some missing link, nagged at his subconscious, but Hunter wasn't awake enough to pay it attention.

"Right, how about an early breakfast?" Hunter threw his duvet over Adam's head and took a moment to pull on his slippers and dressing gown to keep away the chill that permeated through Astley Manor even in summer.

"Yes!" Came Adam's muffled reply, as he shuffled out of the duvet and off the bed. "Can I have Coco Pops? Jack found some and said I can have them."

Hunter and Adam made their way downstairs, the old house was dark and still sleeping. They stopped at the living room, which was illuminated by the crackling fire someone had helpfully lit. There, as Adam had promised, a familiar monk stood. Marcus was inspecting the bookshelf as he waited, his eyes drifting over the British classics.

"Marcus, you're here early." Hunter said pointedly.

"I did not want to miss you, Hunter." The monk said, looking a little sheepish. "I did not know your routine. But you did not have to get up, I wait."

"Adam told me you were here." Hunter explained. "C'mon, kitchen. Coffee."

Hunter yawned and led the way to the kitchen. Adam ran ahead and began rummaging in the cupboards, triumphantly pulling out a bright box of cereal.

Hunter went to get a bowl, but his son snatched it from him. "I can do it." Adam insisted.

Hunter smiled, reluctantly letting his son make his own breakfast, images of the potential mess the Coco Pops would make. He turned to build a fire in the aga and tried to get a match to light. Hunter heard Marcus chuckle behind him, and a fire sprung up in front of him, causing Hunter to fall back onto his arse.

"That's cheating." Hunter stated. "I never managed to learn that trick."

"Hmm, it is strange." Marcus replied, suddenly serious. "That you can shield an army, but you cannot light a fire."

"Yes, thanks – the senior monks enjoyed pointing that out." Hunter sighed at the hours spent in theory and practice as he tried and failed to learn something even the youngest monks could do; and the following, in-depth discussions about possible reasons and solutions. It had all made Hunter's headache; he had never done well with finicky detail. That had always been James' job.

"At least I finally learnt how to make that hovering light." Hunter said defensively, to stop the natural progression of where his thoughts were leading.

"So, this is Adam." Marcus said as Hunter put a pot on the stove. "It is nice to meet you, signorino. I have heard a lot. Biagio ti ha insegnato italiano, sì?"

"Biagio!" Adam started through a mouthful of Coco Pops. "Abbiamo giocato a calico."

"Incredibile." Marcus glanced at Hunter. "Your son has a talent for languages."

Hunter handed a mug of hot coffee to his friend. That was an understatement, to be honest, it worried Hunter a little that his son picked up so much so easily. "Anyway, I though you two had met earlier this morning? Adam was *supposed* to be in bed."

Marcus looked confused. "You are mistaken, Hunter. I see no one this morning."

"But he…" Hunter broke off, frowning. It was too early to work anything out. "What brings you here, Marcus?"

"The Abate wanted to send a message. I volunteered." Marcus replied, pulling a face as he took a sip of the bitter coffee. "He says well done with the… the… macchina."

"Sorry, it's the best we've got." Hunter mentioned, very much aware that he needed to restock his pantry. "Is the Abate and the Donili ready to spread the word?"

"They already do it, Hunter. My wife is with your MMC as we speak. Biagio has gone to Fraulein Kuhn. Luis to South Africa; Anna to America… The list is long, most of the monks have decided to help you."

"Marissa is with my MMC?" Hunter echoed, worried at the idea of sweet innocent Marissa dealing with General Dawkins. "Will she be safe? They won't confuse her for a witch; or view her in ill light because of the connection with me?"

"Marissa can take care of herself." Marcus said with a slow smile as he thought of his love. "We have agreed to meet at the Abbazia de Donili in one week to discuss the next step."

The talk drifted conversationally over life in Donili for the next hour or so. Adam, after his early and exciting start, was falling asleep where he sat, so Hunter picked him up and carried him to the living room, laying him on the settee.

Hunter had made a second round of coffee, and he and Marcus sat in amiable silence by the time the rest of the house stirred. Hunter always liked to hear footsteps and voices filling his house. The Manor, for all that it made him feel at home, could also make him feel cut off from the rest of the world.

Marcus flinched beside him, and Hunter looked up to see Mel enter the room. He could not blame the monk for feeling a tad uncomfortable with a demon around.

Then something clicked.

"Mel, can I speak with you outside?" Hunter said, his voice cold as he tried to keep his temper in check.

Hunter pushed past a dazed-looking Shaun and ignored Kristen as she shouted his name. Hunter threw open the front door and stalked out into the courtyard, the gravel crunching underfoot. Hunter squinted in the bright sun and ignored the beauty of the countryside around him.

Mel followed him, her plimsole-covered feet were feather light and making hardly any noise.

Hunter stopped in his tracks and turned to face her. Her blue eyes were wide, and she looked so innocent in her white summer dress. Hunter pushed aside that instinct to trust and protect her.

"Mel, what is Incy?" He snapped.

Mel looked bemused at Hunter's ignorance. "He's a spider, George."

"Is he a familiar?"

The world was silent, the wind stilled, and the morning chorus of birds quietened. A familiar. Hunter felt sick mentioning it.

The silence seemed to stretch on.

"Yes." Mel whispered.

"You gave my son a familiar!" Hunter roared, his calm breaking. "You gave my five-year-old son a fu-"

"Hunter!" Kristen shouted as she jogged over to them. She looked between Hunter and Mel, hardly believing that Hunter was losing his temper with her. "What the hell is going on?"

"Adam's pet spider is a familiar." Hunter said with disgust.

Kristen paused. "Have you given her chance to explain?"

"No, but-"

"Then don't be so damned hasty." Kristen turned to Mel. "Mel, why did you give Incy to Adam?"

"For protection." Mel said simply, watching as Hunter started to pace in front of her, the energy of his anger almost palpable.

"Is it dangerous?" Kristen asked, forcing herself to keep her attention on Mel. "Will it hurt Adam?"

Mel looked shocked that she would even ask. "No! Incy is there to protect and serve Adam."

Hunter just grunted and kept pacing.

Kristen put her hand on Mel's shoulder. "Mel, why don't you go have breakfast while I have a chat with Hunter."

After taking a moment to work out who Hunter was, Mel turned and went back to the house with all the appearance of a kicked puppy.

"Why are you defending her?" Hunter snapped after Mel had retreated.

"Uh, maybe because I don't need you losing it and accidently blowing something up. Plus, it would be pretty dumb to piss off a demon. And I'm sure it's not as bad as you're making out."

Hunter stopped his pacing and glared at Kristen. He hated that she had made two very good points; and one that was way off the mark.

"I suppose I shouldn't expect you to understand, Miss Davies. You were never educated; you couldn't know what it means."

Kristen nodded, her lips pursed, then reached out and slapped Hunter across the face hard enough to make his head snap back.

Hunter staggered back, surprised. "Ouch!" That was the hardest a woman had ever slapped him, but then again, he'd never been slapped by a 6th gen witch-hunter.

"Be glad that's all you're getting. I don't need you, or anyone, accusing me of being uneducated. I have a GPA of 4.0 and I have the benefit of not being brainwashed by your Malleus Maleficarum prejudices."

"You don't understand." Hunter forced himself to be reasonable. "A familiar is a devil-spawned creature that feeds off witches to survive."

Kristen rolled her eyes. "It's a symbiotic partnership – in return the witch gets a loyal servant. I have done the reading, Hunter."

Hunter swore beneath his breath and stalked away towards the expansive Astley grounds.

Kristen jogged to catch up with his longer strides. "What's really upsetting you Hunter? That Incy's a familiar? Because you've been perfectly fine and accepting that Mel's a demon. Or is it because it further points out that Adam's a witch!"

Hunter stopped. He didn't want Kristen to be right, but he couldn't deny the pang of guilt in his stomach.

Kristen walked round to face him, then stepped closer, her hands running up his muscled arms, her head resting on his chest. Hunter felt the warmth and comfort of her, it felt right.

Kristen tilted her head back to look at him. "There is no rulebook on what to expect where Adam is concerned. Just don't take it out on others." She rose onto her toes and pressed a gentle kiss to his lips.

Hunter responded by pulling her tighter against him. "I'll try. Can I rely on you to step in and distract me when it goes wrong?"

Kristen looked up at him, a blush colouring her cheeks. "I think I can handle that. Come on, let's get back inside, I want to catch up with Marcus."

Kristen slipped her hand into Hunter's and he let her lead him across the long grass. Hunter still wasn't happy, but the initial shock had passed. He wondered if there was any way of guaranteeing Mel was telling the truth, rather than relying on instinct.

As they came back to the front of the house, Hunter glanced warily at the living room windows and surreptitiously dropped Kristen's hand.

She immediately turned to give him a questioning look.

"Sorry. I'm not ready… for 'us' to be public." He explained weakly.

"Way to charm a girl, Hunter." Kristen snapped, her patience suddenly fraying. "And just so you know – most of them have already guessed."

Kristen turned in her heel and marched through the heavy front door, making it slam back on its hinges.

Hunter's old womanising ego savagely kicked him in the head. But it was too late to change how badly that had come out and he had enough to worry about without adding Kristen to the list.

As he walked into the living room, he saw that Adam was awake now. Probably due to the numerous adults gathered awkwardly, waiting for Hunter to return.

"Adam, come with me." Hunter said quietly, nodding to the corridor.

"It wasn't me!" He replied quickly; his big hazel eyes worried.

Hunter smiled. "Nothing's wrong. Just come on, it's secret."

The boy jumped down from the settee and pushed past Shaun to get to join his father.

Hunter didn't go far, leading his son to the empty library. He closed the door firmly behind him, then turned to face the boy.

"Adam, does Incy ever bite you?"

"Yes – but it doesn't hurt daddy!" Adam answered, looking very worried again. "You won't make me get rid of him, will you? Because he's mine. And Mel – Mel says it's normal."

Hunter took a deep breath, reminding himself to stay calm. He couldn't believe Mel would tell his son that; normal – how the hell did Mel know what was normal!

"Adam, show me where Incy bites you." Hunter requested.

Adam hesitated, then rolled up his trouser leg. "There." He pointed to the back of his right calf.

Hunter knelt down and ran his thumb over the area that Adam indicated. His flesh paled and flashed back pink where pressure was applied. Apart from one spot the size of a penny;

it stayed pale and did not change colour, because there were no capillaries to do the job.

The witches' spot. The site on a witch's body where their familiar fed; reputed not to bleed; and one of the signs that medieval 'witch-prickers' used to identify and persecute witches. Hunter knew enough of the history and anatomy attached to the spot, and the truth was that Kristen was right – it was yet another reminder that his son was a witch.

"Daddy, I miss mummy." Adam said as his father's silence continued. "She'd let me keep Incy."

Hunter sighed in defeat. "You can keep the spider, Adam."

The boy sat quietly for a minute. "When's mummy coming?"

Hunter hesitated, it was not a conversation he wanted to get into, how could he tell a five-year-old that his mother was a baddie on the other side? He wondered how Sophie had managed up to now. Hunter had no proof, but his gut feeling told him that Sophie had never painted him as the bad guy in Adam's eyes.

"We'll see her soon, Adam. Soon." He finally answered, honestly enough.

**Chapter Thirty-two**

Hunter tried to concentrate, but throughout his conversation with Marcus and for the rest of the day, his mind kept coming back to Mel. He felt unsettled that he had allowed this demon such unlimited access to his son. When he put it in such stark terms, Hunter could hardly believe it; he had been so quick to trust Mel. Despite every logic, and the warning from the abate, he had continued to accept that she was here to help.

By that evening, Hunter decided that he had to do something. He quietly asked Mel to join him in the library; as an afterthought, he asked Kristen to come too.

The little blonde demon walked into the library with her usual, skipping step, then turned to face Hunter with those big, curious blue eyes.

Hunter waited for Kristen to come in and perch on the nearest table. He closed the door and slowly turned back to Mel.

"Mel… you are my friend, yes?" He asked hesitantly.

"Of course, George." Mel replied, smiling at the easy question.

"I want to be your friend; I want to trust you. But I don't trust your boss." Hunter said, getting straight to the point.

Mel pouted at what she considered unnecessary worry. "Luci is only trying to-"

"Trying to help, yes, I know." Hunter cut in. "When we were in Donili, you said that you weren't supposed to help us. What were you supposed to do?"

Mel chewed her lip, swaying slightly where she stood. "I was supposed to watch. I was supposed to keep the witch-hunters safe until you came. I… I was supposed to stay unseen, but everyone was so nice. I hadn't had friends before."

"So, does that mean you don't have to do everything Lucifer says?" Hunter asked. "You can choose to disobey?"

Mel continued to look uncomfortable. "He doesn't control me. I won't be punished as long as everything happens as it should."

Hunter shivered at the very idea that he was playing into the hands of the devil. "What about Adam? What did Lucifer ask you to do for him?"

Mel blinked in surprise, thinking it obvious. "He asked me to give him a familiar."

"Is that everything?"

Mel was startled by the harshness of Hunter's voice. She nodded. "I am here for you George, not Adam."

Hunter glanced at Kristen, hoping that she would jump in if she thought he was being too harsh, but the American just gazed calmly towards the two of them.

"Mel, you said that you could read the truth. Really look at what your boss is doing and tell me that he isn't interested in

Adam." Hunter insisted. "Tell me that there isn't a possibility that he will try and claim Adam."

Mel looked away, her unease growing. When she turned back to Hunter, there were tears in her eyes. "Yes."

Hunter heard Kristen move from her table. He gave a bitter smile, a silent promise that he wasn't about to lose his temper again.

"And he will use you to get to him." Hunter said, resignation in his voice. "Mel, I can't let that happen. I need you to make a choice. You have to stop working for Lucifer, you have to reject him and all his future plans. Or you have to leave and never come back."

"Y-you don't want me?" Mel stuttered.

Hunter sighed, his heart breaking at the sight of the distraught and innocent Mel. "We all want you to stay, Mel. But I can't risk Adam."

"H-he'll hurt me."

Kristen stepped up and hugged the poor girl. "I'm so sorry, Mel. This is for the best. Why don't you sleep on it and let us know tomorrow?"

Mel shook her head. "No, no, I don't need to wait. I choose my friends; I will always choose my friends."

*****

The following afternoon, and Hunter and his accomplices were sitting in the garden.

"Your English countryside is as beautiful as you say, Hunter." Marcus remarked, glancing curiously at his host. "But this... is this the normale build-up to a war?"

"I don't know what you're talking about." Hunter replied innocently, as he took in the scene. Mel and Kristen sat on the lawn, Mel busy threading daisies into Kristen's hair; Shaun was racing Adam around Mrs Astley's geraniums. Jack sat reading, occasionally looking up from his book to smirk at his younger colleague.

"I don't think this war has any precedent for comparison – unless we go back to the Middle Ages and my records get sketchy that far in the past."

Marcus frowned at the long words and waited for Hunter to repeat his meaning in Italian.

Hunter added more. "These men and women... and demons... they are going to fight with us. I shan't deny them time to relax and enjoy themselves. Besides, don't you know how rare it is for a British summer not to be accompanied by rain?"

Marcus smiled and shook his head but gazed contentedly across the grounds of the Astley estate. The once controlled lawns and hedges looking slightly wild, and all the more beautiful for it.

"I see why you fight, if you come home to this." Marcus observed. Suddenly the monk sat a little straighter, turning his gaze to the house. Marcus relaxed again and smiled. "You have a guest."

Hunter grimaced, wondering whose arrival could amuse Marcus. He really did not want his mother coming out to join them. Mrs Astley would only complain over the state of her garden.

He looked up and was very pleased and surprised to see Biagio walking over to them instead.

"Biagio! I didn't know you were coming."

"Yes, the Abate has given me permission to come here before the official meeting in Donili. Your mother told me you were out here." Biagio replied, faltering a little at the mention of Mrs Astley. "She is… very pleasant."

Hunter recognised the faltering, almost questioning pitch of his statement. "What did she say to you?"

"That I have good diction, for a foreigner." Biagio answered. "Is this good?"

"Yes, that's positively a compliment."

"Better than I got." Marcus contested. "'Dressed inappropriately for my station,' and 'they should insist on foreigners knowing good English before they are allowed to visit'."

"Please take a seat, Biagio, and tell us why you are really here." Hunter said before things could get silly.

Biagio did so and looked rather pleased with himself. "Well, as you know, I have been to see Fraulein Kuhn. She sends her best wishes, Giorgio, and wanted me to convey that no harm came to her after your escape. Actually, she was so impressed that you managed to escape, that she is confident in strengthening the alliance between you!"

Hunter sat up a little straighter – there was an unexpected bonus. When Hunter had escaped with Mel and Kristen, he had been consumed with relief that they had avoided the Shadow Witch; it had not occurred to him that they could have inspired any great opinion.

"Fraulein Kuhn explained that there was an artefact that belonged to Germany. Something that was stolen long ago. The British witches recently returned it to the Witches Rat as an emblem of peace and unity." Biagio went on, savouring every last word and moment of anticipation until his audience looked ready to hit him.

The monk went into his satchel and pulled out an object wrapped in black silk. Putting it down on the garden table deferentially, Biagio began to fold back the covering.

Hunter's breath caught in his throat and he could not tear his eyes away from the object.

Biagio coughed to get their attention, obviously pleased with their reactions. "Fraulein Kuhn expressed that if this knife was to belong to anyone, it would belong to you, Giorgio."

Hunter leant forward in his seat and reached out until his fingers brushed the black silk – he dared not touch the knife itself. It did not look how he had imagined it would, a blunt and chipped relic that betrayed the many years of its existence. The narrow grey blade gleamed in the bright summer sun, and the handle was ivory and simple in fashion. He could not see the words 'For Her Hand Only' etched into it, not on this side anyway.

"The Abate consented that this was a gift for you, from Fraulein Kuhn, and therefore removes responsibility of this item from the Donili."

Hunter looked up at Biagio, trying to work out the Abate's true meaning.

Biagio sighed, having hoped that his more flowery expression would be satisfactory. "Padre said that he agrees the knife belongs with you. He wished for you to have it before the Donili meeting, so the other elders could not interfere with what is a morally grey area."

Hunter slowly let out his breath. Here it was, the one known thing that could end the life of a Shadow Witch. He looked for a certain someone, wanting verified.

"Mel?"

Hearing her name, Mel stopped plaiting Kristen's hair and danced over to the garden table.

Hunter noticed how both monks shrank back at the arrival of the little blonde girl. Hunter stull hadn't forgiven her over the familiar, but he couldn't understand how the monks were so naturally repulsed by Mel.

"Mel, can you tell me anything about this?"

Mel looked down at the table and immediately her normally carefree expression froze. It was the first time Hunter had seen her look fearful.

"It… it is Sabine's, the weapon of the Shadow Witch." Mel answered in a small voice. "When she wields it, it will always claim it's victim. Wiccans and witches, monks and demons…"

"And demons?" Biagio echoed with unnecessary interest.

"It was a gift to Sabine, the gift of death." Mel said quietly.

"From Lucifer?" Hunter asked, filled with distaste that the blade was from Mel's boss.

Mel shook her head. "She was given the gift of death because we knew one day, a hundred years after the witch-craze started, Sabine would grow weary of life. She fell in love with a mortal man, and after he died, she had the one tool that could allow her to join him."

Obviously, content with her part, Mel left and drifted back to here Kristen sat, the American alert and eavesdropping.

"Why do I feel that every time I get one answer, I get a hundred new questions." Hunter muttered, looking at the dagger.

"I concur. I am not happy with the ambiguity of her answers." Biagio added. At the looks he received from Hunter and Marcus, Biagio turned sheepish. "I do not like what I do not know."

"Well, get back to the Abate and inform him on our new mysteries." Hunter said with a grim smile.

Biagio bowed his head. "I shall see you at the meeting in a few days."

"You're not staying for dinner, Biagio? My mother will be disappointed."

Biagio suddenly looked worried at the prospect of upsetting Mrs Astley.

"Go Biagio, I will make your excuses." Hunter insisted.

Nobody particularly enjoyed Mrs Astley's company, but the feeling was normally mutual. Mrs Astley often didn't like or approve of those she was forced to spend time with. Hunter didn't know if he felt sorrier for Biagio for potentially having his mother's favour.

**Chapter Thirty-three**

The morning of the meeting, Hunter blinked over to Donili Village, taking Adam and Kristen with him. Mel travelled using her own method; and Marcus brought along Shaun, who had dropped blatant hints that he wanted to come.

Jack and Mrs Astley had also been invited in the end, but Hunter's mother refused to make a trip abroad on so little notice; and Jack selflessly decided to stay so there was at least one witch-hunter at the Manor. Not that he thought any witch or demon would be brave enough to take on Mrs Astley.

Donili Village was as bright and beautiful as ever, the green of the surrounding forest, and the glint of the nearby lake. The Abbazia stood out on the top of the hill, ruling over the landscape.

Hunter briefly stopped by to let them know of his arrival, then headed to Marcus' house to await the midday meeting.

He didn't know what would happen at the meeting, or what to expect. Impatience burned through his veins, so instead of stopping when he reached his friend's house, Hunter kept going, breaking into a jog.

When Hunter hear another set of footsteps join his, he started to run.

Donili Village was soon left behind, and the track became narrower as it entered the trees. It was simply a blur of green as Hunter ran down the track that weaved between the great trunks. It was not long before the glinting lake could be seen, and Hunter only stopped when he was at the water's edge. He looked out over the peaceful and familiar scene, while he rolled the tenseness out of his shoulders and stretched his stiff limbs.

"Hey Hunter, not running back to England, are you?" Kristen called out as she slowed to a jog and stopped beside him. "You can really run."

Hunter glanced over to her, not sure if he wanted company. "Thank you, Miss Davies. I had already noticed."

Kristen snorted at his lack of humility, making Hunter soften a little.

"You almost kept up." He offered.

"Shut up, we both know that's a lie." Kristen said with a laugh. "You know, I always thought being a 6th gen was pretty awesome, but just a few weeks with you and I'm feeling disgustingly average instead. I wish I had been born a generation later."

Hunter inwardly sighed at her comments – yes, it was just a lucky chance of birth that had given him these powers. Would that he had been born someone else, someone average and non-influential.

"I'm going for a run, want to come?"

Kristen looked at him warily. "How far?"

"Just a lap of the lake."

Kristen smiled at the challenge and took the track to the right.

Hunter watched her disappear into the trees and gave her a ten second head-start, before following her. Kristen may not be as fast as Hunter, but she was easily as nimble as him, not slowing down as she darted between the trees and raced on.

Hunter felt his own pulse start to beat faster, his breaths coarse from the exertion. They had gone over a third of the way round when Hunter finally caught up with her.

"So... why the run... this morning?" Kristen asked between breaths, not breaking stride.

"I had too much energy." Hunter answered. "I couldn't risk getting frustrated by something stupid at the meeting later and potentially hitting someone."

"Well... Colin Dawkins is gonna be there, I'll understand if you want to hit him anyway." Kristen answered, flashing Hunter a mischievous look before concentrating on the path ahead. "What's his beef with you anyway?"

"Pass." Hunter replied. He honestly couldn't think why the now-General always reacted with hostility towards him.

"You know, there are better ways to expend energy." Kristen said, glancing over her shoulder at Hunter.

Before he had a chance to react, Kristen put on the brakes and threw her weight into her shoulder. When Hunter collided with her, she quickly spun him off balance and let the momentum carry them both down.

Hunter grunted as he hit the ground, his hands quickly found Kristen's waist, but he didn't hurry to push her away.

"I think I like your method of distraction."

"I thought you might." Kristen said with a satisfied smirk, before she kissed him.

**Chapter Thirty-four**

The meeting took place in the Abbazia. Hunter and Kristen were ushered into the auditorium where Hunter had once had lessons alongside the young monks. The seats rose in tiered levels on all four sides, so that all could see, and be seen.

The room thrummed with energy, filled with more people than Hunter had imagined. Besides the monks, there were some he recognised – Colin and Theresa, supporting the British MMC; David and Terry from the Australian MMC; Annette and her little assistant from France. And Laura Kuhn. Hunter paused, shocked that the witch should be present. Laura looked up, recognition in her eyes, but before they could greet each other, they were called to take their seats.

"Benvenuto, signore e signori." The Abate took the floor, calmly taking in the crowd with his grey eyes. "Primo, if you do not understand Italian, your assigned Donili monk will translate."

Hunter lowered his head to Kristen's and quickly translated for her. A flash of annoyance crossed her face, and Hunter could only hope that she would be satisfied with his relay of the meeting.

The Abate waited for the murmured conversations to die down, then continued in rapid Italian. "You are all welcome to the first meeting of witch-hunters, witches and wiccans alike."

There was a lull as his words were translated, then the hall erupted. People were on their feet, most looking betrayed, and many looking angry.

Hunter got the impression that the Donili had been less than forthcoming on what this meeting would entail. He looked down at the Abate, who wore that same amused expression he always had at Hunter's outbursts.

"Silenzio!" The Abate finally shouted. "The Abbazia will play a neutral ground for all parties at this and future meetings. As long as you are in these walls no magic will work, and no violence will be tolerated."

As he translated this to Kristen, Hunter wondered if 'no magic' was supposed to include Mel. He'd witnessed the blonde demon break the Donili rules; it would be a shame if she popped up now and ruined padre's speech. Hunter but back a smile and forced himself not to think of Mel, in case that was all it took to summon her.

"This is the future, ladies and gentlemen. Where the Malleus Maleficarum and the Witches Council unite as equals to govern themselves." The Abate continued. "Finer details can be worked out in your own countries once the war is won."

The Abate went on to discuss each country, calling on every representative. Each comment and description was brief, but it still took two hours to complete the hall.

Hunter sat and quietly translated throughout, noting how the stories were all so familiar. Everyone was on the verge of rebelling and only needed the final push. Even the witches were alert and ready for the chance to change things.

Luckily Hunter was not the only British MMC representative, and General Dawkins keenly took the spotlight. Colin said his piece, and Hunter wondered how he'd never noticed what a pompous arse he was. Huh, probably because he'd previously considered Colin a friend, when the soldier had obviously only been humouring him while General Hayworth was in charge.

Hunter was snapped out of his train of thought by a sharp elbow from Miss Davies. He looked accusingly at the American – surely, she didn't need Dawkins translating.

Kristen nodded to the Abate in response, and Hunter suddenly noticed that all focus was on him.

"Signor Astley, if you please?"

"What?"

"Our mission in Washington." Kristen hissed.

"Oh right." Hunter muttered, getting stiffly to his feet. The run this morning followed by sitting still for two hours was not a good idea.

"As you all know, five years ago the witches used a device from the American MMC to disrupt technology to set us all at a disadvantage. I thought you may all like to know that it has been disabled. Everything is still a long way from being restored, but this is more proof that things are moving in our favour." Hunter finished and sat down.

The hall was filled with murmured translations which were followed by expressions of polite interest. Not quite the reaction Hunter had hoped for.

"Jeez, what have you gotta do to impress people around here?" Kristen muttered beside him.

On the floor, the Abate held his hands up for attention.

"I am sure there is much more to say." The Abate continued in Italian. "And the Abbazia di Donili is open to all of you, if you wish to stay the rest of the day. But you must bring the battle back to those that delight in murder and sin. I recommend making a stand at the next full moon. Delaying will likely help no one."

The room became a buzz of voices again, and the Abate waited patiently for his audience to settle again.

"The longer we wait the more chance the Shadow Witch and her council will have to discover our plans. We cannot give them time to corrupt this alliance between hunters and witches."

The Abate paused and Hunter was surprised to see a flash of uncertainty cross the older man's features. The Abate glanced to where the other senior monks sat.

"As many of you have been told, the Donili's interference was only going to extend to playing the messenger and neutral party in this conflict. But we have decided to go one step further."

Despite the crowded hall, the Abate's eyes found Hunter's.

"To reduce the lives lost and to ensure a swift conclusion to the war, the Donili monks will be joining you on the front line; we will block unfriendly magic."

Hunter felt his pulse race. The Donili had changed their minds! It was only Kristen's hand on his arm that stopped him from getting up from his seat as the shock of excitement flooded through him.

Anything was possible now.

**Chapter Thirty-five**

The sun had set, and it was proving to be a warm autumn evening.

News had filtered through to the witches that an opposing force was massing. The spies were all running home with the same information – that the witch-hunters had somehow managed to pull together numbers not seen since Salisbury Plains.

The Shadow Witch was hardly concerned. They had crushed them before; they would crush them again. And this time, she would put an end to Hunter Astley.

The other witches on the council had sent a wiccan servant to help her get ready for the battle. The Shadow Witch looked down at her now as she laced up the sturdy black boots. The Shadow Witch, the most powerful witch for a thousand years, hardly needed a servant to help her dress.

She glanced to her right, to where her full-length mirror stood. Sophie took in the dark circles under her eyes and the drained, pale look despite her summer tan. She pushed back a lock of dark brown hair that had already fallen out of her plait. Sophie was quite sure the rest of the witches didn't notice how worn she looked these days; ever since Adam had been taken, she had not slept and had travelled across the world at the slightest hint of his presence.

As the days had turned into weeks, she had only become more desperate. She could not understand how she was unable to find him, she very much doubted that Hunter had the power to block her son from her. Oh, she was certain that Adam was *with* Hunter, but it made her worry over who else was involved; who had managed to shield Adam from *her*.

Upon hearing the news that the pathetic remnants of the witch-hunters were rallying against them, Sophie was determined to face them. After all, wherever the witch-hunters went, Hunter would surely be involved.

She swallowed down the lump that rose in her throat as she thought of Hunter. She wasn't still in love with him; for the sake of her kin, she couldn't be. Sophie had been plagued by dreams that had allowed her fantasies and delusions to live. But no more. She had to remember that this was George 'Hunter' Astley, killer of witches; the man that dared to kidnap her innocent son.

She thought back to the many times she had given him the opportunity to see sense, to put aside the conflict and live peacefully with her. How many times had his leniency cost her, her reputation and influence amongst the witches had never been lower. She would not give him the chance again.

"Is there anything else, ma'am?"

Sophie was brought back to the present by the timid voice. She glanced over at the wiccan that now stood with her eyes deferentially lowered. Sophie exhaled, trying not to show the distaste she felt for this woman. For all wiccans; the grasping, leeching creatures. She had punished enough of them over the last few years; an example had to be made of those that dared to use magic that did not belong to them.

"No, leave me." Sophie snapped.

The middle-aged woman bobbed her head and darted out. Sophie let out a small scream of exasperation; she could already feel the adrenaline for the forthcoming battle flooding her system. She would kill Hunter; reclaim her son; and then she wouldn't stop until she had beaten down the opposition in the witches' council. It was time they acknowledged who she was – not just some figurehead – but a leader who answered to no man.

*****

Darkness fell over the British countryside; and with it came the witches.

They came out of the shadows like an endless sea, until they filled the valley. On the opposing slope, a mundane army was awaiting them.

The Shadow Witch looked up, her enemy had gone for the higher ground, traditionally an advantage. Her frown deepened; let them cling onto any hope they liked, they would be dead by morning.

"Let Hunter Astley come forward." She called out, her hazel eyes scanning the faces of the mob before her.

Nobody moved. The Shadow Witch hissed her disapproval and turned back to her fellow witches. It didn't matter, Hunter might be hiding amongst the ranks – probably with his new little girlfriend – but she knew him; Hunter wouldn't let people die on his behalf. No, he was the hero, he would come to meet her. As she passed the senior witches of the council, she gave the signal.

The witches around her began casting, the air suddenly thick with magic. Sophie took a deep breath, taking pride in the strength of her allies; allowing their magic to flow softly over her skin, building her confidence. Then she turned to face her enemies and all hell broke loose.

Her army surged forward, racing to meet the witch-hunters that stood frozen on the slope. The distance closed and the magic flooded out before them.

Sophie faltered in her stride as she saw the spells dissipate against a solid barrier. Hunter. The ghost of a smile passed her face as she brought out her own destructive power, aiming it into the masses. Sophie watched as her magic buckled the shield – poor Hunter must be distracted; it was hardly up to his usual strength. Without any further concern, Sophie pushed anew. Shouts and cries rose up around her, the metallic tang of blood filtered into the air.

There was an explosion to her left, close enough for Sophie to feel the heat of it against her bare face. She squinted against the brief brightness and focused on finding Hunter. The person projecting the shield was close and Sophie pushed forward, only delayed by one brave soldier that barrelled into her from the side. Sophie ducked under his clumsy attack and in one smooth motion, spun the man off balance and brought up her knife, letting the unlucky man crumpled to the ground.

Leaving the other witches to do the damage, Sophie pressed on with single-minded determination. She brought her magic close about her, a moment more and she could throw everything she had at Hunter to try and catch him off guard…

But Hunter was not there.

The source of the shield was a grey-haired man, no taller than Sophie. He was dressed in a simple black linen outfit and moved like a man half his age. Sophie stood frozen, lost as to who this man was.

'The Benandanti; he has found the Benandanti.' No sooner had the revelation crossed her mind, the mysterious man turned to face her. His shockingly blue eyes observing her.

"Buonasera Sophie."

"You know me?" She asked. Nobody called her that anymore; enemies and allies alike only saw the Shadow Witch.

The Benandanti hesitated, and Sophie could sense him trying to strengthen his shield as her witches renewed their attack. His focus was then only for her. He bowed his head in acquiescence.

"Signor Astley has told me much about you."

Sophie's frown hardened, but she kept control of the thrashing emotions within. How dare Hunter discuss her with anyone, he had given up that right.

Sophie took a deep breath, ignoring the chaos around her. "Where is Astley? Tell me and I will let you live; I will let you return to Italy and carry on your peaceful existence."

Before the old man could reply, a noise rose up above the din of battle, a horn. The very simple note was taken up across the stretch of the battlefield and even though it was mundane, Sophie couldn't help but be unsettled.

"What mischief is this?" She demanded.

The Benandanti smiled gently. "It is the new world. Embrace it, Sophie, for all our sakes'."

Sophie felt a fracture in the magic around her and spun round. It took her a moment to work out what was happening – it could not be happening! But suddenly, witches were fighting witches. There were patches of rebellion spread across the valley; a third of her forces were suddenly turning on the others, pinning them in against the witch-hunters on the opposing slope. Sophie's eyes tore wildly across the scene – how could they betray her? How could they betray everything they had sacrificed so much for?

This was Hunter's doing – she did not know how, but Sophie was adamant he was behind it. That no-good, deceitful bastard had somehow decided that he would work with witches now. Why not years ago, when she had offered him everything? How could he refuse her then, force the world to make war; then think that this was the right course?

Suddenly overwhelmed with the new targets she wished to punish, Sophie turned back to the Benandanti, who stood calmly observing her.

"Where is Hunter?" She snapped, her calm façade breaking.

When the old man did not answer, Sophie raised her hand, her magic seeping out and curling around the man's throat. She could feel his attempts at blocking it, his pitiful shield designed for lesser witches. Sophie gazed on dispassionately as the man became to gasp as she slowly constricted his airways.

"He's... he's not..."

Sophie sighed and released him just enough for the old man to speak properly.

"He's not here. He never was. Even without him, your side has been beaten, Sophie." The Benandanti's blue eyes glinted. "You have a choice. You must choose to stay and fight, or to go to him. He is in the church hall in the next village – but only for the duration of the battle – after that, he will disappear again."

Sophie released the man, letting him slump to his knees. So, Hunter was playing the coward. She let out a scream of frustration, her magic exploding out with force, knocking over every witch-hunter, witch and monk in her path. Leaving them motionless on the grass, Sophie wrapped her shadows around her and vanished.

**Chapter Thirty-six**

Hunter paced the room, the little ball of light that hovered above his head moved with him, back and forth across the ceiling.

"Will you please stand still?" Kristen begged, from where she perched on an old desk. "Or at least make your light thing stay still – it's giving me a headache, bobbing all over the place!"

Hunter looked across at the girl. "Sorry." He muttered, shoving his hands in his pockets and forcing himself to be still. "I'm just... not used to not doing anything."

Hunter thought of the men and women out there. They were protected more effectively by the Donili than Hunter could have ever managed. The 'good' witches had switched to their side, giving them overwhelming odds. Hunter could already see how it would play out – their enemies would realise the futile situation and flee, or they would make a heroic last stand and be cut down.

Hunter didn't want to be cocky, but the truth was that as long as the Shadow Witch was subdued, his side could not lose.

"George Astley, the famous witch-hunter. Are you nervous?" Kristen asked in wonder. "Proof that you're only as flawed and human as the rest of us?"

Hunter tried to raise a weak smile at her ribbing. "I've never been bait before."

"Don't worry, everything will go to plan. Your witchy lover will be here as soon as she realises, you're not with the others."

Hunter felt his palms sweat at the very thought. "You don't have to stay for this, Kristen. It'll be safer if you leave."

"And you don't have to do this alone." Kristen said, re-stating an earlier argument. "But I want a reward when all this is finished. Two weeks in the South of France – just you, me and Adam."

The shadows in the room started to thicken and congeal. She was coming.

Hunter rested his hand close to his gun, and Kristen got to her feet, moving closer to his side.

The Shadow Witch appeared, the shadows hugging her elegant frame. Her sharp features were framed by her dark brown hair, which continued in waves down her back. For a moment she looked beautiful.

And then a moment later her hazel eyes snapped onto Hunter and every fibre of her being echoed her anger.

"You bastard. How could you do this Hunter?!" Sophie fought to find words, her hands clenching by her sides.

"The battle is over. You've lost." Hunter replied, sounding official to feign calm.

The Shadow Witch looked nonplussed at his statement. "What...? Where is my *SON*?" She screamed. A wave of magic rolled off her, so powerful it blasted Hunter and Kristen from their feet.

Hunter grunted in pain and caught his breath while he sat in an ungainly heap.

"You think that you were dangerous when my witches killed Charlotte? When they killed James?" Sophie purred, looking down at Hunter. "That is nothing, *nothing*, compared to what you have unlocked in me by taking my son. Not even your anti-magic can stand against it."

Sophie raised her hand and Hunter felt the air leave his lungs and he gasped frantically at nothingness.

"Give Adam back to me and I shall show mercy. If not, I will tear this world apart looking for him. Not even your Benandanti monks will be able to stop me."

"D-Donili." Hunter gasped, then realised that Sophie had allowed him to breath to respond. "Donili monks. If you are going to defy and kill them, at least call them by their true names."

"Where is Adam?" Sophie hissed, the threat of her magic welling up for another attack.

"I will take you to him." Hunter said rapidly, still on his knees before her. "On the condition that you are bound. We can be human; we can live together in the cottage in Keswick – I know you've seen it too."

Sophie paused, her eyes glazing over. "That's nothing but a dream, however you engineered it."

Hunter shook his head. "It was not my doing." He thought back to the dreams that had invaded his sleep for the past two years. He had always believed they were real, that he shared them with Sophie, that she was behind them. If not Sophie, then who?

"I seem to remember giving you the same option, more than once. You always refused, insisting that you were on the 'right' side." Sophie replied, her cracking voice betraying how close she was to losing this calm façade. "But look at you now Hunter, uniting with witches, despite all your protestations and morals. What were all those deaths and battles for? You disgust me."

"I'm making a better world." Hunter said humbly, then raised his voice. "For our son; for the people that deserve to be treated as more than cattle and sacrifices; and yes, for the witchkind that are peaceful and want to join that future."

Sophie laughed, but Hunter could sense the hum of power focussing in on a single. "In this you describe one person perfectly. Let me ask you this Hunter: *where is my mother*?"

Hunter's gut twisted at the question. Sophie read the answer in his expression and her calm broke. Her scream was a wall of sound that made Hunter cower on the ground.

Then suddenly the scream stopped with a grunt of pain.

Kristen, forgotten in the background, slowly moved away from Sophie, her bloody hand leaving the dagger hilt-deep in her torso.

Sophie looked down disbelievingly. She weakly smiled and closed her eyes, wavering a little in her stance. The woman took three measured breaths, then yank the knife from her stomach with a scream. The pain dropped her to her knees, but then she gave a bitter laugh, and slowly stood up.

"So, this is the American girl. She is pretty, you're right. Consider me jealous." Sophie flipped the knife in her hand and, spinning quickly to face Kristen, drove the blade deep into her belly.

Kristen's eyes widened and she staggered back until she hit the wall.

"Kristen!" Hunter cried, jumping to his feet.

Sophie held up a hand to stop him. "You will say your goodbyes, and then you will join me." She said coldly.

The shadows in the room thickened and began to curl around her once more.

Hunter stood paralyzed, watching as Sophie left. A whimper from Kristen snapped him out of his daze, and he rushed to where the girl half-lay, slumped against the wall.

"What the hell did you do that for?" Hunter snapped, gingerly moving her blood-stained top away from the wound.

"Well you clearly weren't gonna do it." Kristen said, hissing sharply at the pain of each movement. "And I confess, I got a little jealous, all that talk of happy families."

"And look where it got you. 'By Her Hand Only' Kristen." Hunter said, exasperated. "You could never have killed her. And now…"

"And now I'm the one dying." Kristen finished, very matter-of-fact.

Hunter wanted to deny it, to tell her it would all be fine. "It must always claim it's victim, just like Mel warned: the gift of death."

"T-that's all very well, Hunter. Now do you think you can take this thing out of me?" Kristen grimaced. "It really hurts."

"If I do that you will bleed to death quickly."

Kristen rolled her eyes at his statement. "Die quickly; die slowly; I'm still dead Hunter."

Hunter took a deep breath and obediently pulled the knife out of her with a swift movement. The blade clattered to the floor beside them.

"I'm sorry." Hunter took her hand as he knelt next to her. "I am so sorry for all of this."

Kristen smiled weakly, her skin looking greyer by the second. "I have no regrets. I got to meet you. And I get to die a hero, like my father."

Hunter felt his eyes burn. This was unfair, she was too young, and she shouldn't die for his mistakes. "I wish things had been different – this war, the Shadow Witch rising up. You would always be the one I was meant to meet. You still would have come to England to find your father. Brian would have tried to keep you as far away from me as possible, as any sensible father would…"

Hunter's thoughts followed the alternative life they could have led. He was struck again by how cruel fate was – it should be him dying instead.

Hunter's heart skipped a beat as the realisation hit him. Hunter reached out and put a hand over her wound. Kristen gave a small whimper, barely audible.

"Kristen, I want you to watch over Adam. Let him know I loved him." Hunter stated, confident that he was making a better world for his son.

Through her waning consciousness, Kristen stirred, understanding something serious was happening, something she would not like.

Hunter closed his eyes and focussed on the wound. His power was repelled as it stayed greedily open.

Hunter took a deep breath and opened himself to the curse, the remnants of ancient magic felt the presence of a willing victim and slid happily along into this new vessel. Hunter shuddered in pain, the focussed again on Kristen. This time her wound closed as easily as the practice sessions with the Donili; her flesh knitting together to leave a very sore red scar across her stomach.

Hunter had to steady himself as he felt a wave of dizziness. It was hitting hard and fast, he had to get out of here.

Kristen stirred and weakly grabbed his sleeve. "No." She mumbled.

Hunter grabbed the chain at his neck and pulled it away. He stared at the dog tags in his hand, they had protected him for so many years. He pressed them into Kristen's hand.

"See that Adam gets these. And… ask Toby and Claire to raise him. Don't let my mother get her claws into him."

Hunter leant down and kissed Kristen's forehead, then blinked away.

**Chapter Thirty-seven**

Hunter instinctively followed Sophie. The witch purposefully kept her shields down, and he slipped easily into the space next to her.

Long grass swayed in a sweet-smelling breeze, and the rising sun highlighted the hilly landscape.

Hunter took shallow breaths, careful not to aggravate his new wound. He glanced down; glad he was wearing black. His stomach was already queasy, and he didn't want to see the red stain spread.

"I used to come out here when I was a girl." Sophie said, her voice reflective. "This was always my escape, no one bothered me here."

The witch sighed and turned back to Hunter. She was wearing a mask of calm again, but Hunter could see the unsettled light in her eyes. "Where is my son Hunter? Last chance, or I will kill you."

"You won't kill me." Hunter said calmly.

Sophie looked at him with more than a hint of disdain. "I have killed hundreds of witch-hunters."

"But you won't kill me." Hunter repeated. "You have had every chance these past few years. But you always held back – for God's sake, Sophie, you even rescued me on one occasion."

Sophie grew paler as he spoke. "So, you think I will hold back again, simply because I love you?" She argued, then realised what she had said. "Loved you. You're still living in a dream, Hunter."

"Love, self-preservation; whatever works." Hunter replied with a shrug. "You and I are connected Sophie; in a way I don't think either of us can truly explain. We are linked. You suspected it when you tried to kill me four years ago, when all that pain rebounded onto you. And every time since then, when I have nearly died, you were there. The time nearly suffocated from trying to blink to close to your army – I bet you felt that too. I don't think you will directly kill me."

Hunter felt the energy drain out of him as he spoke, so he slowly sat down, not caring about the dew soaking into his trousers. "And I bet you feel exhausted now, but can't explain why"

Sophie looked down at Hunter like he was a child, her lips pressed in a firm line of disapproval. "Of course, I'm exhausted – I have been fighting this battle whilst you've been hiding away with your tart!"

"I found out how Sara Murray died." Hunter suddenly stated, wanting to shift the focus away from Kristen.

"Killed by your grandfather, I know." Sophie snapped, frowning at the swift change in topic.

Hunter shook his head. "No, she was actually friends with Old George; and he loved her, would never have hurt her. Not that he could have. It turns out that the only way for a Shadow Witch to die is if she uses her own dagger to take her life."

"The dagger... you're lying." Sophie protested.

"The gift of death – by her hand only." Hunter quoted. "I have a letter written by your great-grandmother as proof. It is in the Manor."

Sophie hissed through her teeth. "I bet you would just love to get me inside the Manor. Block my powers, never let me out again, is that the grand plan Hunter?"

"No... we're never seeing the Manor again." He replied with a pained grimace.

Sophie stopped and finally paid attention to him. She slowly knelt beside him, and then gently reached out for Hunter's hand. Her breath hitched as she saw the red stain on his palm, and she felt his black jumper to confirm the source.

"You... you..." Sophie stuttered, her pale face blanching further. "You gave your life for that American bitch? You kill us both to save her? Do you have any idea what you have done?!"

"You inflicted the blow, I just took... took advantage of it." Hunter said, quiet in response to her anger. His hand resting gently on top of hers. "I am making a better world for our son."

Sophie snatched her hand away and without a thought, slapped him. "And you think that makes it ok? You think I'm going to lie down and accept it! Bastard!"

She lashed out again and after the first blow, Hunter tried to stop her. He wrapped his arms about her, struggling as she flailed wildly.

He grunted in pain as Sophie's knee connected with his thigh – clearly aiming for something more painful.

"Change it." Sophie demanded, her voice rougher for her screams.

"I can't." Hunter murmured. "It's too late."

"Adam…" Sophie's body shook and she made the conscious effort to sit beside Hunter with what was left of her grace.

"He'll be fine. Toby and Claire will look after him, as though he were their own." Hunter said, his eyes drifting shut as he imagined his son's bright future. "He will grow up in a world where the two sides of him can be at peace. The monks will see to his training when he's older…"

"And we'll just fade." Sophie said, bitterness clinging to her voice.

"No, not fade; we will exist forever." Hunter replied, his breaths becoming shallower. "No one will ever find us here."

Hunter tilted his head to look up. The misty, pastel clouds were tinged with pink, and the sun was just starting to creep over the horizon. The barren, rolling hills still dark against the sunrise.

He smiled. "A new day."

## Chapter Thirty-eight

Kristen awoke to find herself alone. As she sat up, she felt very sore, but very much alive. As the events of last night hit her, she broke into tearful sobs, curling back up on the floor as she waited for the shock to pass.

Eventually she got back to her feet, wavering a little, but knowing that she had to find the others. Kristen squinted in the bright sunlight that flooded through the windows, a piercing headache from the suffocating build-up of magic in this room. She had to get out.

Kristen stumbled outside, taking deep breaths as she waited for her head to clear. The summer sun beat down, warming her cold limbs, but as she tried to walk, she fell to her knees on the gravelled path. Faced with the challenge of trying to get back to the MMC, Kristen silently cursed Hunter for blinking them here – he should have insisted she drive over if the bastard had been planning on leaving her.

As her thoughts strayed to him, emotion welled up in her throat. Kristen bit it down and concentrated on the basics, of breathing and her dubious balance.

"Mel." She mumbled, then through her head back to shout. "Mel!"

There was the soft sway of a white summer dress beside her as the demon silently appeared. "Yes, Kristen?"

Mel knelt down, her usually carefree expression clouded with concern, as her blue eyes took in the signs of damage to her friend. For once, she seemed at a loss for what to say. Biting her lip, she pulled out a handkerchief and wiped some of the drying blood from Kristen's face.

"He- he's gone." Kristen gasped.

"I know." Mel said quietly.

"Is there anything you can do?" Kristen begged.

Mel put her finger on Kristen's lips to shush her. "Don't let Lucy hear; George said he wasn't allowed to help."

"I don't-" Kristen took a deep breath and blinked back fresh tears. Hunter and the Donili monks had all advised against invoking the devil. But Kristen wondered if it might not be worth it, to bring Hunter back, especially when it was her fault he had gone. Her hand strayed to her stomach, which was tender to the touch.

"I need to get back to the others." Kristen said, before she could be further tempted. "Can you take me to them, please?"

Mel smiled and placed her hand on Kristen's shoulder…

The battleground looked like organised chaos. Those that were able-bodied helped the injured in a makeshift hospital. Some had the unwelcome but necessary task of retrieving the dead, working in pairs as they gently laid the fallen in a line to be identified.

There were not many dead; it looked like the Donili had done their duty well, in discouraging the witches. Then when the rebel witches had switched sides, their once-comrades must have followed suit or scarpered. Fighting on would have been martyrdom.

Kristen got to her feet, taking in the scene. There was still the throb of magic in the air, but it was quickly diluting into the open space. Kristen's headache was becoming a much more mundane thing, no longer a signal that her witch-hunter side should be on high alert.

Kristen spotted a group of men and women surveying the field, and as they moved along, she recognised the distinctive limp of Toby Robson. Ignoring the aching pain and complaints her body was making, Kristen started to move towards them. Mel moved with her, supporting her with a surprising strength.

Toby saw them and immediately looked past the girls for her friend. "Hunter?"

Kristen shook her head. "He and the Shad- Sophie – they're gone. Hunter asked if you would take on Adam." Kristen blurted out, stating the important stuff before her emotions got the better of her again.

Toby froze, his face blanching of colour. "How are we going to do this without him?"

**The new world**

Theresa straightened her jacket as she stood up. "It is an honour to welcome you all to the first meeting of the new Malleus Maleficarum Council. It has been decided that from this day on the MMC will enforce the new laws that give witches the same rights and responsibilities as other civilians."

She paused and looked about the room, taking in the new faces alongside the familiar. "The Council itself will have two representatives from the witchkind…"

Those that gathered were clearly uncomfortable. It had only been a few weeks since the final battle and tensions were still high.

There were many more important things to do in rebuilding the world. Just when there had become a new normal, the equilibrium had shifted again.

The country was busy rebuilding. There were plans for housing and power, for simple things they had all taken for granted before the war.

The Council had agreed that they needed to establish the basics before they could move forward.

The witches had a whole manifest of new rules, as to what they could and could not do. To what influence they were allowed to have. Sacrifices and all other means of unnaturally gaining power were banned. Theresa had the unhappy task of laying down the new laws. She looked around the witches in the council; some had been more vocal than others in the disagreement. She imagined there would be months, or even years before they established real peace and understanding.

The changes the witch-hunters had to bear were equally drastic in Theresa's eyes. They had to open up their operation to the scrutiny of everybody.

The meeting drew to a close with more questions arising than were answered. Theresa picked up her leather briefcase and made her way outside.

The autumn rain had a chill to it, but she turned down her taxi in favour of the walk. She needed it. Theresa turned up the collar on her coat and made her way across the grey courtyard, pausing at a plaque by the main gate.

It was completely blank, the inscription yet to be decided upon.

Honestly, Theresa preferred at as it currently was. She murmured a prayer to the many lost over the last few years. Just considering those she had personally known – the list was too long. She only hoped she did them proud.

Theresa shivered, chilled by the ghosts more than the rain. With one last glance at the plaque, she moved on, to walk the streets of London, to finally go home.

**Epilogue**

Two dark-haired children were rolling over in a heap when the boy suddenly vanished.

"No fair, that's cheating Adam." The girl called out, getting to her feet. She was twelve years old and her lanky limbs had an adolescent awkwardness about them.

Adam, at eleven, was half a foot shorter. He reappeared behind Molly, pinning his arms around her.

"Is not. In a real fight, we have to use everything we've got."

Molly struggled, trying to get free, her face reddening as she tried to resist the temptation to throw her head back and break the younger kid's nose.

"Auntie Kristen?" Molly pleaded.

Their trainer and referee looked up from the book she was reading beside their makeshift training grounds in the garden.

"Adam, let go of Molly." Kristen said, giving him a look to say she wasn't joking. "You are both here to improve, and neither of you is going to get faster or stronger if you keep disappearing mid-fight."

Kristen sighed. Since Mel had taught Adam how to blink for a seventh birthday present, Adam too frequently chose to use his power to get out of many things. More than once, his foster-father had tried to ground him and, instead of staying in his room, Adam would blink away to the beach. Usually taking Molly with him.

"Save your tricks for when you're fighting as a real witch-hunter."

Adam pouted, hating when his auntie labelled his gifts as mere 'tricks'. But he obediently let go of Molly.

Molly rubbed her arms. "I heard Macclemore Senior saying that we shouldn't be called witch-hunters anymore. That it's not politically correct." Molly stated in a grown-up voice.

Kristen snorted. "Sure, whatever."

"You don't think so? I mean, it does discriminate." She said, chancing a glance at Adam. It was no secret that he was half-witch, even if that half had been bound when his mother died.

Kristen shrugged. "It's just a name. Besides, 'witch-hunter; witch-hunter-hunter; and all-round-paranormal-police' is a bit of a mouthful."

Molly and Adam laughed at the face their cool Auntie Kristen pulled.

"Enough, start again. No cheating." Kristen announced.

Molly grinned at Adam, and before the younger boy could move, she flipped him and pinned him to the ground with her knees.

"You ok, little bro?" She asked, batting her eyelashes innocently.

Adam squirmed, then dropped his head back on the ground in defeat.

"You might be bigger and stronger than me now, but just wait. This summer I'm joining the Donili and they're gonna teach me everything."

Molly pushed herself off. "Good, I can't wait to get rid of you, loser." She held out her hand to help him up. Honestly, she was going to miss him. A lot. They had grown up together as one big, dysfunctional family.

But everything was about to change. Adam would go to the Donili and Molly would be starting apprentice duties with the MMC when she turned thirteen in autumn. Who knew when they'd next see each other.

Kristen noticed the flash of depression in Molly's soft brown eyes. "Hey, maybe your dad will take you all on holiday to Friuli for Christmas."

Molly snorted. "Yeah right, he's too busy on the Council these days."

Kristen tried to smile, but it was easily seen through.

There was a part of Toby that had never recovered from the injury that had ended his career in the field. Now he threw himself into his work as an important Council member. Survivors' guilt, they all had their fair share of it, Kristen thought as her hand idly traced the scar across her stomach.

"Ok you two." Kristen said, snapping back to the present. "Again."

Other books by K.S. Marsden:

**Witch-Hunter** ~ *Now available in audiobook*
The Shadow Rises (Witch-Hunter #1)
The Shadow Reigns (Witch-Hunter #2)
The Shadow Falls (With-Hunter #3)

**Witch-Hunter Prequels**
James: Witch-Hunter (#0.5)
Sophie: Witch-Hunter (#0.5)
Kristen: Witch-Hunter (#2.5) ~ *coming 2020*

**Enchena**
The Lost Soul: Book 1 of Enchena
The Oracle: Book 2 of Enchena

**Northern Witch**
Winter Trials (Northern Witch #1)
Awaken (Northern Witch #2)
The Breaking (Northern Witch #3)

Printed in Poland
by Amazon Fulfillment
Poland Sp. z o.o., Wrocław